I0822607

Rise of the Dunamy

Rise of the Dunamy

www.dunamybooks.com

Published by:
Blooming Twig Books
New York / Tulsa
www.bloomingtwig.com

Hardcover: ISBN 978-1-61343-043-9
Paperback: ISBN 978-1-61343-044-6
eBook: ISBN 978-1-61343-045-3

First Edition

Printed in the United States of America.

Rise of the Dunamy

James R. Landrum

2014
Blooming Twig Books
New York / Tulsa

Rise of the Dunamy

1

Any other night, the lights of the Atlanta skyline produced a perfect backdrop to the runners, walkers and passers-by of the downtown oasis known as Piedmont Park. The treetops were bursting with fresh green foliage that rustled heavily in the cool night breeze, creating a soft hum as the millions of leaves brushed against one another. However, on this evening, the thick needles of the tall Georgia pines that hovered above the blossoming leaf-bearers formed a bristled sponge that absorbed any cries for help from escaping out into the city buildings that lie a few short miles away.

Three shadowy attackers ambushed a little man in a poorly tailored business suit, as he hurried down the dark cobblestone walkways of the park towards his home. The man had used this shortcut through the park every day on his way to and from work, but he had never before come through at such a late hour. A last minute conference call from the West Coast office had kept him from leaving until now.

Two large men had emerged and now blocked his path as another stepped in behind him, cutting off all possible exit points. His eyes darted around frantically as they searched for an escape route between or around the brutes. The dense overhanging canopy of the trees and tightly knit trunks he had grown so fond of now created a cell around him with the two thugs blocking the exit. Escape seemed impossible.

Each of the assailants was shrouded in a black hooded sweatshirt and dark pants, cloaking their features in darkness. The leader of the attackers stood directly in front of the frightened man, demanding his wallet, and clumsily waving a large black handgun only inches from his face. Holding the gun sideways and at eye level, he beckoned urgently with his free hand for the businessman to hand over anything of value. The gunman's weapon shook visibly as he made his demands.

The unfortunate businessman raised his briefcase up to block his chest. He looked around desperately at each of the men, grasping the case tightly, too frightened to make a move. The two other attackers remained several feet away, their faces invisible to him at such a distance in the dark. The man before him was well hidden also, but his lower lip and goatee were illuminated by a thin ray of moonlight. A long puffy scar scorched a path through the neatly manicured hair that covered the man's chin.

"Don't look at me, bitch!" the man demanded.

Is this for real? The businessman wondered silently, as he hoped for some sign that this might be a terrible practical joke.

Ok. Never resist, just give them what they want. That's what people are always saying. He slowly reached back to locate his wallet in his rear pocket. Retrieving it quickly, he held his thin black leather billfold out with a shaking hand for the leader to take.

"I…I don't have cash," he said in a trembling voice, afraid of the impact his words might have on the situation.

After snatching the aged leather container from his hand, the scar-faced man fingered through it and quickly confirmed there was no cash. Angrily, he ripped the numerous plastic cards from inside their slips and thrust them into his pocket before flicking the wallet back at the businessman, striking him squarely in the cheek. Raising his briefcase higher as if it might shield him from another attack, the frightened man squatted down slowly.

Scar-Face kicked the man's briefcase hard with his steel-toed boots, sending it flying. It skidded down the cobblestone path a few feet from them, slamming into a large rock and into the dirt that surrounded the walkway. The latches snapped loose, sending documents flying from the case and blowing about in the gentle night wind. With a quick glance, it was obvious there was nothing of value in the briefcase either. The leader grabbed the man by the lapels of his oversized suit, pulled him to his feet, and pressed the cold steel barrel of his gun hard against the man's cheekbone. The businessman caught the unmistakable scent of metal and gun oil. Quickly, the smell was replaced by a different foul mixture. Sweat, cheap cologne, and stale breath assaulted his senses as his attacker came closer, gnashing his teeth in frustration at the lack of valuables the businessman possessed.

Suddenly, a loud rustling in the darkest area of the woods caught everyone's attention. Scar-Face maintained his tight grip on the man's lapel as he swung his weapon around in the direction of the sound. Something had shaken some of the foliage in the woods several feet from where they were all standing. A small sapling swayed about as they all stood and stared. The thick covering of the trees shielded the moonlight from revealing the source.

"Check it out!" Scar-Face demanded gruffly of one of his hooded cohorts. His subordinate complied reluctantly and approached the area the sound had come from, drawing his own gun from his waistband as he approached the woods. As he reached the edge of the woods, he peered in uneasily to locate the source of the noise, holding his weapon out in front of him. Seeing nothing, he turned back towards the others, shrugging his shoulders slightly as he began to speak.

Just as the thief turned his back, his cohorts watched in horror as a dark figure emerged from behind one of the tree trunks. Exploding out from the darkness onto the man's back, like a predator onto its prey, the mysterious figure began beating the unsuspecting thief mercilessly. After a few stunning punches to the face, a solid shot to the back of the head crumpled the legs of the dazed thug. Riding him to the ground, the figure from the shadows was flung forward. The figure moved effortlessly and fluidly, rolling as he landed, and instantly pounced back onto the motionless man. The brutal assault continued.

His movements had been so sudden and so swift, both of the other men were taken completely by surprise. They had yet to react.

Shaking himself from his stupor, Scar-Face violently slung the businessman by his collar towards the third hooded man, who was clumsily unsheathing a large field knife for self-defense. Confused and panicked, the third man saw the approaching businessman as an attacker, and he stabbed him through the chest.

Although things were moving quickly, the small businessman's thoughts slowed as he looked down at the simple black hilt of the knife that was protruding from his chest. He watched the hooded man's hand pull the knife from his body, as all the air escaped his lungs.

The dying businessman dipped his fingertips into the deep gash in his sternum; his fingers instantly sensed the heavy flow of blood that poured out of it.

His heartbeat quickly began to increase to accommodate the amount of blood that was escaping from the laceration. Cold began to creep through his body as blood flowed unabated from the mortal wound.

As his body crumpled to the ground, he lay facing the men as they located and attempted to overcome the shadowy assassin who had emerged from the woods.

The man could see the body of the first attacker lying on the ground, motionless. He was no longer of importance to the mysterious figure, as he had now turned his focus to the remaining assailants. The dying businessman tried to make out the face of the figure from the woods, but he was only able to catch a quick glimpse of its eyes.

However, for one moment a single beam of moonlight snuck through the canopy and shone directly between the other men and onto the figure's face. The businessman was able to capture a brief glimpse into the intense, vivid greens of his avenger's eyes.

Every second seemed like an eternity to the businessman as his life leaked out onto the walkway beneath him. In the second he saw those eyes, they seared themselves into his vision as if he had stared too long into the burning sun. Those green eyes were everywhere he looked for the next several moments: intense, sad, and filled with rage.

Blood began to pool around the dying man as he gasped for air. Each breath sent tufts of dirt from the ground beneath his nostrils. Growing ever weaker from the loss of blood the little man blinked to rest his tired eyes. He waited momentarily in the darkness, listening as the pounding of his heart filled his ears. Fighting the urge to slip into eternal slumber, he felt compelled to look one last time.

Slowly lifting his heavy lids open once more, he set his gaze upon his avenger, now the only remaining fighter on the field. The dead weight of his unsupported body forced the air from his lungs slowly as his brain activity ceased. His empty wallet lay where it had fallen a few feet from his head. The papers from his briefcase continued to blow about the quiet darkness of the park. His glassy stare was now unchanging.

A sigh of defeat escaped the sweaty hulking beast as he met the little man's frozen gaze with his own. The life had left the businessman's eyes and his hollow glare now captivated his defender, and as the beast's chest heaved from the battle, his vivid green eyes pulsed in rhythm with his accelerated heartbeat. He stared back sadly for a moment.

The businessman's unnecessary death caused a sickening feeling deep in the pit of his stomach that drew his attention back to the torturous pangs of hunger that were now upon him. Turning his attention back to the bodies of his victims, he could no longer ignore the growing discomfort that filled his gut. Picking up Scar-Face's limp body, he ripped through the thin cotton sweatshirt that covered him, and began to feed.

2

"Hello, beautiful!"

Lucian's voice jolted Sofia from her daze. She sat in her squad car looking down the cobblestone walkway where a host of officers and crime scene detectives had begun working over the location. He whispered the words into her open window as he passed on his way to begin his examination of the crime scene. That was all it took to pull her from her trance. The sound of his sultry deep voice with that unexpected bit of urban flare was enough to jerk her out of her most intense moments of concentration. She watched him out of the corner of her eye as he made his way around the front of her car. He nodded towards the crime scene and snapped off a subtle wink at her as he smiled.

"See ya out there!" he called back to her as he ducked beneath the familiar bright yellow tape. She continued to watch, as admirers from the precinct quickly surrounded him. She finally exited the car and prepared herself for this grisly start to her day.

"Just one godforsaken clue. That's all I'm asking for on this one," Sofia said to herself, as she climbed under the caution tape that surrounded the perimeter of the scene. The breeze carried the stink of dead bodies. The vivid greens of spring normally caused a surge of energy throughout her body.

Now, the unpleasant smell of blood and decay overpowered the surrounding flowers and trees whose buds and blossoms had begun to burst open. While the chatter of the birds would normally have instantly brightened her day, the laser focus this casedemanded did not even allow her to listen. The all-too-familiar sense of defeat that had begun to accompany each of these recent crime scenes crept into her gut as she approached the pile of corpses.

No one within the department had come up with a single viable witness to any of the murders in this case and this would be no exception. In fact, this crime scene was the most concealed they had encountered so far. However, there was one difference. Most of the attacks had taken place in alleys and abandoned buildings that provided only a moderate amount of cover from nearby areas. This area was different. Sofia glanced towards the opening in the trees that overlooked the lake and out into the distant, bustling downtown area. This location presented a scenic and picturesque setting during the day, but at night, it would have been a prime spot for such an attack. Trees shielded the opening from a nearby road and the nearest clearing was four hundred yards ahead. The path itself was wide and paved with cobblestones, surrounded by a tightly woven tapestry of trees and thick underbrush. Tiny beams of sunlight made their way between the swaying treetops and onto the ground surrounding the body bags that now lay around the area.

Sofia had been working homicide for nearly two years. She had risen to the detective level faster than anyone in her precinct had. She was respected by every single cop on the force. Each one of her peers knew her to be, and openly referred to her as, the best female cop on the force. Each one knew her to be as good, if not better than, every male officer on the force, but refused to admit it. Now, she was dead in the water after weeks working the case everyone had begun affectionately referring to as "The Cul-De-Sac Case". The case had been given this name because each crime scene that brought them to the case led them in circles and sent them away the same way they arrived, clueless and empty-handed. Whoever, or whatever, was committing the murders that had plagued the downtown Atlanta area over the past month hadn't left so much as a strand of hair at the murder sites.

Although she had solved nearly every single case she had been assigned, she had never worked on a case that generated more buzz throughout the department than this one. It seemed like every cop on the force was doing everything they could to keep up with the facts of the case in hopes that they could offer the bit of information that would lead to the capture of the culprits. The amount of recognition and acclaim that was to be gained by anyone associated with this case was sure to elevate any career.

The sudden rash of murders had also drawn a great deal of interest from several local journalists. Typically, they knew better than to try and get a word out of Sofia regarding an active case. However, the lack of information making its way to them about the recent attacks seemed to have driven some of the more well-established reporters to try and press her for anything they could get.

Between the interest around the precinct and the calls from the press, Sofia found it incredibly difficult to keep the details of the case from getting to the public. But she knew that if the specifics of the case happened to get out, the number of phone calls she and Bishop would have to field would be a huge distraction. Whenever case information was leaked to the public everyone from concerned citizens to “helpful tipsters” would begin to bombard the department looking for, or attempting to offer, further information about the case. Every person in the community with a strange neighbor, or that had ever heard a commotion outside their window would call in to report it in an effort to help. That was one interruption Sofia always tried to avoid by simply keeping case information to herself, and Sofia was trying harder than ever to keep distractions to a minimum.

She and Bishop had spent numerous frustrating hours combing each of the crime scenes and hadn’t located a single piece of evidence. The only progress they had made in the case was linking the crimes based on the obvious common traits of the mutilated bodies, and that each victim had a criminal history. They had also determined that, due to the number of victims involved in some of the situations, and given their cumulative fighting experience, the culprits had to be attacking in a relatively large group. It had to be a gang, but no local gang would take credit for the attacks. With each passing day, Sofia became more determined to close The Cul-De-Sac Case as quickly as possible. She saw every life that was lost in her ongoing investigations as a personal failure.

3

After arriving in America, Sofia's parents found a place for them to begin their life in Dover, New Jersey, which was developing a strong Hispanic community at the time. Many of the families that were migrating to the area were coming in from Colombia, just as they had. Sofia acclimated quickly and although she started behind the other students of her age, she quickly caught up in her studies and was able to join her appropriate grade level.

Her passion for police work began when a police officer and forensic expert came to speak to her fifth grade class. She took such an immediate interest in the police officer's presentation, and asked so many questions at the end that he awarded Sofia with a plastic shield and "deputized" her. Sofia spent the following months donning her police badge on every outfit she wore and handing out tickets to other students for perceived infractions. Sofia's ticketing became a game among the children for some time. As the novelty wore off, the other kids moved on to new games, but not Sofia.

As she progressed through school, she would spend any free time that she had reading about police work. When she began reading up on the topic, she would check out children's "detective" books such as Nancy Drew, and the like. She grew bored with the simplicity of such works and began looking into criminology and crime scene inspection. Sofia was quickly hooked on them.

Her obsession was not something that her friends could ever understand, and they often teased her about it. While the other girls of the neighborhood's interests were developing towards boys and socializing, Sofia continued to focus on law enforcement. Her friends all wondered why a girl with Sofia's natural good looks and intelligence would ever focus on going into law enforcement for a living. Sofia never expected them to understand her desire to fight crime. She would simply tell them it was something in which she was interested.

After earning an academic scholarship to a number of excellent universities, Sofia enrolled at the University of Florida and earned her degree in criminal justice in only three years, graduating at the top of her class. A business opportunity for her father brought her parents south as well, relocating them in downtown Atlanta, Georgia. When she finished college, Sofia reunited with her parents and immediately joined the police force in Atlanta, just before her twenty-first birthday. Turning down a higher-level office position offered to her right away, Sofia opted for an entry-level position so that she could learn things in the department from the ground floor. This decision instantly gained her a great deal of respect from her peers.

While she was initially unconcerned about fitting in with the men of the department, Sofia was all too aware of their opinion of her. It was impossible for her to go any length of time without hearing some comment from a fellow officer regarding her looks. She was gorgeous and the effect her natural Latin curves had on men was obvious.

Even when she was young, the boys in her neighborhood, as well as some of the men, began hounding her relentlessly for dates. While she found the attention uncomfortable at first, she learned very quickly how to enjoy it.

During adolescence, Sofia set aside her schoolwork for a time and followed her suddenly overwhelming interest in dating. One of Sofia's most persistent suitors was an older boy named Mateo who lived nearby. Sofia was fourteen and Mateo was eighteen. He had recently dropped out of school. The entire neighborhood disliked him and viewed him as a troublemaker. Everyone made it a point to tell her how shocking it was that she was running around with someone like him. She often found herself defending him as misunderstood and claiming the others didn't know what they were talking about. During their relationship, Sofia completely abandoned her study habits to make time to follow Mateo around, doing everything he told her.

Not until her parents saw one of her midterm progress report reflecting several low marks, and one particularly concerning "D", did they sit her down. Her mother reminded her how much they had gone through in order to give her a better life. They wanted her to graduate high school and for her to follow her dreams, wherever that might take her. Sofia argued with them, but only briefly. Her immense respect for her parents and the thought of disappointing them was so great she decided to rededicate her focus to her schoolwork. She ended things with Mateo and decided to put dating on hold for a while.

Upon telling him of her plans, Mateo backhanded Sofia and knocked her to the ground angrily in the middle of a crowded room. Several people came to her rescue as she scrambled to her feet. Sofia knew Mateo was known for his aggressive demeanor, but it had never been something he had directed at her. She was shocked by his reaction and spent the next day, following the incident, sulking around her parents' small apartment. Sofia dodged their concerned questions by ducking into her room. She had used their concerns with her grades as the reason she was so sullen and removed.

By the end of the weekend, news had gotten back to her father and when Mateo came by to talk to Sofia, her father met him at the door. Sofia sat in her room and listened as her father spoke in a hushed tone to Mateo. Sofia's father was an average sized man of just under six feet tall, but years of hard labor in the village had given him a great deal of strength. As her father spoke, Sofia could hear Mateo squeaking in pain, never quite saying a full word. She was unsure of what was happening, but later overheard men around the community affectionately referring to him as "the old ball-buster" as they greeted him. As he spoke to Mateo, Sofia was able to hear her father mention his connections in the area. Her dad promised he would be keeping an eye on Mateo. There was a brief silence, followed by the sound of the front door shutting softly. Sofia could hear whimpering in the hallway for a moment before her father came into her room. Hugging her gently, he told her everything would be all right. He kissed her softly on the side of her face where Mateo had struck her.

After that, whenever Sofia saw Mateo, his eyes grew large as he left the area immediately. It was comical how quickly and clumsily he would exit. Mateo often knocked things, as well as people, down in order to get to the door. Another side effect of her father's encounter with Mateo was that much of the attention to which she had grown so accustomed stopped.

As she aged, Sofia stayed true to her dedication to her studies. Even though her naturally voluptuous physique, now toned by her various self-defense training courses, continued to draw the attention of every eye in the room, she maintained focus. At times, while she was away at college, she felt great loneliness and considered accepting one of the numerous outstanding dinner invitations with the young men around campus. Instead, those were the times she developed her strongest studying techniques, losing herself in her schoolwork for hours on end. Those study sessions helped form her intense work ethic, which she would later pour into her career.

Sofia's looks only improved as she aged. She was a constant topic of conversation whenever someone believed her to be out of earshot. Conversations with male officers always included at least one reminder for them to stop staring at her breasts, which usually went unheeded. It was common for her to catch a glimpse of men with whom she had just spoken with their eyes glued to her ass as she walked away. She had found such behavior amusing, even complimentary, throughout her younger years. Now, she thought it unprofessional and disrespectful. Sofia often wondered if she truly felt the behavior was unattractive, or if she had just forced herself to believe it in order to keep her mind on her studies. Either way, she found herself outside the limitations of her promise to focus on school instead of dating, while still actively remaining outside of the dating world.

In the few years she had spent coming up through the APD, Sofia had done all she could do to develop a thick skin when it came to comments about her looks among her fellow officers. She tried to play along with their jokes or simply laugh off the comments, but that only seemed to encourage them. Over time, she had simply withdrawn from conversations with the worst offenders. It was not until a particularly bold rookie made a huge mistake, that things began to change.

Trey Parker was young, handsome, incredibly fit, and he was the first to point out those facts to every woman on the force. Some of the women enjoyed his advances. Sofia found him boring, shallow, and unintelligent. Every conversation involving Parker that she had ever heard, ended up with him talking about workout routines or his looks. Whenever he made a comment to her, she simply rolled her eyes and walked away. As the Policeman's Ball approached, some of the other officers she was friendly with talked Sofia into coming. Begrudgingly, she showed up late hoping everyone would have had enough to drink for her to sneak right back out without being noticed. As she arrived, Sofia was greeted by a lively bunch of associates. Parker was the most inebriated in the group, and became quite aggressive.

After saying her hellos to everyone in the bunch, she decided to make a quick lap around the room before leaving. Parker, having already been shot down by Sofia numerous times during the group conversation, reached out and groped her ass as she walked away. This caused a combination of shocked expressions and muffled laughter from the group, including everyone nearby.

Instantly reacting to the situation and the embarrassment that consumed her, Sofia took hold of his hand and pulled him down as she thrust her elbow into his nose. It broke upon impact. Wrenching his arm behind him, she slammed his face into a nearby table, sending various plates and drinks flying into the air as the table flipped upwards. Maintaining the pressure on his arm against his back all the way to the ground, Sofia planted Parker firmly into the tile floor. She held him there as he cried out in pain. Although the music continued to play across the speakers, all of the lively chatter around them stopped as Sofia held Parker in place.

As the rage subsided, Sofia realized everyone was looking at them in shock, but no one moved to help Parker. Mortified by the amount of attention she had drawn, Sofia released him, eased to her feet, and hurried out of the room.

It took months for her to get past the embarrassment she felt because of the incident. However, the early weeks were softened each time she saw Parker's blackened eyes from the broken nose she had inflicted.There was also the huge knot that formed on the side of his forehead from smashing into the table. Everyone that had seen the entire interaction stepped forward to say Parker had been out of line and that Sofia's reaction had been justified. Sofia decided to let things die rather than pursue further disciplinary action against him, so the matter went away. Nevertheless, her confrontation seemed to stop the unpleasant comments.

While she believed she had put an end to inappropriate comments about her, she found out she had merely managed to convince those who made them to do so in private. It had been two years since the incident at the Policeman's Ball and, in that time, Sofia felt that she had done a great deal to change the opinion of the men in the precinct. She had made detective and continued to put in more hours at work than any other officer. She hadn't had to deal with the sexist comments since the event and had even noticed a substantial decrease in the number of times she had to ask the men to stop staring at her chest. She truly believed that she had done enough to earn the respect of the other officers.

Sofia had just left a conversation with a particularly harmless officer, when she realized she needed to turn back for her paperwork. Upon doing so, she overheard officer Eckersley, a husband and father of two, making a comment about "what he would do if he could get Sofia alone" to someone. Hurt, but infuriated, Sofia began to storm around the corner and confront Eckersley when she suddenly heard a familiar voice. She had only recently taken the position of homicide detective and she and Bishop hadn't been partnered up for long. As it turned out, very few people were aware how protective he was of her.

"Oh yeah, Eckersley?" he growled. "Fill me in. Tell me what you think you would do to my partner!"

"No…nothing, Bishop. You know…. She's just so…" Eckersley stammered out. There was a loud thud that Sofia could tell was a body being pushed up against a wall, before Bishop continued.

"You watch your goddamn mouth when you talk about my partner, understood?" Bishop said fiercely.

"Y…yeah…. Sure, Bishop…. I just thought….You know…."

"You thought wrong," Bishop huffed. Sofia couldn't see what was happening, but she could tell Bishop's blood was boiling by the tone of his voice.

"Go call your wife, you piece of shit," Bishop called back angrily, his voice growing more faint as he walked away. Not wanting to run into Eckersley, as he was undoubtedly going to be heading the opposite direction of Bishop, Sofia decided she would return for her paperwork later, and headed back towards her desk.

Sofia never mentioned that she had heard him take up for her, but overhearing Bishop's interaction with Eckersley instantly created a powerful bond for her. Hearing him take up for her meant the world to her. It meant that after years of feeling alone among her peers, she finally had an ally.

4

"I still have no idea how you can eat at these crime scenes," Sofia said with a grimace as she watched Bishop gnawing on some sort of breakfast burrito.

"Ah, don't sweat it, sweetie. Give it some time and you'll be doin' the same thing."

"I've told you about calling me sweetie, and I don't want to get to a point where I'm able to eat around dead bodies!" she proclaimed. "It's disgusting, not to mention the risk you're running of contaminating our crime scene."

Bishop continued to observe the scene as he crammed the final oversized bite into his mouth and licked the remaining salsa from his fingers. She stared in dismay as he scraped the chunks of egg that had landed on his shirt onto the ground.

"Just like that! You're intentionally dropping bits into our crime scene!"

"Calm down, Sofia! I brushed it off into the grass and I'm nowhere near anything relevant. Good Lord, I'm ten feet from anything."

"At least you're finished and we can focus." As she spoke the words, Bishop pulled another silver-sleeved burrito from his pocket and began to unwrap it, crinkling the aluminum wrapper to taunt Sofia.

"You've got to be kidding me," she mumbled to herself in disbelief.

It had been nearly a year since Sofia and Bishop had paired together. She had grown quite fond of him. Beginning with the conversation she had overheard between Eckersley and him, Sofia had always felt that, no matter what, Bishop had her back. The only reservations she had where he was concerned were because of his "old school" detective work.

Going into their partnership, she had heard stories about Bishop regarding planting evidence and strong-arming suspects to gain confessions. Nothing had ever been proven, but she had witnessed situations where she believed she had arrived just in time to stop him from such things. He had always been regarded highly for his detective work, but everyone knew he was a bit of a wild card, willing to do whatever it took to make an arrest. While she had always seen their partnering as an attempt for her to watch over him and keep him in line, Bishop felt he was placed with her as a mentor. He often treated her as his protégé rather than an equal.

Right from the beginning, Bishop became very protective of Sofia and always found it necessary to try to keep her out of harm's way. He claimed it was just "the way he was taught," and that he had been raised to protect women. Sofia spent a great deal of time, in their first months together, explaining that there was no need to be so protective over her. Whenever he would try to step in front of her, if a situation got even mildly hostile, she would explain how difficult it made it for people to take her seriously. Bishop would simply disregard her comments and continue doing exactly what he wanted. Finally, she made her point clear when she was forced to take down a man twice her size. Bishop was attempting to hold down the man's accomplice. After seeing a man that size writhing in pain with Sofia on his back, pinning him to the floor, Bishop accepted that Sofia was able to handle herself. From that point on, he began respecting her requests and stayed out of her way when things got physical.

The difference in their styles was the source of a large number of their arguments. Bishop had been on the force for over twenty years and had entered the Academy right out of high school. Being a third generation cop, he admittedly had no real aspirations of doing anything other than being an officer. He had earned his stripes as a beat cop and had partnered with some of the oldest guys on the force, becoming very well versed in the "old way" of doing things. Bishop's style was like a glance into how police work used to be handled. He had been surrounded by the self-proclaimed "old guard" his entire life. His actions mirrored that mentality.

His old-school, hard-nosed style was a major concern to Sofia. She saw it as a way for corruption to enter into his work. Sofia believed that if he was willing to bend the rules to the point that he was, then there was very little keeping him from doing whatever he felt was within reason to get a job done. Although she had never known him to use such tactics against an innocent person, Sofia knew that his actions could all too easily land the wrong person in jail. Regardless of these facts, Sofia loved being his partner and simply made a habit of keeping an eye on him as often as possible.

"This has to be our guys. Same post-mortem mutilation as the other bodies," Bishop said to Sofia, as she observed the scene, doing little to stop the falling pieces of his burrito from landing on his shirt, much less the crime scene. His thick southern accent was covered by the partially chewed remains, tucked away in his overstretched jaw.

"The muscle has been removed down to the bone on the arms and legs. It's a freakin' mess," he said. He took another large bite out of his burrito even though he hadn't yet finished what he was chewing. "All except this guy. What's so special about him?" Bishop indicated the body of the businessman that lay several feet from the others. "He got to keep all of his body parts. I guess we can rule out 'hunger' as their motivation behind chewin' the bodies up."

Bishop looked over at the businessman momentarily before continuing in a serious tone, "These guys are seriously screwin' with my head, you know? Usually, with serial killers you get a pretty specific type of victim. Similar body type, hair color, facial features, something that every single victim has in common. These perps are all over the map. Different numbers of victims, all completely different looking. They're killing in different locations, no evidence at the scene." Bishop scratched his head anxiously, frustrated at the lack of consistency between the murders.

"And then we've got this guy," he said quizzically, indicating the stabbed businessman once again. "I mean, what's with him? These three were chewed to bits, and this guy gets off scot-free? I see that those guys were clearly up to no good and all, but why not go after the bonus body? Were they full?"

Bishop relaxed for a moment before interjecting one last thought. "Maybe it's that shitty suit," he joked quietly, as a smirk crept across his lips. He resumed his breakfast as he continued to observe the mangled remains, upon seeing his partner's lack of amusement with the commentaries.

Sofia snapped on a fresh pair of latex gloves and was ready to begin making her own sweep of the scene. She moved slowly and deliberately throughout the area, making sure to get a quick scan of each of the body's locations to ensure she wasn't compromising any evidence. Squatting beside the first corpse she came to, she slowly unzipped the large black plastic body bag to reveal the victim. Preparing herself for the putrid odor that she had grown uncomfortably accustomed to, she shielded her nose and mouth with the back of her hand before peeling back the noisy material to reveal the victim's face. The lifeless eyes of a young Hispanic male stared off into the distance down the walkway his head now rested upon. The awkward angle of his head in relation to his body allowed Sofia to easily determine that his neck, like so many of the other victims in the Cul-De-Sac Case, had been broken. Sofia paused momentarily to prepare herself to examine the body for one of the only other similarities between the killings.

Each body in the Cul-De-Sac Case showed very similar signs of severe blunt force trauma. It was determined to be from fighting just prior to their death. In addition, each of the bodies had been mutilated in the exact same ritualistic manner. The beatings were so severe that most of the victim's bones were broken and sometimes even shattered. This body was no different. The shattering of several bones was evident as she looked over what remained of the young man. Most of the bone in the arms and legs was exposed due to the lack of meat and flesh that remained to cover it. Sofia removed a pen from her pocket and used it as a probe to inspect some of the smaller shards to make sure they were in fact bone and not a foreign substance.

"Some of these fragments are so tiny. It's like they're hitting these guys with sledge hammers," she said quietly. "How are they doing this?"

She prodded around a while lifting and poking various bits of mangled pieces of the man's remains before looking around for some assistance.

"Make sure you keep him pretty well covered.The crows got here early today." Bishop was referring to the flock of reporters that had shown up, who were now corralled behind the yellow police tape, kept at bay by patrol officers. Bishop had taken to the idea of referring to the reporters as "crows" in reference to how they showed up wherever there was a corpse. He had become more insufferable with his use of the term since Sofia pointed out the fact that a group of crows is a "murder of crows."

"I know enough to keep them from seeing anything," she replied sharply, as she quickly pulled the plastic back over the remains.

"I know it, kid. I didn't mean you weren't watchin' yourself. It's just those cameras they got now can sneak in places you wouldn't believe."

Sofia continued looking over the corpse, ignoring Bishop's statements.

"No need to get pouty. Just hate for those scavengers to get a single picture."

5

"Hello again, beautiful." The words had become Lucian's calling card to Sofia. He called them out to her as he tiptoed in between and around the various obstructions with his perfect smile shining brightly.

Dr. Lucian Grey was the medical examiner that worked with their department. He and Sofia had been flirting incessantly over the past several months. The sound of his voice was always able to send a shiver up her spine.

"You look a little more alert than you did earlier," Lucian stated cordially as he eased his way next to her. Sofia smiled subtly as he came closer, realizing he could have positioned himself across the body from her if he wanted a better view.

"Looks like our guys earned some fresh ink last night," Sofia said, referencing the manner many gang members went about identifying the number of crimes that they had committed using tattoos to signify the number and severity.

"There you go jumpin' to conclusions again. Funny how you don't know jack about these guys and you just assume they're all good with ink. Maybe they're 'straight edge.' Ever think of that? Maybe they don't believe in tattoos," Lucian quipped. Lucian was, aside from being gorgeous, one of the most entertaining people that Sofia had ever met. He was charming and funny on top of being highly intelligent and an unbelievable flirt.

"Straight edge, huh? So we should be looking for a group of teenagers that murder people and disfigure their bodies, but that don't believe in things like drinking alcohol, doing drugs, or having premarital sex?" Sofia's comments were rife with sarcasm. "That makes no sense, Lucian."

Lucian sat for a moment, squinting and rolling his eyes back and forth as he thought about Sofia's comment. Then he slowly started nodding. "I might be on to something there. I mean, those kids have gotta have some release somewhere, right? I mean, damn. Teenagers that are telling themselves they can't be sexual, can't drink, can't smoke, can't this, can't that; sounds to me like they're off to a pretty weird start to begin with."

"So are you saying that kids that don't want to do that sort of stuff are weird?" Sofia inquired, knowing that Lucian was aware that she had refrained from such things during her younger years.

"Weird might have been the wrong word, but I think it's definitely added stress to an already stressful time. It's hard as hell to get used to your hormones gettin' all crazy when you hit puberty, and to add all those restrictions on yourself! Those kids are probably ready to explode." Softening his tone, he whispered to her, "I mean, not everyone is as amazing as you."

Sofia felt her face flush red as her eyes dashed around to see if anyone had heard Lucian's comment to her. When she realized no one had, she quickly pulled herself together. "As ridiculous as your premise is, my comment still stands because 'straight edge' kids still get tattoos," she joked.

Sofia could hear Bishop snickering behind her at Lucian's comments, which was no surprise. Bishop was, like so many other men in the department, intrigued by Lucian. He wanted to live like Lucian, hang out with him, and do anything he could to let Lucian know that he thought he was cool in hopes that Lucian would reciprocate. Sofia saw it as a full blown man-crush. Anytime Lucian said anything relatively funny Bishop would burst out in laughter, especially when it was at Sofia's expense, which was rare.

Lucian was one of the most beloved people around the entire precinct. Sofia had never heard a single person that had come in contact with Lucian say anything negative about him. He had an uncanny ability that allowed him to know just how to handle each person he came in contact with. He could instantly evaluate a person's mood and knew the best way to address them to disarm as well as enamor them. Even when he was dealing with the most sullen and unpleasant men on the force, Lucian was almost always able to lighten their mood, even if it was only while they were in his presence. He was always fun to be around, but he knew when it was time to get serious and take care of business. He had a keen sense for people, knowing which ones were receptive to jokes and compliments and which ones wanted him to give information and keep quiet if he had none to give. Sofia had never seen Lucian in so much as a brooding mood, much less angry or upset. His charm was undeniable, and he had the looks to match. Sofia often found herself wondering if he was actually perfect, or if she was just ignoring his faults because of her crush.

"Good God. That suit is horrible," Lucian mused as he looked over at the corpse of the businessman.

"That's what I said!" Bishop called out triumphantly, overjoyed that he and Lucian had made the same observation.

"Well, not everyone can have the eye for fashion you do, Lucian." Sofia quipped, smiling as she glanced over towards the man's body.

"Well, that's true," he replied. "Sometimes you just need to bite the bullet and spend some money at the tailor. Maybe I should consider a side job as a fashion consultant for guys like that."

"I bet you could make a killing," Sofia added nonchalantly as she turned her attention back to the body before her. She rarely used humor in the workplace, but with Lucian she made an exception.

"Hell, if that's the case, I should give up this dead body business and go do the fashion consulting thing full-time," Lucian replied, instantly drawing Sofia's attention back to what he was saying.

"Uh…wait…no. Come to think of it, that sounds like a pretty

small market. Seems like you would run out of clients pretty quickly." Sofia wanted to put the thought out of Lucian's mind as she considered that he might be serious. She dreaded the thought of not seeing him on a daily basis. Peeking at him out of the corner of her eye, she could see him smiling at her flustered response.

"Yeah. Plus the perks around here are pretty hard to beat," he said as turned his head and winked at her. Sofia fought to cover up her grin as she cut her eyes back to her work.

While only slightly above average height, his height was accentuated by how slender he was despite the fact that he was constantly eating. Sofia had him sized up at about 6'2" and a lean 175 pounds. He took very good care of himself, and paid plenty of attention to his appearance while never seeming overly concerned with his looks. He was always sporting new haircuts and the latest style of clothes, and had never made a poor choice in either respect.

These days he was wearing his hair in a trendy little faux-hawk that Sofia typically hated, but absolutely adored on Lucian. Although she had never asked, Sofia assumed he was in his mid to late twenties, but could probably have passed for a teenager because of his baby face and perfect skin. While he had the looks, the hair, the wonderful personality, and spoke with the unbelievably sexy combination of southern twang and urban slang, there was something behind all of it that was the biggest reason Sofia was drawn to him. Oddly enough, she had no idea what that reason was. There was something inside that perfect shell that Sofia knew was far more beautiful than anything he could present on the outside. It came across in the conversations she had with him and the care and kindness that he showed to everyone he came in contact with, including the bodies of the victims he came into contact with on a daily basis.

It was that combination of characteristics, and so much more that she could see whenever she looked deep into his beautiful hazel eyes. She had stolen many moments and locked in on his eyes, taking note of the deep browns and pale greens that gathered there. However, there was something there that she couldn't see, she just knew it was present. In Sofia's eyes, as well as nearly every other woman he came in contact with, he was the complete package and she had developed an intense crush on him over the past year.

As Lucian worked alongside Sofia, examining the corpse of the young male, the sweet smell of his cologne caused Sofia to swoon ever so slightly. Blinking her eyes, and with a shake of her head, Sofia was able to rid herself of her romantic feelings for a moment and refocus on the task at hand. Lucian opened up his antique black-leather medical bag and pulled out a very large and very sharp metal thermometer. With a quick jab he plunged the thermometer into the victim's liver. As he waited, he pulled an all-too-familiar aluminum wrapper from his bag.

"The two of you have got to be the most disturbing people on the face of the Earth!" Sofia exclaimed as Lucian unwrapped his breakfast burrito.

He looked at her quizzically for a moment before stammering. "Who…what now?"

"You and Bishop. How can you eat like that when we're examining dead bodies? Mutilated, dead bodies?"

Lucian looked around for a second and located Bishop, who had overheard their little exchange and was now making his way over towards them. The pair smiled and touched their burritos together as if toasting their similar choice in breakfasts.

"You're even more disturbing because of how close you get to them while you're eating. The smell alone should be enough to keep you from needing to eat!"

"I do this all day!" Lucian stated in a comically high-pitched voice. "If I don't eat near them, I'll never get to eat!"

"Well we certainly know you're not going to let that happen," Sofia joked. Lucian was eating constantly. If he wasn't eating when she was talking to him, he had generally just finished eating or was on his way to get something. She had teased him a great deal about the amount of food she had seen him eat and his unbelievable metabolism.

"Aren't you the slightest bit concerned about contaminating the evidence?" she asked, knowing the answer before it came.

"You've seen me eating around these guys before. Ever seen me drop anything?" he asked defiantly.

Sofia shook her head. One thing she had always noticed when she observed him eating was how careful and well-mannered he was. "Besides, I know what I'm eating. If I find any of it inside the body and outside the stomach, I'll know where it came from and discard it.... You know, as long as it doesn't land somewhere I don't think is all that gross.... 'Cause then I'd just eat it," he added with a smirk, causing Bishop to gag.

"Oh my God, dude!" Bishop barked out between dry heaves, which he was struggling to keep the surrounding members of the media from seeing. He walked over to a nearby tree to further shield himself as he tried to compose himself.

"You are disgusting, Lucian!" Sofia said, wincing to keep herself from also gagging.

Lucian laughed loudly as he watched Bishop struggle to regain his composure enough to continue eating his breakfast.

"I got this mental picture of you eating from inside a body." Bishop groaned, holding his fist to his lips as he concentrated on keeping himself together.

"Fresh body, or had it been sitting a while?" Lucian continued, his grin widening as he did so.

"Oh, God!" Bishop groaned again, lurching forward and placing his free hand over his mouth.

"Lucian, stop! You're going to make him throw up all over my crime scene!" Sofia whispered loudly.

“I’m sorry. You’re right, I guess.” Gathering his poise, Bishop moved over to a different area to inspect the crime scene as he allowed his stomach to settle.

“Thank you.” Sofia said in a frustrated tone.

“No sweat. I was going to say something about having to sift through his vomit, but he was really about to lose it.”

“Lucian, stop being so disgusting,” Sofia groaned. Closing her eyes tightly, she began rolling her head around to try and get the mental image out.

Lucian glanced at her out of the corner of his eye and snickered to himself before checking the thermometer for the temperature. “Core temp indicates that this one’s been dead about six hours, putting estimated T.O.D. at around 3 a.m. I’ll have to take them back to get the cause of death, but I think it’s safe to assume that we already have a clue,” he said, taking a much more serious tone as he scanned the scene for the other victims, “except for that guy, of course. He doesn’t quite fit.” Lucian pointed back to poorly dressed businessman who lay several feet away near what was clearly his wallet and briefcase.

6

"What are we missing here?" Sofia asked herself quietly. "Bishop, I know you don't want to, but can you run through them one more time?"

Bishop released a long, aggravated sigh as he flipped through the pages of his pocket notepad and began reading in a dull monotone.

"The first guy was a solo. Thirty-four year old white male. He was found in an alley downtown. Career criminal. In and out of prison his whole life. Seems to have had some ties to the Aryan Brotherhood. Said to have been a potential member that was handling some of the Brotherhood's business on the outside. He had recently beaten a vehicular homicide/drunk driving rap where the victim was a ten-year-old boy. He appeared to have been beaten to death. No witnesses at the scene, and no one has come forward. The marks on the body made by the assailants led us to believe the beating was done by a group. All muscles from the victim's arms and legs had been torn from the body postmortem. No useable DNA located at the scene."

Bishop snapped to his next page of notes. "Second and third victims were black males. Both twenty-four years of age, found at the bottom of an embankment off Holmes Boulevard. Both were suspects in several ongoing murder investigations and appeared to be enforcers for a local gang. Both were beaten to death. Both bodies had the muscles torn from the bone at the arms and legs." He flipped loudly again.

"Next was that really big bastard down in Five Points. Twenty-eight year old white male. Beaten to death, muscles torn from the arms and legs. No known affiliations...."

Bishop looked at the page blankly for a second as if he expected more information to magically appear. "I guess that's it on him."

He then flipped the tiny page again and brought his focus back to the current crime scene.

“Here we have four bodies. It appears that three of them robbed and killed ‘the suit’ over there before they were attacked by our guys. One of the three has this guy’s credit cards,” he indicated towards the body of the man that clearly didn’t belong with the others solely based on his appearance, “and a knife with blood on it. Plus, the stab victim didn’t become snack food. All of his bits and pieces seem to be intact. It would be nice if the blood on the knife belonged to one of our attackers, but it looks like it’s gonna match the unfortunate Mr. Business over here. These three look familiar, but I’m not really sure why. We may have had to take them in a few times. It won’t surprise me if they all have several pings in the system. They don’t have any tats that point us in any way toward any level of gang affiliation. May have been out to make their bones.” Bishop looked over to Lucian momentarily before adding, “You know, that’s how these gangsters refer to a guy’s first kill.”

Lucian looked up with huge smirk on his face, as he bounced his eyes between Bishop and Sofia. “Did you seriously just try to give me a lesson on some street slang, dude?”

Bishop lowered his head to conceal his smile in hopes that Lucian would take it easy on him.

“Im’ma let that go for now, Bishop, but you do know how ridiculous you just sounded…right?” Lucian continued, jokingly.

“And we found out that the third guy had several complaints against him, didn’t we?” Sofia asked, as she stared at the body of the victim that appeared to have been mugged. She was locked in on the specifics of the case and wouldn’t let herself be dragged into their silliness.

“Third scene, fourth victim.” Bishop flipped through the pages in his notebook as he tried to find the specifics on the victim. “Yep. Looks like he’s been brought in a few times for domestic violence. Beat his wife up several times, but she always refused to press charges or even make a statement." Bishop dropped the monotone announcer's voice he had been using to recite the previous information.

"I knew I was forgetting something when I was looking at that guy's sheet. The wife actually came in to identify the body last night. I talked to her for a second, and she didn't look like she had any recent marks on her, but I caught a glimpse of her kid in the car. He looked pretty bad off. His eye was swollen shut. He never got out of the car, so I couldn't tell how bad it was. The wife ran off as soon as she saw me looking at him. Too bad about that guy, he's a real loss to the community," he added, with cutting sarcasm.

Sofia's eyebrows rose quizzically at this new information.

"Sorry, Sofe. I meant to mention that to you sooner," Bishop added, staring blankly into the distance as he remembered the boy's face. As tough a cop as he was, Bishop was as soft as butter when it came to children.

"Seems pretty clear that the guys in this group see themselves as some sort of vigilantes." Sofia didn't realize that she had spoken loudly enough to shake Bishop from his trance.

"Honestly, I don't really see the point in looking for them. I say we let 'em keep going and see how much of the scum they can clean up before they take on someone they can't handle," he joked openly, getting a few laughs out of the surrounding officers. Bishop's comment was just enough to set off Sofia.

"How did I know you would say something like that?" She was enraged at Bishop's callous attitude. "We've had this discussion, Bishop. I don't think that's funny! Accused does not mean guilty. While we believe that the guy is probably guilty, a jury of his peers did not prove him guilty. We don't get to be their executioners; that's not how our system works. That doesn't even begin to take into account what they are doing to these bodies. You've seen what they're doing to these people and you know how deranged they would have to be to do such things!"

She was shouting in an effort to let everyone around her know that Bishop's opinion was completely out of line, and that it was equally wrong for any officer on the force to find amusing.

Bishop began fanning his hands at her in an attempt to calm her as she was drawing the attention of everyone, including a few of the nearby journalists.

"No need to jump on your soapbox, honey. I'm just saying that they're getting results where we aren't. Some of these guys are just slippin' through the system and we can't do anything about it. I'm not sayin' that they're right, I'm just sayin' they're effective." Sofia wasn't surprised at Bishop's backpedalling, given the presence of the media. He knew that anything they picked up might be put into print, and that would cause him a world of trouble.

Bishop paused momentarily as Sofia calmed down. Taking a look around at the bodies, he slipped a pinch of snuff into his lip; wiping the remnants away from his face before continuing, "As far as what's going on with the bodies, yeah, that's a pretty sick little twist." He looked around with a rather disgusted look on his face as he surveyed the grotesque scene.

They continued to work the site, looking for some clue to lead them in any direction. This site was just like the others in that there were ample amounts of blood and DNA from the victims, but nothing usable from the killers. As was the case with the other attacks, the muscles appeared to be ripped from the bone. Sofia could see that the remains were not uniform and didn't show signs of cutting, so any sort of knife or other utensil seemed unlikely.

Each time they looked over one of these scenes, they always came to the same conclusion; the attackers had to be using their teeth to strip the meat away, which should have left at least trace amounts of saliva behind, but hadn't. The fact that none was found on any of the bodies had led Sofia and Bishop to wonder what method they were using to remove the muscle. The jagged tears in the skin seemed to be most consistent with teeth marks, but it would be impossible to do what they were doing without leaving some level of trace evidence behind.

Once more, no eyewitnesses came forward during a sweep of the area, and the evidence at the crime scene was minimal. The evidence they were able to locate only appeared to further link the victims to the stabbing of the businessman. After spending an hour knocking on doors, Sofia and Bishop decided to return to the precinct to re-examine their case files.

7

As she began scanning the first page of the report, Sofia cradled her pen between her forefinger and middle finger and began wobbling it back and forth. The rhythmic wobble of the pen helped her slip deeply into her own thoughts.

Investigators had first begun the case with the attack on the possible member of the Aryans. Due to the type and extent of the damage to the corpse, they couldn't be sure an animal hadn't been involved. At that time, they had begun investigating it as a possible animal attack. The abuse that the body had endured, along with the numerous apparent bite marks that covered the body, would have really only allowed for one type of animal to have attacked them. That animal was a bear. Being that there were no signs of bear tracks or any other forensic evidence indicating the presence of a bear, coupled with the fact that it was highly unlikely that there was a bear in the downtown area, they quickly abandoned that possibility. After their brief consideration of the bear attack, they considered the idea that it may have been an accidental death, not a homicide. They were out surveying the scene to see if the victim could have fallen from a rooftop and then been picked apart by a passing pack of animals when they received word from Lucian. He had determined the cause of death, which instantly changed their opinion of the case.

The man had been killed by blunt force trauma to his neck. Although the cause of death and location of the strike were evident, after much deliberation and forensic examining, they had been unable to determine the murder weapon. Lucian had informed them that he believed that the man had been punched in the neck, based on the bruising. Bishop and Sofia both agreed it seemed a bit far-fetched to believe that someone was capable of doing such a thing with their hands. They continued to search for a more plausible weapon.

The next attack happened a few days later, across town from the first. The attacks were very similar in their surroundings and severity, and the wounds were similar. At this point, Sofia and Bishop revisited the earlier case and began to investigate the two attacks as though they were related. Their suspicions were confirmed when a third attack occurred only two days later.

As they inspected things further, several patterns developed that linked all three crimes. However, none of the patterns would lead them any closer to the killers. Sofia knew that since they had developed a pattern, it wouldn't be long before the FBI got involved. Any time the potential of a serial killer arose, the FBI sent in its own team to handle the situation. The idea of federal agents coming in to take over her case was maddening and had driven her to immerse herself even further.

Although the causes of death in each case had been a broken neck, Lucian had commented that they would all have died from the amount of internal bleeding they were experiencing anyway. The beatings each of the victims received prior to the broken neck were so severe, it almost seemed like the final strike was meant to be merciful. All of the victims had been brutally beaten. Once again, Lucian's findings were that the bruising patterns indicated no weapons were used. The only exception was the victim in the final attack. They believed he had been killed by the other victims that had also been found dead at the scene. He had also clearly died from the stab wound.

All three attacks had been committed close to high traffic areas, which increased the amount of foot traffic through the actual crime scene, so determining the number of people involved was nearly impossible due to the large amount of trace evidence at each scene. In every attack, the victims were armed. Most often, they had guns. In each case, those guns were fired. Yet, they were unable to find any trace amounts of blood from the attacker around the site. Whenever they were able to locate slugs they believed were fired at the attacker, no DNA was ever lifted from them.

Sofia suddenly asked aloud, "Where are the slugs with blood on them?"

"Which slugs? Nothing we've found has had anything on it." Bishop wore a confused look on his face.

"That's what I'm saying. There has to be slugs with blood on them. It's just not possible that these guys are being killed without any of them getting a shot on the attackers. Their combined rap sheets are a mile long! Most of them fired their weapon at some point during the attack, and most of them fired several times. Not one single bullet hit any of the suspects. Even if they missed the person they were aiming for, it seems like they would have hit someone in the group." The frustration continued to mount from the increasing likelihood of FBI involvement.

She knew that the second the FBI showed up, she'd be allowed to only participate in the investigation at a subordinate level. The agents that took over these sorts of cases weren't keen on allowing local law enforcement officers to help in the decision making once they became involved. Sofia didn't want anyone making it look like she didn't know how to do her job well, and that's exactly what they would do.

"These 'cannibal killers' must be well organized. Maybe our victims are firing up in the air or something to try and scare them before they attack."

"Yeah, you've said that already," Sofia said, with a huff, as she angrily flipped through the pages of the case folder. "It's just not possible. Based on the shell casings we've found, there should be a ton of slugs at the sites, but we've only found a handful between all of them. Plus, these guys aren't going to try and scare someone. These guys are going to attack first, if they feel threatened. They all have backgrounds with violence, so they aren't scared of an altercation. Some of them have been involved in shootings before, so I doubt they're hesitant to fire at someone they think is after them."

"Well, I think it's pretty obvious then."

Sofia closed her eyes as she prepared for what she could tell was going to be a stupid comment.

"We're talking about ninjas." Bishop's comments were accompanied by a subtle laugh. This was typical of Bishop. Anytime he couldn't figure something out, or the facts presented to him didn't make sense, he would make a ridiculous joke and laugh the situation off. Sofia could usually find the humor in his jokes, but this was a much different situation because of the FBI timeline.

She looked on in silence as Bishop shuffled through unrelated papers and looked over worthless crime scene photos he had seen several times before. It was all just a show that he was putting on for her benefit, and no one was more aware of that than Sofia. Bishop had focused more attention towards cleaning up his workspace than doing any actual detective work since finding the common thread between their victims. The link was that they were all hardened criminals who had successfully evaded the system several times. If Bishop had done anything to contribute to the investigation, Sofia felt that he was purposely misdirecting all efforts in order to delay the murderer's capture.

What was once a wasteland of unfiled paperwork, half-eaten sandwiches, and empty soda cans, was now a well-organized, easily navigable workstation fit for the lieutenant. The only exception was the oversized Styrofoam cup filled with paper towels that was always present at the left corner of his desk, beside his computer monitor. The purpose of the cup was actually quite disgusting, but something that Sofia had learned to deal with during her time on the force.

Apparently, holding a wad of tobacco between a person's lower lip and teeth produces a great deal of saliva that is filled with tobacco remnants. Once his mouth fills up, that person's only option for dispensing the tobacco-laced saliva was to either swallow the solution, or to spit it out. Bishop was a "spitter." The filthiest part of the whole process was that for some reason, even though there was an endless supply of small cups available in the break room, Bishop preferred to keep the same giant cup for months on end and simply change out his paper towels. The cup would end up collecting a layer of tobacco and saliva all around the inside. The stench that wafted over to Sofia's desk was so putrid, at times, that she would often gag when it reached her. The smell was indescribable, but instantly identifiable to anyone who had ever smelled it. It rated somewhere between raw sewage and month-old dirty diapers.

Sofia had done all she could to get Bishop to stop the filthy habit. She had given him documentation on the effects and probability of oral cancer. She had shown him ghastly pictures of those who had suffered from the ailment. She nagged him incessantly, but nothing she did even slowed him down.Her only recent attempt to thwart the frequency of his habit was to throw his cup into the garbage every time she could get her hands on it. This, too, had proven futile. Each time she returned, she found him stuffing new paper towels into a brand new cup from a stash in his drawer. These days, it seemed like he was dipping far more often as another excuse to slow his work on the case. The only progress she had made was occasionally getting rid of the older, smellier cups. As she looked over to the cup that now sat upon his desk, she could tell she had forgotten to trash his cup recently by the amount of doodling he had done on the sides, using his fingernail.

In the past two days, Bishop had decided that they would follow up on several leads that she knew weren't credible. He had rounded up a list of calls that named the areas where they had found bodies connected to the Cul-De-Sac case. Sofia had believed it to be a creative idea to come up with any information that could lead them in the right direction. She had commended him for his creative thinking up until they went up to the first house to question the caller about the complaint.

When they tracked down the original caller, the woman was confused as to what they were doing there, as the call had been from over three months earlier. Sofia let Bishop slide on mistakenly allowing a call so long before the first body was discovered onto his list. The next caller they tracked down had also contacted the police department several months earlier.

When Sofia asked the woman what her call had been in reference to, Sofia was shocked to learn that the complaint was about the neighbor's dog barking during the night. When she learned that information, Sofia knew that Bishop had put no effort into building his list to find out information about their case. He had simply put together a list where calls had come in and proceeded to reference an area near one of the crime scenes. It was Sofia's belief that he had done so in order to keep her from making any real headway on the case, even though it was highly unlikely that she would anyway.

After spending half the day tracking down some of the calls on Bishop's list, Sofia asked what exactly he had hoped to learn from following up on so many completely unrelated leads. Bishop informed her that he was asking each of the men and women questions related to their case. When she pointed out that none of them had heard anything even remotely useful, Bishop had thrown up his hands and proclaimed that he was "trying to think outside the box!" He felt that these were the type of people they needed to talk to because if they were willing to call about such stupid things, these people would also talk to police and share what they knew. In order to calm him down, Sofia accepted his explanation and they followed up on his list for the remainder of the day.

She had hoped that by allowing him to finish the day on his list, he would drop the idea and they could move forward the next day. Instead, the next morning, he had added more calls to his list. Sofia was forced to waste another day of work following up on Bishop's "creative thinking." Although she hated that another crime scene had been located overnight, Sofia was the slightest bit pleased that she wouldn't be stuck tracking down meddlesome neighbors and "concerned citizens."

"What paperwork are you looking through?" She glared at him, incapable of overlooking the way she believed he had been intentionally sabotaging their case.

"Eh. Just looking through some other stuff to try and get my head clear." Bishop never looked up from the assortment of papers as he gave curt answers.

"How's that working out for you?" she snapped, condescendingly.

"Oh, about as well as that nasty attitude is working for you." Bishop began bouncing the papers on his desk to try to get them to stack neatly as he shot a knowing glance at Sofia. "The difference is, after I'm done, there's a chance I'll have a new idea or different opinion on the case. When you're done with your pissy attitude, you won't."

"Yeah, I'm sure you'll be a wealth of knowledge," she muttered under her breath as she rolled her eyes at him and returned to her case file.

Surprisingly, Bishop chimed in with regards to the case as opposed to returning to his aimless pursuits in his old paperwork.

"I'm telling you, I think these guys are new to the area and trying to build some cred by knockin' off rivals. Maybe they eat the bodies to send a real 'don't mess with us' signal. I mean, if you were goin' around makin' enemies as fast as these guys are, you would have to do something to keep the retaliation down. You eat a person and I think it would keep people off of you." Bishop leaned back in his chair and turned towards his sulking partner.

Sofia grimaced in response to his suggestion. As often as Bishop joked about it, she still couldn't wrap her head around the idea that the bodies were being eaten by the killers. They certainly made it appear that they were eating the corpses, but she just hadn't completely allowed herself to believe it yet. She had almost resigned herself to the idea that it was the only possibility, but she continued to try to think of new alternatives.

"They could make the same impact if they used dogs, or something, to chew up the bodies," she suggested.

Bishop replied with a laugh, "A: I think keeping a group of

bloodthirsty dogs out of the way until time to eat would be another level of difficulty to some already unbelievably difficult work. They would create more targets, more noise, and more visibility. B: We've found no signs of animals present at any of the scenes. Angry dogs drool; that's just a fact. And C: Having a group of dogs eat the bodies does not have the same impact as people who eat the bodies. On the crazy scale, it takes a ten to eat a person; having dogs do it is a five at best."

Sofia knew he was right. She just hated the possibility that they were dealing with a group of cannibals.

"Of course, if they are crazy enough to partake in cannibalism, it's a little hard to think they could be the good guys you were hoping for," Sofia said, with a sideward glance.

Bishop rolled his head back, pretending to be lost in thought as he ignored her comments.

At some point, Bishop had speculated that it could be a gang out to do some good. Albeit, in a very misdirected way. When he first voiced this opinion, Sofia gave it very little consideration before disregarding. Bishop had not given up on his idea as readily as she had, and his detective work on the case had taken a noticeable turn for the worse since making the statement.

Because he believed the cannibal killers were cleaning up the streets better than the police ever could, he was in no hurry to catch them. The only reason he hadn't completely abandoned the idea of bringing them to justice was that he understood that, if left to their own devices, it was possible they could hurt an innocent person.He felt that the best idea was to find out who they were so if they got out of line, he and Sofia could easily bring them in. He also felt there was no need to rush to figure out who they were since they were clearly not endangering the general public. Bishop had all but stated these ideas directly to Sofia during a conversation about the case, where he thinly veiled them as hypothetical questions.

When Sofia called him out on his idea, shocked at his disregard for the law she worked so hard to enforce, he quickly backpedaled, stating, "It was a hypothetical question!" While he continued to operate slower and slower, regarding the case, Sofia had been busy trying to use every outlet she had available.

Although she had used every street resource she could think of, Sofia was unable to locate a single sliver of information that matched up with what they were seeing. No one knew of any gang that was into any sort of rituals that even sounded close to what was happening in these cases. Sofia's constant contact with her street resources, and her knowledge of the street, let her know there were only a handful of gangs in Atlanta who might be behind these acts. Of that handful, there were only two, in their jurisdiction, that might have been out to commit these crimes. The two were the East Niners and Los Diablos.

Sofia had a resource well connected with the East Niners. A locally developed gang imbedded in the downtown drug trade, the East Niners was still relatively new to the scene, having only been around a few years. They had come up in the system quickly, and had made the proper connections with the other gangs in the area. This allowed them to work in certain parts of town while they built their credibility. They had been given more difficult areas to work, and had managed to make it look easy. The men behind the Niners were intelligent. They had developed several new ways of dispensing their drugs in the areas with higher police presence, and faster response times, while managing to keep from drawing the eye of the patrols. The local patrols first became alert to the Niners when Sofia had given them a heads up. She had learned of the Niners from a young man she had met years before and kept in contact with.

She met Dex at a soup kitchen in her first year as an officer and took an instant interest in his well-being. When she met him, Dex was a scrawny, malnourished boy. His big snaggle-toothed smile and poofed out afro had gotten her attention immediately, from across the room, and drew her to him instantly. Although he was bouncing around the system, moving between foster families and occasionally taking up residence in the streets, Dex was a happy boy and always very respectful. Now a teenager that had been through a great deal of struggle and sadness, the happiness still managed to show itself whenever Sofia was around. Over the years, she had maintained a relationship with him and he had turned into her most reliable and well-informed street informant. The word he had been bringing her the weeks before the Cul-De-Sac murders began was that the Niners were becoming unhappy with the arrangement between the gangs. He also mentioned their desire to begin a possible territory battle.

Since the case had escalated and Sofia had decided to check with her informants to see what the word around town was, she had spoken with Dex only once. He told her that the Niners had not been behind the murders and that all talk about a possible territory fight was on hold. They had heard of the killings and realized the connection themselves. Dex also said that everyone in the Niners had been warned of the situation. They had been told to prepare to protect themselves.

Satisfied by what she had heard about the Niners, Sofia had asked Dex about Los Diablos. Dex's answer was the same as it ever was when it came to them: he had nothing. Los Diablos was a gang developed by, and who received its orders directly from, La Eme, or the Mexican Mafia. The members were vicious and did exactly as instructed by their Mafioso leaders. They were infamous for dismembering people that posed a threat. In this case, not a single member of the gang had been killed.

Dex had told Sofia that he had nothing, so to not expect much. They were loyal to the gang, and never spoke of their dealings to outsiders. The only insight he had to offer was that he believed they were not involved in the Cul-De-Sac murders. He said they hadn't been involved in any sort of incidents with other gangs recently, and they had nothing to gain from starting a war.

Sofia thanked Dex and told him to watch out for himself until she found the killers. Although he hadn't made as compelling a case for Los Diablos as he had for the East Niners, Sofia felt like neither was involved. Dex had been right about Los Diablos having nothing to gain from a war, but she also knew something that she found equally convincing. It was true that they had left enemies dismembered, but there had never been any occasion where a member of Los Diablos had been found guilty of eating a victim. There was a very clear distinction between those things to a member of LD.

Sofia knew that in the Mexican culture, cannibalism was as taboo, if not more so, as it was in most other cultures. With the shot-callers of Los Diablos being some of the highest-ranking members of La Eme, a call for such actions would be noticed within the gang, and certainly would not be allowed to continue. The leaders of La Eme were not unintelligent. They knew that such behavior would lead to far more attention to their activities, and that was not good for business. In the end, every direction that Sofia tried to go with this case led her to a dead end. After speaking with all of her informants, every idea was eliminated, and she found herself back at square one.

"You two just getting in from Piedmont?"

Sofia sprang to attention at the question posed to her by the lieutenant. He had snuck up on her while she was lost in thought over the case.

Sofia respected the lieutenant a great deal. He had been the driving force behind some of her recent promotions and he had always pushed her along when she needed it. Coming through the force as a black man in the 70's and 80's, Lieutenant Marcus Nichols had seen enough prejudice towards minorities to make him want to make his own kind of difference within the force. He made it a personal goal to lend a hand to the most gifted officers. Nichols would do everything in his power to assist them in their personal advancement whenever he was able. He had shown a great deal of faith in Sofia's abilities. She was always eager to impress him whenever she was able, which hadn't been too often on this case. Nonetheless, she started making it a point to give him every bit of information from every crime scene. Sofia wanted to make certain that he was aware how hard they had been working on this case.

"Yes, sir! We had four victims. Three possible muggers, one—"

"Don't take this the wrong way, but I need the short version, Milena. Go, Bishop."

"Three guys killed one guy; our guys killed those guys. No evidence. No witnesses. The really short recap is we have a ton of dead people and no leads."

"And you believe this one is linked to the CDS case?"

"Absolutely. The bodies were shredded," Bishop replied.

"What's your next move?"

"Catch the bad guys, boss."

"Your immediate next move, smartass?" their boss asked Bishop gruffly.

"We're waiting for some blood samples to rule out the dude in the suit as being on our guy's tab. That's probably gonna take a bit, so we're thinking of going to check out the scenes again to make sure there's nothing we missed." Bishop motioned to Sofia, as he finished stacking his papers neatly and placing them back into the case file. The unmistakable smell of Copenhagen that was constantly on his breath wafted across the desk towards her. Revisiting the crime scenes was one of his new favorite diversions. He knew that since they found nothing time and time again, that it was a very credible way to keep her time occupied. He did this instead of allowing her to focus on the case, while still putting them in no position to make progress. Sofia hadn't seen it as so much of a diversion when he first began suggesting they revisit the crime scenes. She had been a willing participant in the review of the scenes. Now she saw his suggestions as blatant obstructions, and it was beginning to infuriate her.

"You better make sure you've gotten everything you can from those places. Anything you find at this point is going to be questionable anyway. Too much time has passed and too many people could have gone through there."

"Understood," Bishop replied.

Sofia watched the Lieutenant's white head of hair meander through the crowded room. When it disappeared into his office at the far end, she turned her attention to Bishop. "We've been over those scenes enough times for me to close my eyes and count the blades of grass at each one. There's nothing there for us to find. Whoever is behind these murders clearly took every precaution to ensure that nothing was left behind, Bishop."

Sofia's nerves had been stretched to their limit in this case. She was beginning to find it difficult to put up with Bishop's usual eccentricities, much less his flagrant stall tactics.

"You know I don't like to pull seniority, kid." Bishop sighed as he pushed his chair in neatly. "So just saddle up and let's go."

Sofia rolled her eyes at his comment.

Bishop was the king of pulling rank, and Sofia usually found it quite entertaining. It wasn't something he usually felt the need to do with her, just others around the precinct that had less time on the force than he did. If he was waiting behind someone for coffee that he had rank on, he would make as many gentle sounds as he could to get their attention. If that didn't work, he would simply say, flat out, "Pot's getting pretty low, kid. Why don't you let me get the last of it while you make a new one?" Bishop would call a man twice his age "kid" if he had seniority on him.

Thinking quickly, Sofia came up with another alternative to offer Bishop that she knew he would jump at the chance to take. "Tell you what. I could use a little break from this stuff to try to clear my head. Why don't you go check the scenes again, and I will head over and see what Lucian has found out about the latest victims?" She was actually very pleased with that idea herself. She knew that there was no chance that Bishop would pass up an opportunity to get away from the case, but also away from her, for a few hours.

"You serious?" Bishop gave her a stunned but satisfied look, and never fully stopped his stride towards the door.

"Sure. We can clear our heads for a while and get back to it in a few hours." Sofia assumed he never even heard the final part of her explanation as she heard the front door of the precinct shut behind him.

9

The morgue had become one of Sofia's favorite places to visit. She had entered rooms before where nearly all of the occupants lay filleted open before her, but none was inviting like this. She had to work to hide her excitement each time she entered the room because Lucian was there and he had a very youthful air about him. It was infectious for Sofia. She always felt light and happy when she came into his presence, even when she couldn't show it. He was her first real crush since Mateo, and it was far more intense with Lucian. Nonetheless, she always did her best to remain as professional as possible when she spoke to him in front of the others. She knew that if she acted any differently, it could ruin all the work she had put in with the other officers. Flirting was forbidden, unless they were alone.

Rounding the corner from the staircase to the hallway, she strained her ears to hear Lucian's voice echoing through the corridor. She loved to hear him muttering to himself as he worked, whenever she approached his room. Drawing closer to the morgue, she began to hear his incessant rambling right on schedule. The initial wave of smells always hit her about this time as well. The most overpowering of these was the various cleaning chemicals that sterilized Lucian's tools and tables. While a little strong, the smell always gave her a feeling of cleanliness. It was a welcome feeling when entering a room filled with death.

As she entered the room, she could see Lucian standing over the body of one of the victims from that morning; taking great care as always. He was carrying on a one-sided conversation with the corpse regarding something about his "ridiculously outdated sense of style."

Lucian's faux hawk was hidden by his favorite black scrub cap. His face was covered with an intense, almost intimidating, scowl as he focused on the cadaver that lay before him. A large empty bowl of what smelled as if it once contained chicken parmesan sat near the sterilization sink. Lucian had since moved on to the partially eaten club sandwich that sat on a nearby preparation table. Sofia no longer saw the point in mentioning Lucian's incessant eating. She had mocked him for a while once they had gotten comfortable with one another, but quickly grew tired of his sharp retorts. She imagined he had been defending his eating habits for quite some time, which had given him a response to anything she could dream of to say to him. Nowadays, she was more concerned with keeping their conversations light and flirty.

"Hey, sexy. Any news?"

Lucian looked up from his work, somewhat startled. His face seemed to soften as he realized that she had come alone. Lucian understood why she acted so professional in the field, but greatly preferred their private interactions.

"Well, hello, beautiful. Actually, I have very little for you at the moment. I honestly didn't expect to hear from you so soon. I started with the other victim first, the guy who was stabbed and didn't get eaten. I sent blood samples off to the lab so they could run 'em against what you pulled from the knife, but it looks like he's gonna be the match. The width of the blade is consistent with puncture wounds. Do you need me to hold off on him and get back to the others?" He pointed his scalpel towards the other bodies sprawled out on the other examination tables in the room.

"Nah. No real hurry on that. I just came down to see where you were at on these so I didn't have to rework the crime scenes with Bishop." She playfully knocked out a little tune on one of the empty steel tables before hopping on top of it for a seat. "Anything interesting about that guy?"

"Nah, nothing really. Looks like he was a smoker. Stomach contents were normal, looked like fast food. The cause of death was a puncture wound to his heart, and that looks like the only dent from the fight. From what I can tell, there was very little physical interaction with the exception of the stabbing. Blade punctured the heart along the right ventricle, causing his pericardium sac to fill with blood, which keeps the heart from expanding to fill itself. The only upside is that it was quick. I don't see anything to indicate that this was anything more than just a mugging gone bad. That's really more down your alley though."

Lucian lay down his scalpel and took a break from his autopsy to focus on Sofia. "So, what are you up to? It's not like you to miss a chance to work a case."

"Oh, nothing." She let loose an exasperated sigh. "You know how Bishop is being about this. He keeps trying to keep me from looking at the actual evidence by running back and forth between empty crime scenes." Sofia had spoken to Lucian on a few occasions regarding Bishop's view of the case. She had mentioned on several occasions that she felt he was intentionally taking steps to slow down their investigation.

"That dude is hilarious!" Lucian gave her a sly smile. "Did he pull rank on you again?"

"Of course, and it's not hilarious, Lucian." Sofia's voice filled with frustration.

"He kills me!" Lucian laughed. "He's the king of workin' the system, isn't he?"

Sofia's irritation at Lucian's lack of outrage at the way Bishop had been handling himself in this investigation was evident. "I don't understand you. I know how you feel about solving crimes and I know how you feel about justice, so how can you be alright with his carefree attitude on this?"

"That's where you always get off track, baby," Lucian explained. "You care too much about what he's doin'. I understand being angry about it, I just don't feel the same. I'm not about to let his relaxed attitude about this case get to me, and neither should you. Just keep doin' your thing. If and when you break this thing wide open, make a choice as to whether or not you want to share the glory. It's not as big a deal as you're making it."

It was always the same story with Lucian. He always said, "Never let others be responsible for your emotions." That was how he acted. Even with his youthful air and cultural flare, Sofia often caught glimpses of an old soul in his wisdom. He always acted exactly how he wanted regardless of what might be going on around him.

"But he's directly affecting what I can and cannot do. What you're saying is that he and I can work separately in our own way, but that's not true. He's dragging me all across town on these pointless errands and keeping me from doing anything productive!"

"Where's he at right now?"

"The crime scenes.... Again!"

"And you're in here?" Lucian prompted.

"You know what I mean!"

"No, what I know is that you're a smart girl and could figure out how to get away from him. You just haven't done that until now."

"No! He's constantly doing things to tie up my time, Lucian."

"You know I'm not going to continue to argue with you. Either you can get away from him, or you can't. You're the one with the facts. Only you know whether it's possible or not. I think you finally found out he'll go work without you, now you're just frustrated that you've let him get away with screwin' you over for so long."

"Well, I just think you're afraid to make anyone mad at you, so you just refuse to argue with them." Sofia felt frustrated that he may be right. Lucian simply let out a loud laugh.

"Wow!" Lucian hit her with a well-directed grin. "And the claws come out! The hell was that about? I think I've told you this before, Sofia, but I think that what I believe is my own business. I don't feel the need to push my beliefs on people. When I do bring them up, it's only to let people know where I stand on an issue. Then I listen and consider what they have to say in response. I'm not about arguing just to argue. I'll leave that up to everyone else in the world who thinks that they can actually win an argument."

Sofia knew that there was no point in trying to debate him. She wasn't even sure why she was trying.

"I know," she muttered, embarrassed that she had let her frustration out on him. "I guess you're probably right about me being aggravated with Bishop and this case. I can't find anything on these guys. No evidence is ever found, no witnesses ever come forward. There's nothing that can lead us anywhere. What do you think?" She asked Lucian for his thoughts in a desperate attempt for a fresh look at the case.

"Oh, no. Not me. If I'm going to lead you anywhere, it will be based on what I find here." He stood up from his resting place and approached the victim on the table. "You guys are trained to think on a whole different level than me. I can only tell you exactly what this evidence indicates, and that's the way I like it." Lucian began to look the body over as he leaned against the table.

"You know, you may need to try and step away from the case so that you can take a fresh look at it. You've said before that it's the best thing for you to do when you're stuck," Lucian suggested.

"I know, but I can't let this one go for some reason. I try to get away from it and it just keeps creeping in somehow. I even tried working an old case to try to get my mind tied up in that, but I couldn't focus on it. I just kept thinking about this." Sofia began lightly bouncing her palm off her forehead in frustration.

"I'll tell you what, lemme take you out tonight. I'm the king of mindlessness."

Sofia stopped bopping her forehead, leaving her hand placed firmly in the middle of her face. She slowly raised her eyes to bring him into view and peered at him around the edges of her wrist. She was not paying attention to his face when he made the comment, so she was unsure if he had been kidding. Whether or not he had been joking, he looked serious now, although a little comical since he was ducking down to look at her beneath his surgical light. She was now staring at him and unsure what to say.

After staring at him for what felt like an eternity in Sofia's mind, Lucian smiled softly and said, "I guess I'll take that sweet smile as a yes."

Sofia suddenly realized that in the time that she had been sitting and staring at Lucian, a soft grin had spread across her lips. She quickly looked away from him in an effort to conceal her excitement, but knew that it was obvious. The smile, the staring, and the unintelligible stammering that followed, were all very clear signs. Being the gentleman that Lucian was, he didn't give her any grief about it. He simply continued to smile back at her for a short time before slipping his mask back over his face, returning his focus to work in an effort to make her more comfortable. After a few moments of gathering her thoughts, Sofia was finally able to speak.

"Well, you don't have to take me out to take my mind off of things." As the words came out of her mouth, she screamed at herself in her mind, What are you saying!

"Oh, I'm not. I want to take you out. I have for a while." Lucian wasn't lying. He had been trying to work up his nerve to ask her for quite some time, but the timing never seemed right. Sofia was the first woman in quite some time that he felt might actually turn him down. He knew she was interested in him, but other factors had always worked their way into the equation.

"I just think that this is the perfect time to ask, because you're less likely to say no since it could potentially help you on the case," he continued.

"What makes you think I would have said no either way?"

"You just have a ton going on right now. I thought I would wait until after the case was over." He looked up at her. "But now there's this opportunity.... So I took it."

"So you've been thinking about this for a while? How much time are you spending thinking about me?" she teased him with an uneasy smile.

Each time she spoke, she heard that voice in her head screaming for her to stop, but it was useless. She felt consumed with awkwardness and completely out of her comfort zone. The very limited experience she had consisted of boys and men who approached her, but she had no interest in dating any of them, with the exception of Mateo. She was just as awkward about it back then. She hadn't spent the years perfecting flirting that others had, which stunted her growth in the area. In every situation since her high-school crush, she was perfectly capable of keeping her cool as she shot men down. The three experiences she had allowed since finishing college hadn't been with men she was so enamored by. Those interactions had done nothing in the way of preparing her for what she would do if confronted with someone she actually found interesting.

Sofia didn't even feel like she knew how to stand normally, and kept twisting her toes into the ground like a child. In an effort to stop her toe twisting, she began moving around the room, which produced a new nervous twitch. As she moved about, she began touching anything that she could reach and either stroking it or playing with it in some way. Everything that she was doing now felt very uncoordinated and strange. She was keenly aware that it looked even worse than it felt to her.

Realizing how awkward things could become if he didn't allow her an easy out, Lucian continued to keep his eyes down and focused on his work. His efforts paid off as they effectively kept him from seeing Sofia make a complete fool of herself.

Sofia finally regained some level of composure when she realized that Lucian's averted eyes weren't due to his concentration on his work, but that he was keeping himself occupied in order to keep from watching the train wreck that was taking place. She snapped herself out of the awkward meandering and tried to regain a tiny bit of dignity. She straightened up and cleared her throat.

“What I meant was, that is very nice of you and I would love to.”

Lucian finally seemed comfortable enough to take his eyes off the victim’s intestines. Pulling down his mask to expose a comforting smile, Lucian continued trying to ease Sofia’s nerves. “Good deal. I’ll swing by and grab you at your place, if that’s cool. Does six o’clock work for you?”

“Perfect,” Sofia responded quickly. She was now eager to leave the room. Hopefully, she’d leave behind the embarrassment she now felt.

“Just text me with your address, when you get a chance. I can’t really write right now.” He explained by holding up his bloody, gloved hands.

Still mortified from the scene she had just put on in front of him, Sofia became completely focused on keeping her answers as brief as possible to keep from recreating that moment.

“I’ll see you tonight.” They politely each gave one another a nod of agreement before Sofia turned to leave.

“And Sofia?” Lucian faced her as she turned to leave.

“Yes?”

“Don’t sweat it,” he said, with a wink. Lucian left his comment vague in order to keep Sofia from feeling even more embarrassed about the way she had just reacted to the situation. It had worked. A tight-lipped smirk slid up the corner of Sofia’s lips as she turned to leave once more.

Sofia wanted so badly to skip gleefully out of the morgue, which she actually would have done had she not allowed herself to act like such a child only moments ago. She did allow herself to burst through the swinging double doors that led into the hallway, though. Something had to be done in order to release some of her excitement.

10

Upon returning to her desk, Sofia did everything that she could to try and get some work done. She was able to get some paperwork taken care of which was normally something that she would never even bother with until a job was closed, but she couldn't concentrate enough to do anything else. Going through pages of documents, she filled in her name, badge number, and any other generic information that she could as she began creating a mental checklist of things she needed to do in order to get home and ready by six o'clock. This went on for the remainder of the day.

Upon returning to her desk, Sofia did everything that she could to try to get some work done. She was able to get some paperwork taken care of, which was normally something that she would never even bother with until a case was closed. However, she couldn't concentrate enough to do anything else. Going through pages of documents, she filled in her name, badge number, and any other generic information that she could. She began creating a mental checklist of things she needed to do in order to get home and ready by six o'clock. This went on for the remainder of the day.

Sofia hardly noticed when Bishop finally returned from whatever ridiculous escapade he had gone on without her. He, on the other hand, was paying plenty of attention to how much busy work Sofia was doing.

"What are you doing?" He looked puzzled as he passed in front of her desk.

Sofia snapped her head up at him, and looked almost shocked to see him. She had been running through all of the possibilities in her mind that the night could hold. She had been focusing so much on them that she had all but forgotten where she was.

"Oh, you're back! Sorry, I was just kind of zoned in on this stuff, I guess." Sofia returned to her paperwork, not wanting to miss a second of mental preparation for her date.

"What case are you doing that for? Did you close something today?" Bishop knew all too well what Sofia's routine was, and found her current actions highly peculiar.

"Oh, nothing. I mean, no. I mean, it's not for anything in particular. No. I didn't close anything. I was just trying to get ahead. I'm just trying to get my head straight so we can figure this thing out." This was entirely true, although not her main reason for doing the ridiculous task.

Bishop remained bewildered by Sofia's break from her usual routine, but decided to let it go since she wasn't hounding him about where he had gone or what they could do next to further the case. Watching her out of the corner of his eye, Bishop began quietly checking his desk to see if anything was out of place. The only explanation that he could think of for Sofia's odd behavior was that she was about to play a practical joke on him and was trying not to alert him to what was about to happen. After searching every possible place that could have been sabotaged, Bishop decided to check with one of the other detectives to see what information he could come up with. Walking over to Detective Welsh's desk, Bishop sat down on the edge with his back facing Sofia.

"Hey," Bishop muttered in greeting, with a nod, interrupting the middle-aged detective's review of one of his current case files. The deep, permanent creases in Welsh's face intensified as his brow furrowed into his normal scowl. He was quick- tempered, especially when interrupted. Bishop, however, had a bad habit of not caring about that sort of thing, especially when he outweighed Welsh by thirty pounds.

"What?" Welsh asked angrily, shaking his head a bit to make his aggravation clear.

"Any idea what she's up to?" Bishop asked, nodding his head

back towards Sofia's desk, and completely disregarding Welsh's attempts to drive him off.

"Looks like she's working, Bishop—just like I was trying to do. Maybe you should try it," he replied gruffly. "It's funny how much detective work you want to do when it comes to seeing what your partner is up to, but how little you want to do on your cases."

Continuing to ignore Welsh's frustrated comments, Bishop's questioning of Sofia's actions persisted.

"She's doin' busy work. She never does busy work when we're workin' a case like this. How long has she been at it?"

"I don't know, ever since she got back a little while ago, I guess. Why don't you just go ask her?" Detective Welsh replied, with an exasperated sigh, before turning his back to Bishop entirely. He attempted to return to his own work.

Bishop took a second to think about where she would have gone and remembered what she had said before he left. He couldn't help but chuckle to himself as he put everything together. Bishop nearly burst out in laughter as he watched Sofia mindlessly filling out needless paperwork. He could tell that she was nervous, but rather than pester her and possibly get her started on something that might keep him there late, he just went back to his desk and found his own project to waste time on. The two worked quietly for the remainder of the day. Sofia focused on her mindless busy work and worrying about her evening. Bishop dodged the higher-ups and anyone else that might question why the two weren't out canvassing scenes and searching for clues. Finally, the day came to an uneventful close. Bishop shook Sofia from her trance-like state with a booming 'good night' as he passed her desk. As Bishop left the station, Sofia was still looking around the room as if she had just awoken from a deep sleep. As she finally became aware of her surroundings, she snatched up her belongings and made her way home.

11

Sofia maxed out with adrenaline and excitement. She felt as though she had been pounding energy drinks all day as she prepared for her date with Lucian. The anxiety crawled through her skin like a million tiny spiders. It had been years since she had actually gone out on dates, and those hadn't gone well.

After her brief dating experience with Mateo, Sofia focused much more on her studies and her extracurricular activities, and made no time for dating. She went to her proms with dates, but since they were with groups of other people and had always ended with a giant party, she had never felt that they were representative of what a real date was like. Since high school, Sofia had gone on only three dates, and each one was its own level of terrible.

The first date she went on out of the academy was the one she considered to be the first of her adult life. Several times, men asked her on dates while she was in college and the academy. Sofia never felt like taking the time away from her studies to go out. She was still deciding whether to follow her parents south, when she accepted a date invitation from a charming young man with whom she had attended college. He had been after her for months prior to her graduation, and Sofia felt good around him.

Her low expectations were still not met. The majority of the date took place at a noisy bar, where he proceeded to drink so heavily Sofia had to take him to the hospital before calling it a night and heading home alone. His intoxicated state being as debilitating as it was, the drunken Casanova still managed to make several half-coherent attempts at fondling her during the drive to the hospital. Upon arriving at the hospital, alcohol poisoning and the broken wrist Sofia had given him as a parting gift for his unwanted advances, were his diagnoses.

Her second dating experience occurred several months after the incident with the drunk. She had decided that moving to Atlanta to be near her parents would be a nice change. Sofia immediately began attending the Police Academy upon her arrival. During her training there, she met another cadet who had just moved down from Pennsylvania. They decided to get together to check out the town together. He managed to do a little better with his selection of locations, taking her to a quaint, undiscovered café that he said a friend had suggested to him. Although she expected their discussions to include something about getting used to the cultural differences they each experienced since moving south, the dinner conversation revolved around their experience at the Academy, and little more. At the end of the date, Sofia lowered her guard and agreed to look at his apartment. Although well-versed in the enforcement of the law, and identifying predators, she had never had personal experience with one.

After looking around his shabby bachelor's pad, Sofia decided to make her exit. Being that she hadn't been in the situation often, she felt a goodnight kiss was expected, so she granted him one. Sofia's attempt at a sweet, soft, goodnight kiss turned into a sloppy, one-sided, face-rape that she attempted to endure. When he started trying to remove her clothes, Sofia tried to pull away from him, but he pulled her back tightly and became more aggressive. Sofia's repeated warnings that she was not interested in him went unheeded as he pushed her towards his couch.

Clearly unaware of Sofia's years of extracurricular study and proficiency in self-defense, he quickly ended up face down in his cheap, dirty carpet. Her knee sat firm in his spine after a solid knee to his groin. Sofia pounced on his back and placed him in a tight chokehold as she pulled his arm halfway up his back. After some not-so-gentle coaxing, Sofia got him to admit that he had been completely out of line and recorded his statements on a mini recorder she kept in her purse at all times. After playing it back for him, she informed him that he would keep any comments regarding her or their date respectful and truthful. If he did not obey, she would gladly take the recording to his superiors. The two were assigned to different precincts, and Sofia made sure to check in with his fellow officers from time to time to see what was being said. She was surprised to hear that none of them had ever even heard him mention her name.

Her third, and final, attempt at dating happened a few months after meeting Bishop, but well after his protective instincts for her had taken over. She had met a cousin of his, named Denny. When they stopped by his house for Bishop to drop something off, he asked her out. They went out a few days later, but Bishop followed them in a patrol car to each location. He used the spotlight anytime they were getting "too comfortable." The siren sporadically sounded to interrupt any conversation where Sofia was reacting positively. A fiasco from the start, they called it an early evening and agreed to try another time. The next day, Denny called Sofia to tell her that he was sorry, but he couldn't continue to see her. He and Bishop were very close, and he thought it would be too weird for her partner to see them together. Sofia agreed, and they ended things.

Those three occasions had created a serious aversion to the dating scene. Nevertheless, she felt compelled to look past that for a chance with Lucian. Luckily, she picked up several hints during her unbelievably uncomfortable interaction with Lucian in the morgue. They let her know that he was very excited about their date, too. There were so many things that were coming together to make this potentially the greatest date of Sofia's life to this point. Although, the bar was not set very high.

The most obvious and overwhelming difference between her previous experiences was how attracted she was to Lucian. She had never really dated a man with whom she was truly smitten. Mateo would have been the closest, but that was on such a juvenile level. Besides, she had never really gone on a date with him; not to mention that she didn't find him nearly as attractive as Lucian. For that matter, she couldn't even remember a time when she had been this attracted to a man, period. This was a fact that Sofia had wondered about on several occasions during their casual conversations around various crime scenes and during her visits to the morgue. That unknown factor that she still couldn't quite pinpoint pushed her infatuation with him.

Lucian's classic good looks were undeniable, but she could never figure out why it was such an overpowering connection that she felt to him. The looks were there, but his physique wasn't what she normally would have been drawn to. The reasoning she always gave was that, while he may have fallen short in an area or two, his charm and confidence were off the charts, which more than compensated for any deficiency. There was also a great deal to be said for how wonderful Sofia felt when she was with him. Lucian was able to take her mind away from work, which was completely out of character for her. He made her feel like a different person.

Sofia had always been driven to succeed at her profession. It brought her great joy to enforce the law and make it safe for decent people to live. But the way that she felt with Lucian was different. He was fun and exciting. He had a way of saying things that made even the most ridiculously boring activity sound energized. He had a brand of humor that everyone enjoyed, and Sofia was no exception. She knew several of the men on the force that would find a reason to go see Lucian when they were having a rough day, or if the job had gotten to them. His humor, mixed with his wild bachelor lifestyle, always did the trick. He was always able to bring their spirits up.

One thing that Sofia found to be most impressive was Lucian's outlook on life. It remained consistently upbeat and positive, even though he faced so much death on a daily basis. He was the most fun-loving and optimistic person she knew. Whenever he faced a difficult time or had a run of bad luck, he would somehow turn it into a positive. He did so by claiming that it was an opportunity for him to learn from his mistake or situation. He didn't seem to be afraid of anything and found joy in everything. The only time that she ever saw him without a smile on his face was when he was meticulously dissecting a victim in search of evidence.

In most cases, he was able to observe a body faster and more closely than even the most veteran examiners. However, in some of the more violent and heinous cases, she had seen him focus on a single body or case for days on end. He had a way of taking care of his victims that showed how much he cared about finding those responsible for their deaths as much as Sofia did.

All of these factors were coming together to create the extreme levels of angst that she was struggling with. Oddly enough, even though she was struggling with her anxiety, she felt confident that this night was going to go wonderfully. She had attempted to manage some of her nervousness by downplaying the likelihood that this would become anything serious due to Lucian's reputation as a ladies' man.

Lucian regularly had women that he had dated coming around the office to see him, which was shocking, considering where he worked. Sofia would see gorgeous women come in the precinct and instantly knew whether or not they were looking for Lucian. While the spectrum of women that came looking for Lucian was vast, ranging from very posh, extravagant women, to successful businesswomen, to twenty-something club girls, they all fit into the "perfect 10" category for the men of the office. What made it clear they were there for Lucian was that they, without fail, would overlook every man in the room as they made their way towards the morgue.

The men around the office loved to talk about, and speculate, about Lucian's sex life far more than Lucian himself did. They would constantly compare his conquests as if they were playing a game. Any time the subject came up, one of the men would mention a name, description, or sometimes just a date that one of the girls had come by, and the other men would try to make a comparable selection. All the men within earshot would start grunting, and smiling, and laughing, as if they had been involved in some way. They did the same routine every time a name was entered.

The most interesting thing to Sofia about the women that came to see him was not their physical appearance, which was always the most impressive thing to the men around the station. The fact that Lucian had been with so many women, and seemed to remain on such good terms with all of them, seemed impossible. It was something that always struck Sofia as odd when she first began working at the precinct, but had now become quite common to her. The girls would come to see him, sometimes staying for an hour or more to talk to him. They would blaze a path to his door, turning the head of every male officer in the building as they did so. They would often leave while reapplying makeup or primping their hair, leading the men in the office to speculate about the activities that had just occurred. It was funny to Sofia that so many of the women seemed completely oblivious to the fact that they were in a morgue, although in some cases it was completely believable that they had no idea where they were.

On more than one occasion, she had witnessed two (and on one occasion, three) girls arrive together and leave together. Each seemed to have her own encounter with Lucian, and yet none of them appeared to be jealous of the others. One time, Lucian caught Sofia making an odd face as the girls passed her while leaving the morgue. He vaguely addressed the situation by stating, "Oh, they're all roommates." She hadn't inquired further, and he hadn't offered any more explanation. Sofia had accidently let slip what Lucian had said in their brief exchange about the girls being roommates, and the men ran with that information. Their stories about Lucian became wilder after that.

They always implied that the girls had been involved in some sort of group sex situation with Lucian, or that he had talked them into some "girl-on-girl action." The stories always made Lucian sound so seedy, and conniving, that Sofia would usually walk away whenever the others began telling them. She had spent more time with Lucian one-on-one than any of them and couldn't bring herself to believe he was the man they made him out to be. However, Sofia had to admit his situation was intriguing. The idea that Lucian was even half as sexually active as her fellow officers made him out to be was exciting to her on some level, and terrifying on another.

Sofia's virginity had never been something she had to talk about with people. While she assumed everyone knew she had remained a virgin, people actually assumed just the opposite. Anyone who saw Sofia instantly pegged her as a sexual goddess because of her exquisite body and gorgeous looks. It was a foregone conclusion with everyone that she was a phenomenal lover based solely on her looks and ethnicity. She knew the stereotypes about Latin lovers. She just thought people knew she had put more effort into her studies than into sex.

Now, she faced the possibility of losing her virginity to a man with such a sexual pedigree that he was the envy of every man she knew. It was very intriguing. However, every time she considered how awkward or unsatisfying she might be to him, she would cringe and become unbelievably uncomfortable. Each time it happened, she shook her head quickly and told herself out loud, "Not thinking about that!" As the time for Lucian's arrival drew closer, she had to tell herself more and more often not to think about it.

Given the amount of anxiety Sofia had built up over the event as she scrutinized every detail throughout the day, she remained incredibly excited about their date. Her only fear was that, in the event that something went wrong, things between Lucian and her may become strained and cause things at work to become difficult. She had considered this possibility for the better part of the past few months as her infatuation with Lucian grew. She had told herself for some time that they were better off keeping things professional, but she couldn't stop playing out different scenarios in her head where they were together. As it turned out, it was the constant parade of women who dropped in to see Lucian, which changed Sofia's mind. She figured that if he was able to maintain contact with so many of the women he had dated, it would be possible for her to continue working with him if things didn't go as well as planned. In the back of her mind, Sofia knew the chances of her reacting well to being rejected weren't good. She also knew she wanted to date Lucian really badly.

12

Sofia began thinking about what to wear since the second she nervously accepted Lucian's dinner invitation. She finally decided to go all out and wear a dress that made her feel as exciting as Lucian did. It was a beautiful, sexy, feminine dress, which was not at all her style. She had managed to talk herself into purchasing it by swearing she would one day use it for some sort of undercover work. She didn't know when she would be doing any or whether she would be doing any, she just knew that she was going to buy that dress. Sofia realized the second she put the dress on that she was going to buy it because it would make her feel like a woman. She saw it and knew that wearing a dress like that would make her look and feel amazing. That dress would make people look at her in a different way than she had allowed anyone to look at her in quite some time.

Growing up, she had never fully embraced her good looks. She had certainly taken advantage of them for a short time in her youth, but she hadn't ever gone out of her way to learn how to enhance her looks. She had learned the basics of using makeup, but after the incident with Mateo, she gave up on such pursuits in order to spend more time on her studies. Her natural beauty was always present, but she stopped putting in extra time to accentuate it. Blue jeans and t-shirts were the dominant fashion trends throughout the scrapbook of her life. Her look had been one of the easiest ways that she could go about keeping from attracting too much attention from boys, which left her with even more time to study.

he had done what she could to mask her natural beauty at times, which often proved to be a difficult task, but tonight was different. Tonight, she wanted Lucian to see just how enchanting she could truly look. Her only concern was that she wasn't extremely comfortable wearing makeup, or its application. Rcalizing she could do far more damage by trying to overdo, she decided it was best to stick with the basics she was comfortable with, and hope for the best.

Just as Sofia finished sliding her dress into place and adjusting all of her voluptuous parts, there was a gentle knock at the door. From the instant that his knuckles made contact with the metal of the door, she began to tingle with excitement. She couldn't help but smile as she made her way through her apartment towards the door. She tried to control herself, and made every attempt to force her face to stop making a corny little half-grin, but it was futile. Not wanting a replay of her earlier embarrassment in the morgue, she gave in and allowed her brightest smile to take over her face.

She swung the door open, and there he stood. He was wearing a pair of designer jeans with a tailored blue silk button up with the cuffs rolled once. His hair was gelled up in his faux-hawk. His head was down, as he had been staring at his two-tone blue and black dress shoes while he waited for her to answer. He looked up at her with his perfect smile, his eyes lighting up as she came into his view.

"Wow, you look insane! That dress looks amazing on you." He gave a wide smile as he leaned in, giving her a gentle hug. "And damn do you look nice with so little makeup!" Sofia's heart fluttered as Lucian successfully eliminated her biggest concern.

"Well, thank you. You look great, too."

"Are you ready to get going or do you need a minute?"

"No, I'm ready. We can get going." She closed the door behind them as she moved out into the hallway. As they headed down the hall towards the elevator, Sofia stopped abruptly and began searching her purse.

"I just need to head back really quick. I need to grab my gun." Sofia had not left her apartment without her weapon since the time she received it in the academy. "I'd hate to think of what might happen if we ran into the cannibal gang and I didn't have it."

"How about you leave it behind? You just relax, and trust that we're going to have a good time, and that we won't need your gun. I promise I'll take care of you. You just need to trust me." Not wanting to make him think that she didn't trust him to take care of her, and feeling pretty confident in her hand-to-hand skills, Sofia opted to move ahead instead of going back to her apartment.

"And let's try and keep the shop talk to minimum tonight. It's gonna be impossible for me to keep your mind off of things if you keep talking about them." He smiled as he extended his hand for her to hold. Sofia nodded in agreement, as she interlaced her fingers with his and they continued down the hall.

As they approached the opening for the elevator, Lucian reached out and thumbed the button. Sofia was becoming increasingly more uncomfortable about not having her gun with her, and looked back over her shoulder to her apartment door. Lucian, noticing her tension, gently caressed her chin and guided her eyes to his, saying, "I promise you'll be all right. You don't need to be nervous. We're going to have a great night." Lucian held her face there for a moment as they gazed into one another's eyes. He slowly leaned in and gave her a short, sweet, soft kiss. As their lips parted, the elevator arrived and their evening began.

13

"Is it cool if we walk?" Lucian asked as they stepped out into the warm evening air. "I figured it'd be a good time for us to talk a bit. Plus, I'm not a big fan of driving." He scrunched up his nose a little at the very thought of the idea. "Too many people out there that should never even be allowed to look at a car, but they're out there driving like jackasses."

"I don't mind. It's a nice night for it."

"I did tell you how good you look tonight, right? You really do look great. I feel a little underdressed."

Sofia felt her cheeks begin to glow brightly. She just smiled back at him. "Thank you," she said shyly, "You look great, too. Although, I imagine you can probably fit in anywhere you go no matter how you dress."

"Well, that's true," he said unabashedly. "It's pretty easy for any guy, I guess, assuming he puts some level of effort into it. If I put on a pair of nice shoes and my shirt is ironed, I'm pretty much good-to-go for every occasion."

"Pants probably help."

"Well…I guess that really depends on the scene." He raised his eyebrows at her humorously.

"You go to a lot of places where pants aren't a requirement, huh?"

Lucian pretended to think it over for a moment before replying, "Nah. I suppose not. You're right. Nice shoes, ironed shirt, and some form of lower body cover, and I'm on point for any party."

"Well, that, and that pretty boy smile of yours," she said, coaxing a confident smile from Lucian.

"You like the smile, huh?" He pointed to his mouth. "This business right here took some work, you know? Back in high school, my smile was busted. It was all, awkward and forced, way too toothy at first, then no teeth at all. Embarrassing as it is to admit, I used to practice smiling in the mirror to try to get it right. This ain't natural." He flippantly pointed again, as he flashed his beautiful smile.

"Oh, I'm sure," Sofia replied sarcastically. "I doubt there was ever a time when you weren't adorable."

"Oh you better believe it. I was a big ol' nerd in high school."

Sofia made a strange face at him, unable to envision him as anything but the most popular person in any situation.

"I still am, actually. I just do a better job of hiding it than most. Back then, I was very advanced in terms of height and stuff. I was just never drawn to sports all that much, so I didn't really bulk up. I was good at sports. I just didn't feel the need to play them. My mind was more geared towards science. It didn't help that I was unbelievably socially awkward. Damn near socially incompetent. I really think that's the best way to be, anyway. I mean, who wants to peak in high school, right?" He chuckled. "Plus it pushed me into my studies since I wasn't wasting my time with ridiculous extracurricular activities."

"I agree with that, about peaking in high school. I was pretty much the same way. One thing I find very hard to believe, though. I find it almost impossible to believe that you weren't cute in high school. I mean, you look like you could still pass for a high school kid now. I'm definitely going to need some visual evidence."

"Good luck with that. Let me know what you come across. Don't be surprised when you don't find anything. I may have been the only person you'll ever meet that successfully dodged every possible picture in high school. You should just take my word on that. I was really good about not letting people get pictures of me." Lucian had a very pleased look on his face as he recounted some of the moments of his youth.

"What's with the smile?"

"Ahh, you know, memories from back in the day. Good times."

"So high school wasn't the hell for you that it was for so many other kids that weren't all that popular?"

"Well, I was a nerd, but I wasn't really all that unpopular. My friends and I didn't really get picked on all that much, except for like, ninth grade. Even then, we actually did a pretty good job of sticking together and staying off the radar of the older kids and the bullies. Made us more difficult to attack. It's a popular method in the animal kingdom, you know. Like with antelope. The way they travel in large herds for protection from lions. The size of the herd acts as a natural deterrent to attackers, and when the herd is attacked, the percentage of survival for each of the members goes up. Plus, we weren't afraid to bite back, you know. We could handle ourselves if we really had to. Anyway, that only lasted for about a year. Once we got to sophomore year, we all started filling out pretty good. When that happened, people just kind of backed off."

"What were your friends like?"

"We were all pretty similar. We were into games and science stuff. There was me, Matt, Dave, Pat, Tommy. That was our core group. We always had a few other people around. Matt was a real outdoorsy, woodsy kind of guy. Dave was really bright, and artistic as hell. Pat was off-the-charts smart. You couldn't beat that kid when it came to anything having to do with thinking. Scrabble? Trivia? Whatever it was, he was gonna beat ya. Tommy was a combination of everyone else really, just probably nicer than any of us. One of the sweetest guys ever. Everyone really had lots of different people they hung out with. We just always ended up together. The times we spent together outside of school were some of the best times I can remember."

"Well that's nice to hear. You hardly ever hear about people enjoying their time in school anymore. Kids are so caught up in cliques and drama that they forget that it's the only time they will ever have so little responsibility. Do you ever talk to them?"

"We try, but it's tough. Tommy and Matt moved off. They both got married and have families. Dave is off trying a little bit of everything. Pat's probably curing cancer or something," Lucian said, with a chuckle. "How about you? Did you realize how great those times were, or was it all drama and cliques?" he prodded.

"Well, for me it was more responsibility than most. I did have a good time though. Probably not as many as you, but some definite good times. So where are we headed?" Sofia asked.

"I was thinking we could go catch a flick." As quickly as she could process the words, her stomach began to tighten. Things had started out so well and now he was going to drag her to some ridiculous movie where they would sit in silence for hours? Was this to be the bulk of the evening's plan? Why had she gone out of her way to get dressed up for this? Sofia considered going back to change clothes for some more appropriate attire as she slowly stopped walking and began looking back in the direction of her apartment. Lucian continued walking past her a few feet before turning back to her, his face baring a mischievous grin.

"Totally kidding!" He raised his hands in defense. "You look like you're ready to knock the crap outta me." She realized that she must have been showing her displeasure more than she thought. Sofia tried to mask her surprise as best she could.

"No!" She shot an embarrassed smile up at him as she began walking again, giving him a gentle shove as she passed. "Jerk," she exclaimed softly as Lucian began to laugh. "Stop it. You're not as funny as you think you are," she said playfully.

"Sure I am!" he proclaimed. "It was funny to me, and that's what's really important."

Sofia let out a sigh of relief as the tension that had begun to build in her neck now released. There was still some hope that the date would go as well as she had imagined.

"I was actually thinking of heading over to the Fernbank Museum for martinis. How does that sound? I know it's a bit of a hike, and you're dressed a little too amazing for a train ride, but I think we'll make it. Trust me, it's well worth it."

"Much better, actually. I don't mean that to sound ugly, but the movie thing set the bar pretty low."

He laughed. "I know. I thought you might at least get a little kick out of it. I guess not. Made me laugh, anyways."

"Well, I guess it's funny now, just not so much a minute ago." The two continued on, each laughing a little to themselves as they thought about Sofia's reaction.

"So, I guess questions about what you do in your free time are a little unnecessary," Lucian said jokingly.

"Why do you say that?"

"Well, I've seen how much time you spend at work, and how many times you've come in after a day off with a better idea of what you should be doing in a specific case. I assume that means that any time you spend away from work is spent thinking about work, if not actually doing work."

Sofia had never really thought about how little time she spent not doing work.

"Well, I guess that when you love what you do, it's really not an issue to just keep doing it when you aren't getting paid for it. I really love making things safer. I like that I'm spending my time making the world a safer place for the people I care about. If you think about it, I really don't spend as much time working as I do indulging in my favorite past time. The only part of it that I consider work is when I'm filling out paperwork. I even get into that a little sometimes. It's a way for me to relive solving the case."

That was the first time that she had ever thought of her job in that way before. She always just thought that she took her job very seriously, but it really was the thing that she enjoyed the most. She didn't feel that she was missing out on anything by having such a lack of a personal social life. What she truly enjoyed, and wanted to do at all times, was make the world a better place.

"I mean, even with the trouble we're having with this cannibal gang, I enjoy the chase. All of the trouble we are having right now is just going to make it that much sweeter when they slip up and we catch them. Which reminds me, I thought of something today I meant to ask..." Glancing up at Lucian as she spoke, she realized she had allowed herself to meander into a conversation about work. "Oh, right. Sorry."

"It's cool. I know you can't help but go back to it. I was just hopin' I could keep your mind off it for a little while."

"Just interrupt me when I start doing it, or make a noise or something."

"Does that sound like me? Interrupting, makin' some rude ass noise to stop you from talkin'? Nah, I ain't doin' all that. You talk, I'll listen. If I can't get your attention off dead people, I'm not a very good date anyway." In typical Lucian form, he had made something she had done seem like something he was responsible for. His comments also successfully caused Sofia to make a conscious decision to resist the urge to talk about the case for the remainder of the night.

14

"You're a nerd, too. You know that, right?" Lucian mocked Sofia after a few seconds of silence.

"I'm not a nerd!" she whimpered, sticking out her bottom lip as she pouted momentarily at his observation.

"Sure you are, but don't get so upset. It's not a bad thing to be," Lucian said.

Sofia replied, "I know that, but I'm not a nerd. If anything, I'm more of a jock."

"First of all, ew. Never say that again. The connotations that go with being a jock are so much worse than being a nerd. Second, no one said the two were mutually exclusive. You're very athletic, but nothing like a jock. Jocks are mean, and you are anything but that."

"Fine," she partially agreed, "I'm not a jock. But I'm definitely not a nerd."

"Do you read a lot?"

"Well, yeah. But mostly just about work-related stuff."

"But other people in your line of work don't read that stuff and they still do fine, right?"

"That's true I guess…."

"And you're pretty well-educated, right? Didn't you mention something about being in the top of your class and catching up in school really quickly, even though you were way behind when you got here?

"That was just…necessary."

"So, when we take out the factors like the fact that you're athletic and gorgeous, we're left with: you felt socially awkward in high school; you skipped several grades and made excellent marks in school; and you have excelled in your chosen field through additional, and completely voluntary, research?"

"I'm not a nerd," she whimpered, sticking out her bottom lip.

"You're a huge nerd!"

"I'm such a nerd…" she conceded, lowering her head. Lucian wrapped his arm around her as he laughed loudly, which brought the smile back to her face instantly.

The two turned the corner and entered the MARTA station and started towards the escalators that took them to the trains.

"So who is it that you're protecting?" Lucian asked, as they waited for the train to arrive.

"What do you mean?" She turned her attention from watching a group of young girls who were having an overly loud conversation nearby. "I mean, I'm protecting everyone that the person that I arrest would have hurt in the future, I suppose."

"No. You said you are protecting the people that you care about. Is that your parents, or siblings, or what?"

"Um, I don't really know. I guess I didn't really mean it like that. I mean, I'm an only child, and I've never really known any cousins or other relatives. But, yes, I suppose I did start out with my parents in mind. They had a very hard life when we lived in Colombia. We always lived in fear of what might happen if we didn't do as we were told by the men who ran our village. When we came to the United States, I expected things to be much different and I worked to make sure I was doing my part to make that hold true."

"Are you saying things aren't better here?"

"No, it's very different here. In so many ways, it is better, but I can see similarities. We moved to an area filled with immigrants who had survived similar experiences to ours. Some of those immigrants saw the new conditions as a time for them to start their own version of what we had all already experienced. Although they would never have tried to enslave us the way that the drug lords in Colombia had, they did form gangs that tried to run our neighborhood. While they were unable to terrorize us the way we had been in our villages, they were still able to impact our lives and force us to do things we didn't want to. I knew at a very early age that I wanted to make my neighborhood a safe place for my parents. I wanted to make their lives better because they deserved some happiness after so much suffering. So, I started doing everything that I could to learn about becoming a great police officer."

Lucian listened intently as she continued.

"I read a number of books on how to correctly inspect a crime scene as well as how to conduct an interrogation. I saw the police officers as heroes. They actually made me feel safe. They would come to our schools, talk to us in the streets, and ask how we were doing. They cared about our safety, and they didn't have to. Sure, they were paid to do it, but they chose to step into harm's way to keep people they didn't know safe. From what I grew up with when I was very young, you don't know how different that was. I thought that was the most amazing thing I had ever seen. I already knew I wanted to enforce the law, but those officers showed me how honorable the profession could be. So, I devoted my time to learning how I could become a great police officer so that I could make a difference."

Sofia stopped. She realized that she hadn't shared that much personal information with anyone in her entire life, and yet it had come out so easily with Lucian. She always kept her personal life very personal. She always thought that sharing information like that might show a weakness to someone, and she never wanted anyone to see a weakness in her.

As she focused on how readily she had offered up some of her most personal thoughts, the train approached. With a gust of wind that blew her flimsy dress back tight against her body, the train eased to a halt and everyone boarded. The pair found a few adjoining seats, and prepared for their ride.

"Okay! So, I just unloaded an awful lot of info on you there. Sorry about that." Sofia uncomfortably thought back to their previous conversation.

"Don't be silly. Why do you think I wanted to walk? Besides hating to drive, I mean. I'm very interested in knowing about you. I love hearing about that sort of stuff. How are we ever going to be a couple if we don't know things like that about each other?"

Sofia couldn't stop herself from smiling. "Couple, huh? So you're not hoping to make me one of your little girlfriends that stop by the office to flirt with you all of the time?"

Were it possible, she would have snatched those words from the sky and stomped them out before they could reach his ears. The corners of her smile began to drop slowly as she realized that she might have just sent their evening into a blistering nosedive. Lucian raised one eyebrow and looked at her with a smug little smile.

"Bold comment!" Lucian declared with a laugh. "But, I think you know you're different than those girls. They just weren't what I was looking for. Without getting into it too much, I enjoyed spending time with them but they weren't in the same place that I am. I've met plenty of really sweet girls, and things always end well when they realize that I sincerely enjoyed my time with them. I'm looking for more than just night after night of going out and partying. I guess I'm growing up."

Sofia wanted to breathe deeply so she could let go of the nervous knots that she had worked up in the muscles of her stomach after her comment. Not only had it not ruined their evening, it successfully caused Lucian to answer some lingering questions that she had about all of the girls that she had seen visiting him. She had wondered how she was going to get over that, or how to bring up such a matter without sounding jealous, but she had done it. Although completely by accident, she had resolved one of her major concerns with only a few seconds of discomfort.

With the question of his philandering addressed to her satisfaction, Sofia now faced a new issue. Lucian was becoming too good to be true and she had to fight the urge to start looking for his hidden flaws. As the thought crossed her mind, Sofia dismissed the idea immediately. That wasn't something she was going to allow to happen. She had never felt so comfortable around another person, and she refused to let herself sabotage something so enjoyable. Lucian was wonderful. He was fun and funny, exciting, smart, kind, and gorgeous. Sofia knew that she couldn't allow herself to begin looking for flaws. Any time that she allowed herself to do so, it was a guarantee that she would find one, and she really didn't want to find one. Instead, she decided she would focus on all of the things that he was doing so right that made her think he was the most interesting and enchanting man she had ever met.

15

As they reached the end of the long walkway that wound between the fields of luscious green grass that led to the museum, Lucian walked ahead and held the door for Sofia. As they entered, he gently guided her by the small of her back over to the dining area. The inside of the museum was immaculate and the dining area that had been set was very elegant. The tables were set beneath the bones of a variety of historical creatures, the most impressive of which were the fully restored skeletons of numerous dinosaurs. As she looked at the giant jaws of the beast, her mind drifted back to the bodies in the Cul-De-Sac Case. Quickly, she banished the thought from her mind as she continued to take in the scenery.

A live pianist peppered the room with delicate melodies from afar, and the low hum of conversation filled the air. Marbled rose linens covered the intimately arranged tables. Terra-cotta colored brick walls surrounded them, leading to a glass ceiling that allowed for a magnificent view of what had turned into a beautiful evening, without a cloud in the sky. The walls had numerous windows of reoccurring patterns that looked out onto the overwhelmingly luxurious grounds. The bottom row was a series of arched doorways. Stacked four feet above them lay the second row of windows, which were roughly six-foot tall rectangles. The uppermost window levels were sets of circles, broken up by a single rectangle, matching those on the row before it.

The largest focal point in the room was a full sized tyrannosaurus replica that stood across the back of the room. His tail wrapped down along the winding staircase that led to levels containing unknown exhibits, while his neck extended up to the top of the room towards the glass ceiling. His head pointed out towards the seating area, his jaw positioned so that it cast an eternally silent roar over the elegant room. Altogether, the setting was truly magnificent and easily surpassed anything Sofia had envisioned.

The maître d' guided them to a secluded table on a landing overlooking the rest of the room. As she looked out over the other people enjoying their meals and conversation, Sofia couldn't help but feel somewhat nervous that things were going entirely too well. Absolutely everything about the date was going beautifully. Happy endings weren't something she was familiar with seeing. As the feelings began to creep up her spine, she remembered her promise to herself that she was going to have a great time tonight, no matter what. Even if things could never work out between herself and Lucian, she was going to enjoy herself. As she focused on that thought, she felt the nervousness slip away.

As they approached the table, Lucian pulled out Sofia's chair and seated her before making his way back to his own position across the table. Each of them ordered a martini as they admired the scenery.

"I've never been inside here. This is absolutely amazing, Lucian!" Sofia exclaimed softly. Sofia had seen the signs for the museum several times, but never really felt the desire to seek it out. "I never really cared much for the past. I figure, it happened, let's move on," she joked. "But this gives me a very different perspective."

"I never really cared for it much, either. Then, a few years back, I started taking a bigger interest in it."

"Any particular reason for the sudden interest?"

"Actually, yes. I met a guy who's really become a good friend of mine now, and he kind of introduced me to it. He showed me the significance of knowing where you came from and what secrets our personal histories hold that can help determine our futures."

"Sounds like he had quite an impact on you."

"Ummm…yeah. He really has. He's a good guy. Very big into history. He's a great big nerd, so you would probably get along very well." He smiled coyly, causing Sofia to nearly spit her water out all over the table.

"I'm still a little surprised to find that out about myself," she proclaimed as she wiped her mouth. "Well, I talked about my family some, so what's your situation?" She sat back in her seat to give the waiter room to place her martini as he approached.

"My situation, huh? Well, I'd say it's pretty typical. My parents have passed. They were a huge part of my life and my two greatest influences. They were the greatest people I've ever known. I still think about them every day and try to do things that I think would make 'em proud. I got a brother that I used to be very close with, and still am to an extent."

"To an extent; how is that?"

"Well, he's doing his own thing right now, and I'm lettin' him figure out who he is without my input. I was a big influence on him for a long time but I realized that I tend to try to make him think like me. I think it's really important right now that he learn to think for himself and make his own decisions without my influence. But, when we do get together, it's as good as it ever was. Honestly, we're best friends. We just don't see or speak to each other all that often right now."

"That sounds nice. I always really wanted a brother or sister. Being an only child isn't all it's cracked up to be."

"Well, having a sibling doesn't always end up that great, either. In my case it's clearly worked out, but I see tons of times where that closeness is just not there and it turns more into a hindrance than anything."

"How often do you two get together?"

"Less often in recent years, but always on the major holidays. We've actually been talkin' a lot more lately. Seems like we're probably gonna be back to our old ways before much longer."

"Well, I hope I get to meet him some day." Sofia slowly sipped from her martini to hide her mouth as she waited for his response. She didn't want to show any sign of surprise if his answer caught her off guard.

"We shall see. Thanksgiving is right around the corner." His eyes smiled at her over the rim of his glass as he lifted it to his lips. Something about the way he looked made Sofia feel like they were the only two people in the room. That look cast away all remaining doubt that this would end up being the most wonderful evening she had ever spent in the company of another person. Lucian had created a perfect setting for taking her mind off the crime scenes and the all-consuming Cul-De-Sac Case that had been gnawing on her.

The time seemed to fly past as they talked about what seemed like every topic imaginable. Lucian was so open and unafraid to completely expose himself with regard to any subject. At the same time, he was a wonderful listener and seemed utterly intrigued by everything she had to say. Sofia had never considered her life or her views on any topic that interesting, but when she explained things to Lucian, she felt like the most interesting person in the world.

One thing that Sofia had noticed several times as the evening went on was that many of the women in the room were staring in their direction. She had never been with someone that commanded so much attention from others. So many people were looking in their direction that she felt compelled to ask him, "Do you come here often?" She felt silly asking the question, but even the staff seemed to be preoccupied with him.

"Not at night like this, but my friend and I have been here a few times during the day." He glanced around the room. "It's a really cool place; I dig it. There's so much to look at. I would think that if you weren't so hot at casual chatter, this would be the perfect place to go. There's so much stuff to talk about here. I mean, there's a damn dinosaur in the room! Where else can you hit a lull in the conversation and be like, 'So dinosaurs are pretty awesome,' and not be looked at like a nutbar? You know?

Everyone has an opinion about dinosaurs, I would imagine, it's just not that easy a thing to bring up in conversation. Well, right there is your way into that little caveat of chit-chat." He gestured towards the monstrous exhibit, much to Sofia's enjoyment.

"I can't imagine that you've ever had any difficulty with casual conversation," Sofia said earnestly through her laughter.

He focused back in on Sofia for a second before searching his thoughts. "I don't guess I've ever really had a problem with that. Even back in my socially unaware days, it was more the inability to hide my thoughts than an inability to convey them." He paused momentarily. "Wait. Are you trying to say I talk too much?" he asked jokingly.

"Not at all! I'm having a wonderful time talking to you," she said, with a glowing smile. "I always do."

"I'm glad to hear that. You strike me as someone who could use more good times. I just hope that I can think of some more interesting things to do." Sofia couldn't believe how perfect everything that he said was. He had been saying just the right thing, at just the right time, all night.

"Do you ever get tired of being the center of attention?" Sofia finally asked. The question had been something she wanted to know the answer to for quite some time.

"Wow! First, I talk too much. Now I'm this attention starved prima donna. I'm starting to think you're not such a big fan of mine."

"No, no, no! Nothing like that. I just meant that you're someone that people are drawn to. Don't even sit there and tell me that you're unaware of how people look at you. I just wondered if it bothers you or if you have just gotten used to the attention?"

Lucian inconspicuously glanced at the faces of some of the other patrons, sipping his martini as he did so.

"I suppose I am…used to it, I mean. I do notice, but it never has really bothered me. And don't be so sure that all of these people are looking at me, honey. I would bet that you have more fans in here than I do."

"Oh stop. You're being ridiculous. People don't look at me like that."

"I'm telling you, you're a far cry from your usual look tonight. You're not Officer Milena right now. I mean, I've always known how beautiful and sexy you are, but tonight you're really making a statement. You may not draw that much attention when you have your hair pulled up and you're hidden in your work clothes, but you seem to have forgotten how you look tonight." Lucian was right; she had forgotten how she looked.

"And now I'm completely uncomfortable. Thanks." She began to fidget about in her seat and became increasingly anxious.

"Calm down," Lucian coaxed. "There's nothing to be uncomfortable about. Just relax. You look great and people are noticing. Just don't think about them, and try to focus on me." It took a great deal of concentration on her part, but Sofia did just as Lucian suggested. Once she was able to focus in on him and stop surveying the room to see if people were looking at her, they were able to continue their conversation. Slowly, she became less and less aware that anyone else was even in the room, and was once again lost in Lucian's presence.

Sofia loved that Lucian was so at ease with everything that he did. She had never met anyone as confident or as easygoing as he appeared to be. The remainder of the evening went on just as smoothly the first half. Sofia was entranced by Lucian's charm. She could have sat and talked with him forever and never hear enough.

The museum created the perfect atmosphere for them as they continued their evening. The two were so enveloped within their conversations that they didn't even notice that the museum was closing down. The sound of a vacuum cleaner broke the silent background. They promptly paid their tab, apologized for staying so late, and made their way back onto the train towards Sofia's apartment.

16

Locating their seats quickly, Lucian strategically placed himself with his back against the window, which allowed Sofia to rest her back against his chest. Although it wasn't the ideal position due to the immovable plastic hump that was supposed to prohibit anything more than standard, face-front, non-contact seating, it was made slightly more bearable by Lucian's narrow build. Sofia believed that she might be causing him some level of discomfort, but each time she asked him he would simply kiss her on the top of her head and squeeze her tightly. They rode that way the entire ride home as they watched the free entertainment that the train ride offered.

The first few stops allowed enough time for the pair to look on in disbelief as two gentlemen, who had clearly spent the past few hours saturating themselves with alcohol, carry on an entire conversation that could only be deciphered by the two of them. Had they been speaking a foreign language, it would have been easier to tune them out. Because they were speaking their own personal version of English, it was impossible to turn away.

Lucian and Sofia giggled and whispered softly to one another, as they would attempt to decipher a sentence for the other. Mostly, they were just creating their own little story in place of the one the men were telling. The men might have kept them entertained the entire way home had Lucian not scared them off when, in an effort to determine the word that one of the men had been stammering and stumbling over for over a minute, got the word correct and let slip an excited, "Got it!"

The exclamation was enough to draw the attention of the men, who seemed to realize what had been going on. They decided to make their exit despite Lucian's pleas for them to stay and his promises to stay out of their business. The only other people on the train were another, younger couple that Lucian quickly directed his attention to.

"What the hell was all that about, you think?"

The young couple looked a little startled that Lucian had asked for their take on the situation. Nonetheless, the young man quickly chimed in with his opinion.

"Dude was pissed," he said, with a laugh. "You saw him 'bout slap ol' boy in the head? If he was seein' straight, he might of took him out."

"Was that a swing? I thought he was tryin' to catch his balance.... That or he was trying to smack him on the back? I honestly had no idea. I thought they were crackin' jokes, man." Lucian laughed at how differently they had seen things.

"You stupid," the young man replied, joining in Lucian's laughter.

Sofia simply smiled and remained quiet as Lucian made fast friends with the man at the other end of the train. The pair chatted the remainder of the trip about the men, and the evening they had just spent with their respective dates. At one point, Lucian even had him talking about his hopes for his and his girlfriend's future. It was only that they had recently started talking about marriage and hoped to have a date set by fall, but it was more information than Sofia had ever seen divulged to a complete stranger on an empty train before. It was truly an amazing thing to watch Lucian's personality take hold of another person. It occurred to Sofia how unbelievable it was that she could be witness to the horrific events that she had exposure to in her life. At the same time, such simple and pleasant occurrences could be happening in the same city. As her thoughts began to drift into the slideshow of heinous crime scenes she had encountered in past weeks, Lucian's comments from earlier about "being a good date" came to her.

As the words echoed in her head, she forced herself to forget about work and return her concentration to the conversation so she could be present in the moment with Lucian. Focusing back in on the conversation, it seemed as though Lucian and the man had been lifelong friends. Sofia watched Lucian's infectious spirit take over the young couple as they were now both engaged in the conversation with him. As the train pulled into the station at Sofia and Lucian's stop, Lucian exchanged pleasantries all the way to the doors until they closed behind them.

"You amaze me with how you interact with complete strangers." Sofia divulged her feelings as they made their way from the station.

"How so?"

"It's just a foreign idea to me. To think that someone would join me in a conversation when they don't have to; that just seems strange to me."

"I guess I get that. I guess it's just kind of the state of things these days. People don't want to engage other people. Probably more like they don't want to be bothered. I don't know. I just like to try and have a good time."

"Maybe. I just don't have the nerve to strike up a conversation with a perfect stranger is all. Plus, I don't really have any desire to talk to other people."

"Says the woman who makes her living knocking on doors, and asking perfect strangers question after question."

"That's work. That's not the same. That badge makes it pretty easy because you know most people are going to respond."

"I guess. But have you considered that it might just be your way of breaking out of your shell a little?"

As Sofia pondered the answer to his question, she suddenly started to become very aware of the situation that she was about to be in. In her wildest fantasies, she had not anticipated the evening going as well as it had. She had thought about what she would do once things progressed to this point and had come up with two scenarios. If the date had gone poorly, she was going to use the case as an excuse to get out of having to invite him up. Lucian was aware of her schedule and knew that she was off the following day. Knowing this, she had decided that she would say that she was going to put in some overtime and following up with some of the victim's acquaintances if she needed a way out of the evening. If the date went well, she was planning to ask Lucian if he wanted to come up and then see where things progressed. What she had not considered was what she would do if the date had exceeded all of her expectations. There was little doubt in her mind where she wanted the date to go at this point, but she suddenly became very nervous about the prospect of a physical encounter with Lucian.

Sofia had a very limited amount of experience when it came to such things and it was clear to her that Lucian was exactly the opposite. The front of her building was now visible, and hundreds of awful scenarios began running through her head. In none of these scenarios was she unexpectedly amazing in bed and none of them ended with the two of them dating beyond that night.

As they entered her building and headed towards the elevator, Sofia realized that while she had been obsessing over the situation, Lucian had continued the conversation and was now looking at her as if he expected an answer. Flustered, Sofia smiled and nodded. "Yeah," she said uncomfortably, hoping she had answered to his satisfaction.

"Oh," Lucian replied with a surprised look. "Well, what is it?"

"Wha....uh..." she babbled, as she pressed the button for her floor. "I'm sorry. I zoned out for a second. What were you saying?"

"I was just asking if something was wrong. You looked like you were gonna be sick."

Not wanting to let him know how close he had been to being right, Sofia replied, "Oh, no. I'm okay. Something just kind of caught my attention."

"Ah, no! Was it the case?" Lucian asked, in a defeated tone.

Not wanting Lucian to know the case had slipped into her thoughts a time or two, Sofia decided to fudge the truth a bit. “You know what? I really haven’t thought about that all night.” Even with such a tense situation growing closer with every ding of the elevator bell, Sofia smiled gratefully at Lucian. “Thank you for that.”

17

The elevator finally eased to a halt and the doors opened onto Sofia's hallway. After her brief moment of satisfaction as she realized Lucian had successfully kept her thoughts off the case for the majority of the night, Sofia's mind quickly resumed its panicked state. She stared hollowly down the hallway as if she was unsure where she was. Lucian looked down at her as he reached out to keep the door from shutting. Seeing that she was once again zoning out as she looked towards her apartment, Lucian understood that their impending arrival at their destination might be the cause for her change in behavior. Sofia jumped as Lucian took her hand in his and eased her out of the elevator.

"I'm sorry," she laughed. "I'm not sure what's wrong with me all of a sudden."

"I think I do," Lucian replied with a smile. "Don't sweat it."

Caressing her shoulder gently as they reached her door, Lucian looked deep into Sofia's eyes as he spoke. "I couldn't have imagined a better night, Sofia. Thank you for making it so perfect."

Lucian stroked her hair softly with his fingertips, leaving the bulk of the strands resting behind her ear. Sofia simply stared back at him, lost in his beautiful hazel eyes. Placing his hand behind her head, Lucian pulled her towards him. Sofia melted as their lips met. This kiss was far more passionate than the one they had shared to begin their evening. Sofia could feel the blood flowing through her, warming her entire body as it surged to every extremity. Her mind cleared and she was able to stop thinking about what would happen next, and just live in that moment with Lucian.

She couldn't remember a more exciting moment in her life. Nothing she had experienced had ever gone so absolutely perfect, while being so effortless. From the moment she had seen him in the hallway, every single second had been exactly what it needed to be for the next to happen. As their lips parted, Sofia stood silently for a moment as she gathered her thoughts. Turning to her door, Sofia began searching her purse for her keys to lead Lucian inside. Locating her keys, she reached towards the door but stopped short as she felt a tug at her arm. Sofia turned around slowly to see why he had kept her from opening the door.

"Listen, Sofia," he began softly, "I've been in this situation before and I've always made the same decision. My decision to move too fast too soon has never led me in the direction that I want to go with you. I want to follow you into that room more than you can imagine. I just know it will be better for us if I don't. If I want things to end differently with you, and I do, then I have to do something different. So I want to tell you goodnight now and end our evening on the best possible note."

Sofia was stunned. She wasn't sure whether it was Lucian seemingly rejecting her that was causing her to pause, or that he seemed to be saying that he was more interested in having a relationship with her than with anyone he'd ever dated before. Nevertheless, she was indeed stunned.

Lucian spoke quietly to her, saying, "Don't take this as rejection, please; that's not what I'm doin'. It's actually the exact opposite. This is me trying to let you know how serious I am. But I absolutely cannot go inside with you tonight if I want for that to happen." Lucian leaned in and gave Sofia one final kiss. As he backed away, he whispered, "You have no idea how bad I want to go in there with you.... I'll call you in the morning."

Lucian turned abruptly and headed back down the hallway. Reaching the elevator, he leaned his forehead against the cold metal doors as he smacked the down arrow. As he waited for the elevator to arrive, Lucian peeked back over his shoulder to see that Sofia was still standing in front of her door watching him.

"Please...go...inside," he urged loudly, in a halted, half-joking manner.

Sofia turned her attention back to her door and quickly unlocked it. She took one last look at Lucian before she entered.

"You're not making this easy!" Lucian cried out, as the elevator bell sounded and the doors slid open. Smiling brightly as he entered the elevator, he winked at her.

"Goodnight, beautiful."

"Night," Sofia replied softly, ducking into her apartment slowly, intentionally teasing him. She now found it much easier to toy with him as the pressures of a sexual encounter were off the table. She wasn't sure how she would react if he actually made a move to get off the elevator.

As she closed the door behind her, she leaned back against it for a moment as she replayed everything that had just been said. When Lucian was talking to her, she was so preoccupied with what was happening that she was unable to comprehend what he was saying. She had heard everything that he had said, but hadn't processed the meaning until just then. As the words came to her, the smile that was tattooed across her face the entire evening until her concerns about the evening's end had arisen, now found its way back. Her heart began to pound inside her chest and she let out a shrill squeal before she could stop herself. She reached up and covered her face with her hands in order to muffle herself so that the neighbors wouldn't hear. There was no hope that she was going to stop. Sofia tried using several breathing techniques to calm herself down, and was finally able to quell her excitement somewhat. Diving onto her couch and planting her face into the cushion, she began giggling uncontrollably. She spent the next few hours rerunning the night over and over in her head. Sofia repeated her favorite parts out loud, to herself, before finally dozing off in the early hours of the morning.

18

The little amount of sleep that Sofia actually got that night was filled with images of the evening she had spent with Lucian. She had finally fallen asleep as the sun had begun to creep around the edges of her tightly shut blinds at six thirty the next morning. It was little more than a catnap, because her phone began to vibrate on her nightstand. She groggily rolled over to see who would dare bother her so early on her day off. Her lack of sleep was no match for her excitement as she saw Lucian's name on the text message. Lucian had texted simply, "You sleepin?"

There were no signs of fatigue as she eagerly replied, giddy with excitement. "Nah, just layin around."There was no need to inflate his ego by letting him know that she had spent the hours since he left pining for him. The seconds crept past as she waited for his response. She could hardly contain herself as she awaited his next text message.

"How is this better than a phone call?" she wondered aloud, as she sat impatiently, strangling her phone as if his message were waiting to be squeezed from its insides. She knew that she hadn't even given him enough time to receive the message, much less read it and reply, but she didn't care. There was no room for logic here. She nearly fell off her bed when the phone finally buzzed into action.

"Wanna do somethin?" he asked.

She hastily typed away, "I will do anything you want for as long as you want!"As she read the message back to herself, she realized how desperately love sick and corny it sounded. Deleting the message letter by letter, she harnessed her excitement and reworked her thoughts. "Sure. What u got in mind?" It was then that she realized how superior texting was to talking in this situation.

"Nothin major. Eat and hang out. You still in?"

"Sounds good. Where r we meeting?"

"Up to you. Thought you could meet my roommate. Near my place, if that's cool." Sofia had heard Lucian talk about his roommate on several occasions. From what she had gathered, they were very close. This was as close to meeting his family as she was going to get, until she had the opportunity to meet his brother. This was huge! Sofia knew that Lucian lived near an area known as Atlantic Station, which was a very exciting part of town filled with assorted shops, eateries, and bars.

"Sure. Somewhere in A Station?"

"Good deal. Let me know when you leave. Be careful :)"

Sofia leapt from her bed and made a mad dash for the shower. She was overjoyed that Lucian had called her so soon. She had been concerned that his ego would get the best of him and he would make her play the waiting game. She dreaded the thought of having to wait. That had been the only negative feeling she had felt in the past eighteen or so hours that had passed since he had asked her to dinner.

Not wanting to waste time drying and fixing her hair, Sofia frantically jammed her dark locks into a shower cap as she cranked up the water. After feverishly brushing her teeth, she jumped into the cold shower, bathing herself so quickly that she barely noticed that the ancient pipes in her apartment hadn't yet allowed the water to warm up. Sofia was determined to spend absolutely every second that she possibly could with Lucian. She slowed down long enough to shave her legs without causing herself to bleed out on the shower floor before exiting, realizing that some things just could not be rushed. After successfully applying her makeup in record time, Sofia dashed out the door and down the hallway to the elevator.

19

As she reached her car, Sofia sent Lucian a quick text to let him know that she was on her way. Not wanting to waste a single second waiting for the train or any of the stops, she opted to take her car. Atlanta traffic was relentless. However, there were a series of opportunities that opened every day, which allowed for a reasonable drive. Since it was nearly ten o'clock, all of the morning commuters were at work. All of the morning's wrecks should be cleared away. Sofia cranked up her car and exited the parking deck.

As expected, the traffic was light. During her drive, Sofia began to take note of all of the idiotic things that other drivers were doing that she usually didn't pay any attention to. It's no wonder Lucian doesn't drive, she thought.

Suddenly, the car that she had been stuck behind released a large cloud of thick, black smoke and began to slow.

"Oh, no. No, no, no!" Sofia said to herself, as she realized exactly what was happening. The car that was in front of her was an ancient, rusty, bucket of a car that had no business being on the road. She was in such a hurry to get to Lucian, she had employed the "tailgating" technique to try to persuade the car to speed up. She was traveling so closely that she now had no room to go around as he came to a halt in the middle of the interstate. Sofia began to panic as she looked up to notice the never-ending stream of traffic that was swerving around her, making escape impossible.

She watched with great frustration as the people behind her continued to jump over into every available spot before speeding past her. Each car replaced a previous car, and the cycle continued. She could see freedom just beyond the hood of her rust colored captor, but knew all too well how far from that freedom she was.

From what she could see, the man behind the wheel was very old and doing everything that he could to try to restart the car. This consisted of turning the key, holding it in place, and bobbing his head in an effort to "will" it to work. Realizing that there was no chance of him trying to push the car out of the way, or doing anything to help himself, Sofia angrily squeezed her steering wheel, and clenched her teeth so hard she thought one might actually crack.

After what seemed like an eternity of trying to find a chance to get past the scrap pile that had imprisoned her, Sofia finally placed her car in park, turned on her flashers, climbed over to the passenger's seat, and out into the emergency lane. She approached the vehicle and tapped her shield on the glass.

"What!"The man was startled by Sofia's presence.

"I'm just trying to help you, sir. Roll down your window." She shouted back.

"Can't! Handle's broke. Door handle, too! What do you want?"

"Of course it is," Sofia muttered to herself. "Well, I'm in a hurry. I'm just going to push; you steer the car over to the emergency lane!"

"I got no power steering, do you know how hard it's going to be to turn this thing!?"

Sofia's usually calm demeanor in these situations instantly turned to anger as she shouted out, "I'm about to push your giant, rust covered, trash heap of a car with no help! Do you know how difficult that is going to be?! Now either get ready to push or get ready to steer!" She was generally exceedingly polite to those in need, but this was no time for niceties. This man was costing her precious time with Lucian, and that was about to end. Knowing the great amount of risk she was taking on rather than just waiting for help to arrive, Sofia propped her feet on the front bumper of her own car and placed her hands firmly on the trunk of the jalopy.

“Should’ve taken the train,” she grumbled, as she prepared to manhandle the beast. Lowering her head, Sofia eased into a strong, steady push. The car lurched forward for a second before coming to an abrupt halt. Sofia nearly face planted into the back window of the car. Slamming her hand down on the trunk, she screamed, “Come on! NEUTRAL!”

She saw his little head pop above the headrest. The sound of her hitting the car had clearly startled him once again. He began to flail about as if he couldn’t find the gearshift. Locating it, he slammed the handle into neutral and Sofia again began pushing.

The sound of the rubber pushing the loose pieces of asphalt, and the creaking of the ancient axles under the weight of the car, were two of the greatest sounds that Sofia had ever heard. The ground was flat enough so that the car gave very little resistance and began to coast rather easily once she got it moving. Sofia felt the sweat beading up on her forehead as she continued to work to get the car off the bustling interstate. Sofia tried not to laugh as she looked up and saw the little man struggling feverishly to turn his dilapidated wreck into the emergency lane.

The little man finally straightened his wheels and pulled the car completely out of the way of traffic. Sofia ran up to the driver side window, which he promptly opened for her. “I’m going to call you a tow truck.” She huffed as she attempted to catch her breath. “Don’t you EVER bring this car back out on the interstate, again!” she yelled over the traffic noise. Normally, Sofia would have waited around to make sure that the tow truck had found the man and gotten him home safely. This was not a normal day. Jogging back to her car, Sofia climbed back over to the driver’s seat and started back towards Lucian.

20

It was no surprise to Sofia how crowded things were when she arrived at Atlantic Station. It was a beautiful day, and everyone was taking advantage of the sunshine. The warmth of the sun was increasing as it climbed higher into the cloudless sky, but a delicate breeze found its way down every avenue, helping maintain the comfortable temperature.

Upon arriving and parking her car, Sofia texted Lucian to let him know that she was pulling in. Lucian responded by telling her that he was running a little behind and asked that she just come and meet him at his apartment. She agreed. He texted the directions.

Sofia took a brief second to look around the beautifully secluded little community. Elegant shops lined the streets in every direction. The sidewalks were packed. Window shoppers, and a number of other people, ate at the outdoor seating areas. The air filled with the smell of freshly cooked bread from the bakery across the street from where she stood. Unable to stand in the same place too long due to the heavy foot traffic, as well as the desire to find Lucian, Sofia decided it was time to press on.

Before heading in the direction of their meeting area, she ducked into a restroom to freshen up. Her encounter on the interstate had left her a bit sweatier than she had hoped to be. Taking a few minutes to clean her face and hands, and retouch her makeup, she checked to make sure she hadn't damaged or dirtied her clothes while in contact with the disgusting pile of rubble she had encountered on the interstate. She then dashed off once more. The only thing keeping Sofia from breaking into a dead sprint to get to Lucian was the fear of showing up for their day together stinking and sweating through her shirt. She accepted the fact that she was nearly there and carried on at a modest pace towards Lucian's condo. Finally, she arrived at his building and couldn't help but be impressed by what she saw on the other side of the lobby doors.

"At the door," she texted, not wanting to deal with the call box. The buzz came shortly after and Sofia entered. She was instantly impressed as she entered the lobby of the building. The sounds of a running fountain caught her attention. She glanced around, her mouth slightly agape at how elegant the building was. The room was full of various artworks, placed with inspired precision. From where she stood, Sofia could see into a large common room filled with bookshelves. A pedestal chessboard sat in front of an unlit fireplace inside the room, which created an unbelievably comfortable appearance. She continued to scan the room, taking note of each of the corridors that led off to unknown areas. She could only assume they contained equally mesmerizing amenities. As she scanned around to her left, she made eye contact with a surprisingly underdressed young woman sitting in a second, smaller seating area. The woman appeared to have been reading a book as she relaxed in her terrycloth robe, her crossed legs fully exposed through the opening beneath the belt. She was now staring at Sofia with a smirk.

"First time here?" she asked Sofia, knowingly.

"Is it obvious?" Sofia replied.

"Yeah. That's a very common look from people who have never been here. I did the same thing when I first came in." Her warm smile helped make Sofia feel more comfortable in the posh surroundings, and made her feel slightly ashamed that she had thought anything negative about her. "Anything I can help you with?"

"I'm really just looking for the elevators." As she spoke the words, the familiar ding of an arriving elevator drew her eye in its direction. Lucian emerged from the elevator with a huge smile and approached Sofia.

"Hey, Lucian!" The woman who had been talking with Sofia chirped. Sofia was looking right at Lucian as the woman spoke.

His eyebrows rose just a little, in a look of surprise, as he heard her voice. Turning his head slightly, but never slowing his progress, Lucian took Sofia's hand and pulled her back towards the elevator.

"Hey, Sandra. Sorry, I don't want to miss this elevator. Good to see you this morning," he replied quickly, as he hurried over and pressed the button to re-open the doors. The doors didn't immediately open and Lucian's mouth curled down into a comical frown as he stared up at the rising floor counter. Pulling his attention back to Sofia, he realized he had yet to greet her. "Hello, beautiful. You look lovely, as always." Sofia was excited to see him but couldn't help but notice that Sandra was paying particularly close attention to their conversation.

She said, "You look really nice this morning, Lucian." The other woman's voice was no longer pleasant to Sofia, as it had been when she was trying to help her before. It now seemed shrill and desperate, even though she was almost certain nothing had actually changed.

"Thanks, Sandra. How's Eddie doin'?" Sofia could tell that Lucian was uncomfortable with the conversation, but he seemed to be trying to cover it as he spoke to her.

"Eh. The same, I guess." The woman's face soured as she spoke about whomever they were referring to.

"Well, tell him I said hello," Lucian continued plainly, still trying to be as pleasant as possible. "I'm gonna…" he said, indicating towards Sofia in an effort to end the conversation.

"Oh, sure! Sorry. I was just saying hi. I haven't seen you in a while," Sandra added, uncomfortably.

"It's good to see you, Sandra." Lucian gave the woman a final smile before turning his attention back to Sofia. "Anyway. You look great this morning."

"Thanks." The awkward conversation had torn Sofia from her joyful state of excitement at seeing Lucian. Now, she felt uncomfortable and awkward as she and Lucian both stared up at the floor counter as it descended. After a few more excruciating moments waiting for the elevator, the doors finally opened. The pair snuck in as quickly as they could once the occupants emerged. Lucian began pecking at the button, trying to close the doors as quickly as possible. Sofia looked up one last time when the doors finally lurched back to close. Sandra sat on the edge of her seat trying to get another peek at Lucian before they left.

The elevator began its ascent and Sofia looked over to Lucian to see if any sort of explanation was coming. She couldn't help but wonder what must have happened to cause Lucian to act so unlike himself. Usually his interactions with others were so smooth and pleasant. He always tried to make other people feel comfortable. While he had been pleasant with Sandra, he did not attempt to make her feel comfortable. Lucian looked down to Sofia and smiled innocently.

"I'm really glad you came over. I'm not really sure what we're gonna do, but I'm guessing we'll have fun." Sofia was a little surprised he didn't even address the odd encounter from the lobby. Not wanting to take away from their time together, Sofia tried to put Sandra out of her mind.

"I'm glad you didn't feel the need to play games," she replied.

"Yeah, that's not really my style. Either you like someone, or you don't. Either way, you make it obvious. I've had girls tell me to do the whole 'not calling for three days' thing. When I hear that, it's a dead giveaway that someone is into games. When someone tells me that, I don't call…ever. You like someone, you spend time with them. That's just how I do it." Lucian was definitely straightforward, which was a quality that sent a surge of energy through Sofia's body. Each time Lucian said something about, or insinuated that he liked her, it gave Sofia chills and an instant rush.

As they exited the elevator, Sofia turned to him quickly and put her hands around his neck. Lucian wrapped his arms around her and lifted her gently off the ground. She was surprised at how easily he picked her up. As thin as he was, Sofia had always assumed that he would be very weak, but he made lifting her seem effortless. The thoughts fled from her mind as quickly as they came, as excitement and joy at being in Lucian's presence again overtook her.

"Sorry I was running late this morning." He craned his neck to kiss her.

"It's okay. I got a little sidetracked, too." They kissed several more times, as Lucian held her there, but his hold remained steady.

"You got here quicker than I thought you would and you had a holdup? Good Lord, woman! How did you get ready so fast?" He lowered her slowly back to the ground.

Not wanting to make her frantic race to see him sound too crazy, Sofia decided a little white lie wouldn't hurt. "Oh, I was already out of the shower and getting ready for the day when you called."

"Oh, wow. You get going early on your days off? What was the holdup that made you run late?"

"Oh, some little old man's car broke down in front of me on the interstate. I got out and helped him and I think I scared him a little." Her mouth curled back into the same playful smile she had approached Lucian with moments before.

"You scared a defenseless little old man whose car was broken down in the middle of a busy interstate, while you were helping him? You're terrible!" Lucian tried to refrain from laughing.

"He had it coming," she mumbled, before straightening her face back out and saying rather seriously, "Plus, his car was a hazard. He should never have been on the road with that thing. And, he was driving super slow. I almost plowed into him while his car was actually still running!"

"Oh, well, in that case, I'm glad you lit that old man up! That's exactly what I meant about people having cars that shouldn't be driving. You know full well he probably hops in that car every day knowing it's probably gonna break down on him. But, does he care? Hell no, he doesn't!" Lucian stopped himself for fear that he might begin to rant, which would detract from their afternoon together.

"Sorry about that. I really get worked up about traffic sometimes." His face softened as he cut his eyes towards Sofia. Opening the door to his condo, Lucian rolled his arm through the doorway. "Well, let's get in here so you can check this place out," he said warmly, as they entered his home.

21

Sofia knew that Lucian was a playboy, but never really understood to what level until she saw his condo. From the outside, the building was nice enough. It was a very new, very clean building that sat towards the center of the quaint community. The top floor appeared to have been split into two penthouse condos. Each had a balcony that ran the full length of the short side of the building, around both corners, and halfway down the front and back sides of the building. The most appealing quality was really the location. The building was walking distance from nearly everything anyone could need. There were numerous restaurants, a grocery store, and a pharmacy. Nearly any other shop or store that she could imagine was nearby. However, it wasn't until Lucian took her into his half of the penthouse floor that she realized how spectacular the building was.

The doorway opened into an enormous living room. To the right was where the sofa and two large recliners sat, each with a perfect line of sight to the huge flat-screen television that hung on the wall. To the left was what appeared to be a dining area that had been converted to a dedicated computer space. A large desk housed an oversized monitor, a keyboard, and a mouse. Various nooks held a variety of speakers and plastic covers to a multitude of games and programs. A door on the bottom surely held some elaborately built computer.

The most impressive piece in the room was a huge salt-water aquarium that teemed with a variety of beautifully colored fish. Based on the appearance of the tank, it was clear that Lucian took excellent care of it. There was hardly any sign of algae and the glass appeared beautifully cleaned. Sofia marveled at the tank for a few moments before turning her attention to the rest of the apartment.

A row of large windows and a sliding glass door led out to the balcony that provided both rooms with a beautiful view of the bustling community below. The kitchen was beyond the computer area. Beautifully stained cherry cabinets and granite counter tops lined the space. One thing Sofia found to be impressive was how clean the apartment was. There wasn't a sign of even the first piece of stray clothing lying about. Sofia was truly in awe as she looked around the elegant space. She hadn't even realized that she had allowed her mouth to drop open as she panned the room.

"Lucian, this is beautiful," Sofia gasped.

Lucian looked around as he nodded his head. "I agree. Thank you for noticing." He replied so casually that Sofia laughed quietly at his response.

"How very modest of you," she teased.

"Well, I'm not going to sit here and pretend that I live in some shack. I mean, I know this place is amazing; that's why I live here. At least I said thank you." Lucian's response was very deliberate and seemingly well thought out. It was just the sort of response that Sofia expected.

"I'm not about to get into how much money you make, but I will say that I am very surprised that you can afford this," Sofia joked, as she continued to peruse the knick-knacks that drew the room together.

"Well, I really enjoy the work that I do with the medical examiner's office, but that isn't really the only work I do. They allow me some flexible hours and I do some freelance stuff that pays pretty well. Plus, Shane does what he can."

"Is he here?" Sofia wondered.

"He is. If he's not out by the time we roll back through this room, I'll go get him. For now, we can take a look at my room." Lucian held his arm out to direct Sofia to the hallway across the room that ran beside the kitchen.

Judging from what she had already seen, Sofia's expectations for the master bedroom were extremely high, and she was not disappointed with what she saw. The first, and most obvious, feature of the room was the amount of space. A king-sized, cherry wood sleigh bed sprawled along the wall to Sofia's right. Across from it was yet another oversized flat-screen television, which hung neatly against a large section of wall that jutted into the room. Past the bed, the room opened into a large sitting area, decorated with two beautiful dark-red, leather antique reading chairs that shared a small, marble-topped pedestal table. They reminded Sofia of the type of chairs two old Englishmen might have in their office. They might smoke their pipes and read the news. The chairs faced the large windows, which continued the pattern from the kitchen and dining area. The treatments, pulled to the sides, framed the stunning view of the tiny community and the more distant high-rise towers of downtown Atlanta.

Sofia couldn't help but wonder about the need for the additional chair. Was it so common for Lucian to bring women home with him that it justified an additional piece of furniture to accommodate them? Maybe it was simply there for a sense of symmetry? Sofia realized that it was highly likely that Shane had spent more time in the extra chair since he and Lucian were so close, but she couldn't shake the idea of how many other women had shared that view with Lucian. She continued to debate the purpose as she continued her tour of the stunning room.

As she rounded the corner of the large portion of wall that came into the room, its purpose was unveiled. Two large Venetian doors allowed a glimpse into the most immaculately organized walk-in closet she had ever seen. Everything in the closet was neatly arranged, including exquisite mahogany organizational boxes that had been filled by various odds and ends. There were numerous individual shoe racks, all filled with designer dress shoes and sneakers. Sofia had always admired Lucian's sense of style, but hadn't really noticed how extravagant his wardrobe seemed to be. A number of built in drawers housed various different undershirts, socks, and underwear, as well as an extensive collection of both watches and sunglasses. A large tabletop surface was fitted with a personal mirror that made for an ideal grooming station right inside the closet. An impressive collection of neatly pressed clothes hung above it all. Everything was sorted according to a variety of different specifications and spaced the perfect distance apart, keeping them in pristine condition until the time they were worn. Above all of this ran a shelf filled with designer hats and baseball caps. The shelf sat at a downward angle, allowing for maximum visibility as well as accessibility. The hats spanned the color spectrum several times over and included a number of different styles to fit any occasion. All in all, this was truly the most amazing room that Sofia had ever seen in any home she had ever entered.

"My God, this is a nice closet," she said, as she stepped inside to inspect it more closely.

"I know, right?" Lucian was fully aware of the effect that his elaborate closet had on women.

"This is so much nicer than any room in my entire apartment, let alone my closet. I mean, I don't wear that many different outfits so I don't really need much, but this really makes me want a nicer closet. I could put so much stuff in here." Sofia thought back to her own closet and how much junk she had shoved into it. She had never been very organized away from work, and her closet was a clear representation of that. Most of her work clothes ended up scattered throughout the room on every clean, flat surface she could find when she returned from doing laundry. Her closet was more of a place she packed with every random item she had accumulated over the years, rather than clothing.

"On second thought, it wouldn't matter how much space I had. It would probably end up filled with junk."

"Oh, like hell it would!" The thought of his closet in a state of disarray made Lucian cringe. "Mmm, mmm," he said, shaking his head slowly with a scowl. "Nope. No junk makes it in there. Honestly, it wouldn't even be up to you. I'd have your stuff straightened before you knew what was going on. I can't stand a mess in my house."

Sofia felt a thrill as she considered the possibility of living with Lucian. As they left the closet and entered the master bathroom, Sofia could see what Lucian meant. The entire bathroom was spotless. The tile, the sinks, the Jacuzzi, and stand-alone shower, were cleaned as of recently. The smell of cleanser was still lingering in the air.

"Someone was trying to make a good impression," Sofia joked, as she looked around the room.

"How so?" Lucian responded flatly.

"Everything is spotless. Not just in here, but the whole apartment."

"Oh no. Don't get me wrong, I want you to like it, and I definitely cleaned a few small messes today, but I clean on the regular. I wasn't kiddin' about not being able to stand a mess. I clean this place every four or five days. I'm not full on OCD about it, but I like the place to stay tidy." Sofia thought for a minute and realized she couldn't remember the last time she had cleaned her apartment and couldn't imagine what Lucian would say if he saw the piles of clothes and dishes that had accumulated there.

"Anyway, it's a bathroom; not much to see." Flicking the lights off, they turned around and headed back towards the living room. Sofia took another glance at the closet as they passed, shaking her head at the level of detail that had gone into the setup.

"There's no way you're already done," a voice from the kitchen spoke as they exited the hallway. Sofia's head snapped around quickly to find the source. A lanky, clean-cut black man stood in the kitchen preparing coffee.

"There you are," Lucian replied, with a smile. "Sofia, this is Shane." Each extended their hand over the bar as they greeted one another.

"Shane Betts. It's a pleasure to meet you." Shane extended his beautifully manicured hand in Sofia's direction. Sofia instantly realized how much more attention Shane paid to his hands than she did.

"I'm Sofia. Very nice to finally meet you, Shane."

"There's just no way you're already past that closet. I just heard you guys come in a few minutes ago."

"Yup. She didn't really dig it, man."

"I liked it!" she protested. "I've just never really paid that much attention to that sort of thing. I could definitely get used to a closet like that, though. Especially if you're going to be the one keeping it clean."

"No doubt about that," Shane replied smugly. "That man is nothing if not orderly. I'm clean and all, but I only wish I could be as organized as Luci. So, what are you guys going out to do?"

"Are we done with the tour already, Lucian?" Sofia asked quickly.

"Yeah. I think for now we're good. I showed off my half. I'll let Shane show you his spot whenever he's ready," said Lucian, with a wink.

Shane added, "I've got some projects going on right now that have it a little junked up. Maybe next trip. It was really nice to meet you," Shane nodded as he approached Sofia. He shook her hand gently, with a warm smile, before taking his coffee back to his room.

"So, we have the whole day, what would you like to go do?" Lucian asked.

"We could take another look at the bedroom," Sofia said softly, as she eased in for a passionate kiss, only hoping to tease Lucian. After only a few seconds, Lucian began to massage her butt and inch his hands towards her inner thigh. He slowly pushed her back towards his room.

Panicked, Sofia's eyes popped open. She believed that he would remain firm in his decision not to have sex too soon and had only hoped to tease him. Her eyes darted back and forth between Lucian's eyes and his hallway, as he proceeded to guide her back. The feeling of panic and excitement she had experienced several hours earlier in her own hallway began to come upon her as she envisioned what was to come. Suddenly, Lucian stopped kissing her as his lips hardened into a wide smile. He began laughing as he peeked through a single squinted eye at her. Sofia pulled her head back quickly with a confused look.

"What?" she demanded.

"I can tease too," Lucian replied, with a sinister grin. "I gotta say, you picked a really bad spot to try and play chicken."

"Wha.... Well.... What makes you think I'm playing chicken?" She tried to regroup, but she was still too flustered.

"You're eyelashes were batting around like a pissed off hummingbird's wings!" Lucian demonstrated how fast she had been blinking during his tormenting.

"Well! I was just messing around!" Sofia hid her blushing face behind her hands.

"Whoa, whoa, whoa. Don't get embarrassed. It's cool," he urged soothingly, as he pulled her to him and hugged her. "I get that you're nervous about it. You've told me before how little you've dated, and I can tell that this isn't something to take lightly. I'm not pushing you for it, okay? It'll happen and it will be great. Just calm down and stop thinking about it so much." His words eased her thoughts considerably. Realizing that he was aware of her nervousness regarding the issue of sex seemed to take all of the pressure off. "But," Lucian continued, "that teasin' business is gonna have to stop. My mind is in the right place, but my penis and my brain don't talk all that often. Ya feel me?"

Sofia laughed as she pressed her face into Lucian's chest. Releasing her from his embrace, Lucian kissed her on the forehead and took Sofia's hand as they exited the apartment.

22

After another whirlwind day with Lucian, Sofia returned to work the following Thursday. She was making a conscious effort to hide her excitement about her blossoming relationship with Lucian as she entered the precinct. She had already spent most of the morning in a rush as she prepared for work. She had spent the night at Lucian's after falling asleep in his arms. They lay in the bed talking for hours after their day of running around Atlantic Station. She hadn't paid attention to the time, but knew it was past midnight when she had last checked. Lucian was good enough to make sure she was awake with plenty of time to get going, but she had found it difficult to leave his apartment right away. She ran down her mental checklist of things she needed to do to get ready for work and steadily marked off the least important things as she continued to delay leaving. It wasn't until she got down to "change clothes," that Sofia finally pulled herself away from Lucian and rushed home.

Now, she began feeling the effects of the limited sleep she had received over the past two nights as she approached her desk. The adrenaline was wearing off from being in Lucian's presence, and Sofia's eyes began to feel heavy.

Bishop started in on her right away as she sat down at her desk.

"Whatta ya think about getting a win under our belt before we get back to work on the people-eaters?" Bishop asked, eagerly. Sofia didn't have the energy to argue with him and was considering following his lead when the call came in about another set of victims that was being linked to the Cul-De-Sac case.

Sofia read over the rap sheet of the victim who had been identified by the patrol officers that were already on the scene. He had only been out of prison on parole for a few weeks. The victim had been convicted of vehicular manslaughter. He killed a family while driving under the influence two years back. Granted an early parole, he had offered up some information that was going to help in an ongoing RICO case.

As they pulled up to the crime scene, another call came across the wire that there was a second location for them to check out across town. Sofia and Bishop's inspection of the first crime scene revealed very little evidence, once again. The only difference that Sofia could tell was that he didn't have a record as a violent offender. With the exception of the offense he was released for, he had a clean sheet. Although he wasn't known to have been involved in any other criminal activities, the man had been beaten just as severely as the other victims in the case, if not more so.

Sofia looked over the gruesome remains, making a mental note of how much of the beating seemed focused on his face and head. Sofia pressed gently against his cheekbones and eye sockets, as well as all around his skull. The areas were soft, and gave way under the pressure of her gloved finger as she did so. Sofia knew this meant that the bones had been shattered. She had seen such severity in the beatings of the other victims, but it was usually in the ribs, arms, and legs. While the other attacks were all equally lethal, this attack seemed much angrier.

As usual, no physical evidence had been left by the attackers. Other than her observations about the victim, Sofia was unable to determine any other useful information. As tired as she was, Sofia hadn't even felt the need to inform Bishop of what she had noticed about the victim. She assumed he would never make the same connections as he rarely looked over the remains for any extended period of time anymore. He was busy making small talk with the patrol officers, so Sofia handled most of the investigation before motioning for him so they could move on to the next scene. Slightly more hurried than usual, Sofia and Bishop were moving on to the next scene before Lucian ever showed up, so she was unable to get any further information about the body. Normally, Sofia would have slowed down the investigation of the site until he arrived, but today there was a second place for them to get to, so they went ahead and packed up to leave.

The second crime scene was a little more secluded than the others had been. The bodies were covered up causing more difficulty than usual in their discovery. The stench that accompanied these bodies was much stronger and more potent than was common in this case because of the amount of time they had decomposed. This wasn't the first time they had found victims in the Cul-De-Sac case in an alley, but the attackers had never felt the need to conceal them as they had this time. They weren't well-hidden, they had simply been covered by large bags of trash from a nearby dumpster. It was much cooler in the alley than it was out in the open streets, which only helped to conceal the bodies since the sun could not reach them in the shade. In the summer months, in full exposure to the sun, it wouldn't take much time at all to identify the putrid odor of decay.

The bodies had been uncovered that morning by the trash collectors. The trash collector was still slumped over, receiving oxygen and attention on the back of an ambulance, due to the stress caused by the gruesome scene. Sofia felt a small glimmer of hope as she began to look over things. There were still no signs of any physical evidence, but it was encouraging to her that the cannibal killers had deviated from their normal habits on these two attacks. The small amount of hope she was feeling on the situation was still no match for how tired she was, so she again kept her thoughts to herself as she surveyed the location.

The victims were two more low-level gang enforcers and one well-known dealer from the area. The enforcers had been brought in before on some battery arrests, but the pusher had proven to be a much more difficult target.

He had been operating in the area for quite a while and had developed a system that kept the product completely free from ever being traced to him. He had even incorporated one particularly bold step into his process so that every baggie, which was used to package his drugs, was marked with a symbol that was identical to a tattoo on top of his hand. The mark was his way of slapping the police in the face and daring them to try to come after him. Sofia hadn't heard much about the guy lately until a few weeks earlier when she overheard some of the VICE cops having a conversation about him. VICE was the division of the police whose responsibility it was to handle drug related crimes, even at the juvenile level.

Most often, juvenile offenders found with small amounts of marijuana faced minimal penalties. Lately, however, a large number of middle-school-aged children were caught with drugs such as cocaine and ecstasy. The cellophane baggies the drugs were contained in all bore the same emblem. This was the worst fear for police in every district. No officer wanted the children in their jurisdiction getting addicted to drugs. It was true that it looked bad on the officers that patrolled the area, but their biggest concern was much more benevolent. None of them wanted to see a child hooked on drugs.

Dealers were always trying to get their drugs to the youngest possible clientele, and even though most of the schools in the area had adopted numerous programs to keep the children safe from this filth, they were still finding a way in. When the "victims" of the cannibal killers were scum like this, it made it harder and harder for cops on the force to want to find those responsible for their murders. Sofia, on the other hand, still believed that it was crucial that they make absolutely certain the accused was given a proper trial.

After combing through yet another evidence-free scene, Sofia and Bishop loaded up and headed back to the precinct. As they started off down the road, Bishop finally addressed Sofia's quiet mood.

"Not that I'm complainin', but you've been really quiet today."

"I was beginning to think you hadn't noticed," Sofia replied softly as she rolled her head on the headrest to face him.

"Ha!" He laughed with a grunt. "You don't think too highly of my detective work, I guess. Anyone would have noticed how quiet you've been. You're normally yammerin' my ear off with every single thought you have throughout the day."

Sofia smiled weakly as she replied, "I'm exhausted. I didn't get much sleep the past few days."

"Gross! Stop talking!" Bishop exclaimed. "I don't need to know anything about what the two of you did." Sofia looked over at him, surprised by his response.

"Who…wha…what are you talking about?" she asked, somewhat embarrassed by Bishop's implications.

"I know you and Lucian went out, and I don't need to hear anything more about it. I don't need the visual."

"Wha…" Sofia hadn't mentioned their date to anyone and was shocked that Bishop knew about it.

"The way you acted the other day; that was weird. It didn't take much to figure out what had you flustered. Just don't expect me to sit here and listen to how he defiled you." Bishop was doing everything he could to keep from looking at Sofia as he spoke. He had hoped to make her uncomfortable, but hadn't really anticipated how awkward the conversation would make him feel.

"Well…. It wasn't like that at all. We went to dinner and spent our off-days together. He was a perfect gentleman and nothing sexual even happened." Sofia felt incredibly uncomfortable talking about such things with Bishop, but felt the need to address everything right away before any rumors got started. Bishop shuddered at Sofia's comment and the pair spent the rest of the ride to the station in silence.

23

Upon entering the precinct and getting everything set up at her desk, Sofia made a quick call to Lucian to check on the status of the man from the first crime scene that morning. Normally, she would have walked down to the morgue so she didn't miss an opportunity to flirt with Lucian, but her legs wouldn't allow that today. She leaned back in her chair and closed her eyes as she waited for the call to go through.

This was the first time she had actually called Lucian's phone since they normally texted one another or spoke in person. His ringback tone caught her off-guard. Her chest heaved gently as she laughed to herself about the classical music that was playing in her ear. It was a piece she was not familiar with that featured a soft, slow violin solo. The melody had nearly carried her off to sleep when Lucian's sultry voice interrupted the beautiful composition.

"Well, hello there beautiful." Sofia had to jerk her thoughts back to the present and collect herself for a moment before she was able to respond.

"Hey…" she responded weakly. Her voice had already grown hoarse from not having spoken since her conversation with Bishop as well as the near-sleep-experience she had just encountered. She cleared her throat sharply before continuing. "Hey, Lucian."

"Good Lord. Are you just wakin' up?" he replied, jokingly.

"Oh, no. I'm just a little tired." Sofia was still struggling to wake up, but couldn't help smiling as she spoke to Lucian.

"I tried to tell you to go to sleep last night. You work too hard to stay up that late."

"You stayed up later than me…" Sofia caught herself as she began to raise her voice playfully. “You stayed up later than me, and you got up earlier,” she replied, in a hushed voice.

“I’m used to it. Plus, I don’t really work all that hard. I’m my own boss and can take a nap if I need one.”

“Oh stop. You never sleep,” Sofia joked.

“Anyways, I imagine you’re calling about the dude from this morning?”

“I am. Did you find anything?”

“Oh, just that his blood alcohol content was nearly twice the limit. It’s hard to be sure from the beating he took, but there are some signs that he may have been in a car wreck recently. Some glass shards in his skin and a little bit of a burn on the facial tissue that’s probably from an airbag.”

“Wonderful. Considering the way these guys operate, we probably need to be on the lookout for anyone hurt in a car accident in the past twenty-four hours,” she said, with a sigh. “Alright, thanks Lucian. Have you gotten to the other two yet?”

“I’m headed there now, sweetness.” Sofia glanced over towards Bishop to make sure he couldn’t see her grinning. He was sufficiently busy with his own phone conversation, giving her ample privacy to finish her conversation.

“What time you comin’ to see me tonight?” Lucian asked confidently. Sofia snapped her head back over to make sure Bishop was still busy with his call before answering.

“I will be there as soon as I swing by my place for a second,” she replied, in a firm, quiet voice. Lucian laughed loudly on the other end at her attempt to hide their conversation.

“Sounds good. I’ll see you in a bit. Goodbye, gorgeous.”

Just as Sofia was about to reply, Bishop chimed in loudly.

"Who's that? Why are you bein' all quiet?"

His brash interruption startled Sofia, causing her to jump. "Okay then, Lucian. Thanks. Sounds good. Talk to you later…tomorrow. I'll talk to you tomorrow. Bye." Her awkward end to the phone call was far more embarrassing to her than how red her face had gotten. She didn't want anyone at the precinct knowing what was going on with her and Lucian and didn't appreciate Bishop drawing attention to her conversation or her actions.

"Why do you feel the need to be so loud when other people are on the phone? Did I scream at you while you were on your call?" Sofia replied angrily.

"What's your problem? I was just asking who you were talking to." Sofia found it impossible to believe that he had no idea who she was talking to and thought he was trying to draw attention to her.

"It was Lucian," Sofia said sternly.

"Oh. What did he say? Did he see our dead guys?" Bishop asked, still unaware that the nature of the call had been mostly personal. Sofia took advantage of the opportunity to direct the conversation towards Lucian's findings. Shaking her head to rid herself of the frustration Bishop had caused, Sofia passed along the information.

"The victim was drunk…really drunk. Twice the limit. Lucian thinks the victim was in a car accident earlier in the day."

"Oh yeah? Probably killed some innocent people to draw our guy's attention," Bishop huffed beneath his breath. Sofia felt the urge to fight him on the issue, but she couldn't muster the energy. She let out a heavy sigh as she leaned back in her chair, placing her arm over her eyes.

"I'm done for today," Sofia called out to Bishop.

"It's five till. What's the hurry?"

"I'm exhausted."

"Oh, so you're not headed to Lucian's after you pop by your place for a second?"

Sofia snapped her head towards Bishop to see him smiling at her.

"That is no one's business!" Sofia exclaimed quietly, as she looked around nervously.

"Oh relax. I checked. Nobody's paying us any attention."

"I don't care! Don't talk about it around here! Please, Bishop." Sofia hated the idea of the men around the office talking about her personal life. She had heard how they talked about Lucian's love life, and she had no intention of being the object of those discussions.

"Fine. Calm down." Bishop dismissed her with a wave of his hand.

"Thank you," she replied, as she scanned the area one last time to make sure no one was eavesdropping. After looking over her surroundings as inconspicuously as possible, Sofia gathered up her things and headed for the door.

"Have fun." Bishop called out across the room. Sofia glared at him as she backed out the door.

24

As another morning rolled around and as Sofia rushed to get ready for work, she found herself struggling with a feeling she never thought she would have. As her relationship with Lucian continued to blossom, she found herself growing angry whenever she had to leave him to go to work. She realized that her frustration was with leaving Lucian and not her job. She was always able to cast aside her frustrations and get her mind ready for work by the time she arrived, but it was still a very strange feeling for her to arrive at work and not be excited to be there. As she strolled in towards her desk this morning, she heard the other reason she was none too excited about being at work.

"Oh, good, you're here. I'm ready to get going so we can catch some of these assholes that are ruining our city." Sofia knew what Bishop was up to, but decided to play along.

"Awesome! Get your stuff and let's stop these guys before they eat some more people. I'm glad to see you're ready to solve this case, Bishop."

"Oh... Wait... Nope. I meant, I was ready to catch some of the real criminals. You know, like the guys we keep finding dead all over town." Bishop sat back in his chair, folding his hands behind his head, sending a clear message that he didn't plan on going anywhere. Sofia fumed to herself for a moment before Bishop continued. "I mean, what are we talking about here? We've got eleven dead ex-cons who were up to no good, right?" Sofia sighed deeply as she stared at him.

"So, eleven dead drains on society. The one drug dealer they took out would have affected hundreds, or probably thousands of lives and more than likely would have been responsible for a number of deaths. I just can't believe that you won't, for one second, consider that these cannibal guys are saving lives."

“They are taking lives, Bishop! I can’t believe that you are forgetting that fact!” The blood surged through Sofia’s face as she began to raise her voice. She had refrained from allowing herself to say the words, although she had been thinking them for weeks.

The fact that she now realized how alone she was in searching for these men was only fueling her anger. She stopped holding back and allowed herself to scream the words that she hoped would point some of the other officers in the right direction.

“I know how you feel about this, and you don’t get to decide which lives are more valuable or important than others! We protect, and we serve! That is what we do, and we do it for everyone! Try not to forget that, Mr. High and Mighty.”

Bishop never flinched. He never so much as looked up from his paper during her entire rant, which was not the case for everyone else within earshot. Most of the department was now looking towards Sofia. She had hoped to see some shame in their faces as they realized that she was right about everything, but the most common expression that she saw was one of disbelief at her inability to understand their point of view.

“Not what you were looking for, huh?” Bishop seemed smug as he turned the page of his paper, pausing only long enough to glance up at her for a moment. “Look, kid, we all know the job and we all do it the best we can, but you haven’t seen it as long as we have. It makes you hard. It makes you hate. I’m not gonna sit here and pretend like I’m not going to continue looking for these guys. That’s my job, I get that.”

He eased towards her and lowered his voice just above a whisper, “I’m just thinking that maybe these guys could clean a little more scum off the streets before we get too serious about findin’ ‘em.”

Sofia was not at all surprised at what he was thinking, but she was shocked that he had finally said it out loud, without even acting as if it was a joke.

"And what if someone innocent dies while that's going on?" she asked, in a hushed voice. "Can you live with that?"

Her harsh whispers had little effect on Bishop, who again simply glanced up at her as if to say, "Do I really need to answer that?" He cut his look short before replying, "You've seen the same thing I have. They aren't going to kill anyone that doesn't have it coming. It seems to me that they have a better eye on these people than we do. I mean, that jackass who wrecked on the playground would never have been on our radar, and they got him the first time he slipped up!"

Bishop was referring to the drunken victim they had found. His car was later located abandoned a few blocks away where it had been driven into the center of a playground. While no evidence from the scene indicated any additional victims in the accident, the fact the car had ended up in a location where children could have been harmed only fueled the anger of her fellow officers.

"At least, we think it was the first time. Hell, he was out for a few weeks. He could have been responsible for God only knows what since getting out." From the look on Sofia's face, Bishop realized what thought he had just put into Sofia's head. "Craaap!" He moaned in a low, deep voice.

The comments Bishop made had only helped to push Sofia towards an idea she had been considering for the past few days. She believed that the reason no evidence had been located, and the reason the victim list focused on ex-convicts, was because the cannibals they were looking for were police officers. Grabbing his can of snuff off his desk, Bishop walked off to replace his depleted supply of tobacco, angry with himself for pointing Sofia in the direction he had.

Days earlier, Sofia had begun to look into the number of victims that had complaints against them, which never resulted in arrests. Every single victim had a record showing complaints that were later either dropped, or never taken further for whatever reason.

These were facts that very few people would know about, outside of the police force.

The corruption Sofia had seen in her local law enforcement in her village in Colombia had caused her not to trust the police and, occasionally, that crept back into her thoughts. Her experience with police corruption early in life made it very easy for her to believe that this sort of operation could have been orchestrated by someone within the police force. From the time that they started linking the jobs together, Sofia's mind had gone to the possibility that it could be an inside job. She refused to allow herself to think that way, as it was not abnormal for her mind to go there. Every time they came across a case like this, where evidence was scarce and the case was difficult, Sofia's mind would instantly consider the possibility of it having been an inside job. She couldn't help herself.

In her mind, she could still see the faces of the policemen that used to drive through the village, their arms loaded with gifts and money. Every other time these thoughts had come up, she dismissed them almost instantly. She had developed a deep level of admiration for the law enforcement officers in the States, and knew that they always deserved the benefit of the doubt. The difference in this case was the level of involvement that went into the covering up of evidence as well as the analysis of each of the victims. This difficult case could be explained much more easily if this was all being planned and carried out by people on the inside. The fact that no DNA from the perps had been found at the scenes of any of the crimes had been bugging Sofia more than any other part of this case, especially since numerous weapons were fired just prior to a few of the murders.

Sofia believed that had a group of men appeared on the scene, dressed as officers, there would definitely be a decreased chance of any attempts at fighting back. Not wanting to confirm Bishop's suspicions about what she was considering, Sofia decided to go bounce some of her ideas off Lucian. Although she had just left him a short time before when they had arrived at work, and she had yet to begin any actual work on the case, Sofia headed off to see what Lucian thought.

25

Even though they were spending so much time together, both at work and away from it, Sofia felt the same level of excitement when she entered the morgue that she had before they started dating. Although she wanted to burst through the double doors that led to his room, Sofia restrained herself each time she visited. She had considered the possibility that anyone could be in with Lucian at any time. She hated to think of how very unprofessional it would seem for her to do such a thing. Therefore, she eased her way into the hallway to his room once more, pretending to focus on the paperwork that she had brought with her for exactly that purpose. Sofia was so caught up in her nonchalant act, she plowed into a young woman who was leaving the morgue. The force of the collision sent them both sprawling to the ground.

"I am so sorry!" Sofia exclaimed, believing that her ruse had been the sole contributing factor to the accident.

"No, no. It's my fault," the young woman replied. Sofia looked up from gathering her papers and realized that she had seen the woman before. She was one of the women that came around regularly to see Lucian; she was one of his exes. Sofia froze, as she looked at this beautiful woman in her tight red top and black micro-skirt. The girl may have been old enough to purchase her own alcoholic beverages.

Her stomach churned as the possibilities of what could have been going on sped through her mind. The girl was speaking to her, but Sofia could hardly make out her words because of the roar of the blood rushing to her brain, filling her ears.

"I'm so sorry. I wasn't paying any attention to where I was going." The woman picked up Sofia's papers.

Sofia stood still, staring at the woman, unsure of what she might say if she opened her mouth.

“I’m just a mess right now,” muttered the flustered young woman. From her frantic movements and hurried demeanor, Sofia could see that something bothered her. “I’m so sorry,” she said, again, handing the atrociously stacked pile of papers back to Sofia.

“I’ve got to get going.” She quickly got to her feet and scampered off down the hall. Sofia held her poorly stacked paperwork in her hands and slowly proceeded towards the large metal double doors. The urge to turn around and walk out of the room was almost too much for her. She prepared herself for the aftermath left from whatever had just transpired between Lucian and that woman. She couldn’t stop the questions from running rampant through her mind:

What was she doing here? Had she been wrong about what went on inside the morgue when those girls came to see Lucian? Was Lucian still seeing her on the side? How many others were there? Had Lucian gone back to these women because they weren’t sleeping together? He was the one that was holding out! She had been willing on more than one occasion and he had been the one that stopped things! If anyone should be looking for affection elsewhere, it should be her!

Blood continued to surge through her veins as her mind was flooded with thoughts of what Lucian had been doing. She quickly rounded the corner with a scowl on her face and stormed down the hallway. As she approached the door, Lucian’s voice began reverberating off the walls, and what she heard only caused her to become angrier. He was singing! He was singing some stupid song that he was undoubtedly making up, something he did when he was especially happy. As he reached one of his beloved high-pitched portions, Sofia made her way through large metal doors of the morgue.

As Lucian came into view, her anger subsided moderately as she expected to find him dressing himself, or basking in the glow of his conquest, or at least putting on his clothes. Instead, he was standing at one of the tables performing an autopsy. Half of what appeared to be his hoagie sandwich rested on the paper cloth that covered the cadaver's lower half. Sofia's abrupt entrance caused Lucian's head to snap up from his cadaver, and although she couldn't see his mouth through the mask, his eyes smiled at her.

"Hello, beautiful!" His deep muffled voice came from behind the thin, paper barrier. A look of surprise came into his eyes as he noticed the disheveled papers. Pulling his mask down to reveal a curious smile, he asked, "Was your excuse this time that you needed me to help you stack up your papers? If so, we're gonna need to work on getting you some better excuses. I mean, they are detectives." Sofia had told him how silly she felt going down there all the time and about the various different reasons that she was always giving everyone. At that moment, it was the furthest thing from her mind.

"No." She looked down at the mess that she was holding. "This is because some woman just ran me over as she flew out of here like she had been doing something she shouldn't have been." She made little attempt to mask the contempt in her voice as her Colombian accent began to shine through. Lucian leaned forward against the metal table.

"Yeah, sorry you had to see that." He sighed, looking down at the table.

Sofia couldn't contain herself and blurted the first thought that came into her mind. "So you're not denying it!" Her face became more intense with every word, never realizing the absurdity of what she was asking.

"Denying what, exactly?" He fixed her with a knowing grin. "That the woman that you just ran into in that hallway was in this room? No. I don't deny that the person you just saw coming from here was just in here. I would actually like to go on the record as saying that that woman was just in here." Realizing that she had jumped the gun with her question, and that maybe she was further along in the argument in her head than in reality, she began again, this time much more directly.

"What was she doing here?" she demanded, her accent in full Latina swing.

"She comes here a lot. We went out a few times, and she comes by to visit from time to time. Until today, I usually just listened to her go on and on about what she had been up to."

"Until today?" she asked, angrily.

"Oh, yeah. Today I asked if she could quit coming by. I told her that I thought it might bother my girlfriend."

Sofia's cheeks felt as though they were on fire due to the amount of blood in them, only now it remained out of pure, gut-wrenching embarrassment. Dropping all of her papers on the table in front of her, she hid her face in her hands.

"Oh, God. No," she muttered to herself. Lucian came around his table and approached Sofia. Pulling one of the nearby stools from an examining table, he sat down in front of her and waited patiently for her to look at him. It had become painfully obvious that Lucian knew what she had been alluding to, and was trying to give her an escape. Finally, after a few minutes of hiding, she peered at him through the cracks between her fingers.

"Do you hate me?" she whimpered.

"Very much the opposite," he whispered back at her. "I just thought it might make you uncomfortable for those girls to be coming in here, so I've been asking them to stop."

Sofia was mortified, but opened her hands to meet Lucian's kiss as he leaned in to greet her. "Those girls are your friends. I can't let you do that." Although she felt horrible that he was doing it, she truly didn't want them around. She hoped that he wouldn't call her on her bluff, but knew that she couldn't allow him to do such a thing without at least pretending to show some concern.

"I have plenty of friends, and now I have you. Don't worry about it, I'm good with it. Hell, I'm great with it! Do you have any idea how much that crap slows me down? I don't need people stopping in here all day buggin' me."

"Oh really," Sofia raised her eyebrows slightly, but Lucian didn't even allow her the time to comment on what he had just said before correcting his statement.

"At least with you, you let me keep working. Not only that, but you usually talk about work so I'm not missing a beat." Lucian was truly a master of covering his tracks whenever he misspoke.

"Oh, so you mean....they just came in here and talked to you?"

"Well, yeah. Tell me you didn't believe what those guys have been saying? Is that really what you thought I was like?"

"No! Well, not until just a minute ago...I just got a little jealous," she said weakly, mortified once more by her earlier actions.

"Well, that's a little saddening. I mean, this is a morgue.... That's disgusting, don't you think?"

"Yeah...I just didn't know what to think. And we haven't really talked much about that kind of stuff."

"What stuff?"

"You know...Our exes...Sex stuff."

"Good God, why would we?"

"I just thought that was typical stuff to..."

"Why on Earth would that be something you want in your head? Me with another girl? I mean, unless that's—"

"No!"

"What gets you—"

"No, Lucian."

"Going. I mean if you want me to tell you about—"

"Stop please."

"Alllll my sexual encounters—"

"Lucian, stop."

"I could go on and on and on…."

"I get it! You can stop!"

Lucian finally relented. Removing the latex glove from his hand, he took Sofia's hand and looked directly into her eyes.

"We don't need to do that. The most important thing about me that you need to know is that I'm not a cheater. I find no use for it and have no desire to do it. We're together because of everything that has happened to us at this point, so it was worth it. As far as the other stuff is concerned, I'm no saint and never pretend to be one. I know what I like, and I like you." He kissed her hand and backed away from her as he joked, "Plus, you know, practice makes perfect."

"Stop it!" she shouted, smacking her leg and scrunching her face in displeasure.

"I'm sorry! I just mean you will benefit…from all my experience."

"Lucian!"

"Kidding!…But seriously…you'll enjoy yourself."

Sofia tried to keep from smiling because it was truly frustrating, but he was just too irresistible.

"Now, what brings you down here today?" Here was another place were Lucian reigned as king. He had completely let her off the hook for her little jealous outburst. This was one of his traits that she was all too happy to take advantage of each and every time that it was available.

"Uh…" she stammered, struggling to get her thoughts back on work.

"I recognize that folder." He said as he strolled back over to his autopsy and shoved a large bite of his hoagie into his mouth. "More thoughts on that one, huh?" The words would have been difficult to decipher for someone that hadn't become so familiar with someone so unafraid to speak with a mouth full of food. The folder was easy to spot. Sofia had written notes all over the cover in various different colors of ink. She had a habit of making her notes as they came to her, and she often found herself without paper. Bishop rode her several times for doing it, but that never stopped her. Sofia looked at the atrocity that was once her case folder.

"Oh, right! I had to come and talk to you about it because there's no chance that Bishop is going to even consider it. You tell me what you think." She attempted to reconcile the papers in the correct order as she began.

"So, you know that I kind of considered that it was an inside job from the beginning. Well, I pretty much let that go until today."

"What happened today?" Lucian asked, as he replaced his paper mask and resumed his work.

"It was something that Bishop said. He mentioned how much effort was going into the selection of these victims, and how some of them were low-level criminals. Our guys knew that and were apparently watching them."

"Mmmm hmmm." Lucian bobbed his head in agreement, as he inspected his corpse.

"The only way for these guys to know these things is if they are getting information from someone on the inside. Now, it doesn't necessarily have to be being run by someone on the inside. There really doesn't even have to be a great amount of work being done on the inside, but there is definitely some inside work going on somewhere for these guys to know everything that they know." Sofia was very pleased with herself as she finished her explanation and smiled to herself as she finished straightening her papers. This was the first potential lead on this case to date, and she knew that she would be the only one in the department to follow up on something of this nature. Between their loyalty to one another and their admiration for the work that these vigilantes were doing, none of the other officers would even consider making such a move.

"Gotta be careful with that one. You know if you're wrong and you make a big deal out of investigating other cops, you're done." Lucian stopped working for a moment and looked over to her. "I think it could be the right idea, but you've got to be super careful. Know what I mean?"

Sofia knew all too well what he meant. The common perception among police officers for the internal affairs investigation squad was nothing short of hatred. They were seen as rats, or even cannibals by some. They were willing to go after the guys that were out there every day seeing the worst of the evil that people were capable of doing. Sofia had always seen them as the part of the police department that her country had always lacked. She knew that their job was just as important as what she did, and in many ways more difficult. Although she had a healthy respect for what they did, she had never considered doing what they did. It wasn't until then that she realized that if she didn't handle this angle with the right amount of care, joining them may be the only option she had left.

"Yeah, I probably need to make sure that I throw out some different ideas in front of Bishop. I think he had a pretty good idea of what popped into my head earlier."

"Uh, yeah!" Lucian exclaimed. "I would definitely make sure he was way off my scent before going ahead with that. Bishop would be the absolute worst person to let find out. I love the guy, but you know he loves to talk."

Lucian was absolutely right. Sofia would have to make it very clear that she was pursuing an entirely different idea when she was around Bishop in order to keep him from knowing what she was up to.

“I better get back and start working on him now.” Sofia glanced around the room quickly as she made her way towards Lucian, scanning for any living bodies. She stood beside him, her lower lip set to full pout.

“Sorry I was being so jealous,” she whimpered. Lucian was still focused on his work, but Sofia could see his face shift into a very large smile behind his mask. He quickly changed his expression to one of feigned distress.

“I don’t know, Sofia. That was pretty ridiculous behavior. I’m thinkin’ you may need to do some serious convincing later tonight.”

Sofia’s lip leapt back into place as her face jerked into a look of utter shock. Lucian hadn’t even hinted at being ready to take things to the next level before now. The two were very affectionate with one another, but things had remained at a very PG level until now.

“Oh, really!” She was doing all she could to contain her excitement, but she knew that her eagerness was splashed all across her face. Her face became hot as she began to blush bright red.

Lucian peered at her out of the corner of his eye, adding a subtle shoulder shrug. He pulled his mask down to expose his beautiful smiling face as he leaned over to give her a gentle kiss.

“You better go work on getting Bishop off your back.”

Sofia was speechless. All she could do was smile at him as she turned to recover her case folder, heading towards the door.

“Do you want to grab some dinner after wor…?”

"Nope, not especially!" She looked back adoringly, her face still beet red with anticipation. "I would like to walk home with you, though."

"Oh yeah? Not gonna make your nightly stop by your apartment before trying to beat me home again?" Lucian asked.

"Nah. Clearly that point has been made."

"Not sure I see the 'point,' what with us getting there at the same time every night, but sure."

"The point is I make it to my apartment and on to your place in the same amount of time it takes you to just get to your place." Sofia smirked.

"But I don't need to go to your place, and I bet you're breaking your neck to beat me while I'm just cruisin' along and in no hurry."

"Anyway!" She needed to stop this conversation as it was detracting from the positive feelings she had been having only moments earlier. "I would like very much to walk with you tonight."

"Sounds good. Just come and get me whenever you get done today." He looped his mask straps back behind his ears.

"I will," she assured him. For now, the excitement outweighed the nervousness that Lucian's suggestion brought on. She felt the same surge of adrenaline now that she had felt when Lucian asked her on their first date. Only this time, she realized how long the day would feel if she failed to focus on something other than the evenings plans. She instantly began thinking of ways to approach Bishop so that she could ease his concerns about her looking into cops. She knew she had to do something to keep her mind occupied until their evening together.

26

Sofia was beaming as she bounded towards her desk. She was doing all she could to tone down her excitement and keep a low profile, but it was nearly impossible. She hadn't really admitted it to herself, but all of Lucian's efforts to improve their relationship before they got to a physical relationship, while noble, had taken a small toll on her ego. The news that he was ready to move forward was exactly what she had needed. Feeling particularly playful, she knocked the pile of case files over that Bishop had been using as a little makeshift wall between their desks.

He was on the phone, so he was unable to yell at her. The puzzled look on his face accompanied by the hand gesture directed at the sprawled pile of folders on his desk sent a clear message of, "What the hell are you doing?!" He tied up his conversation and hung up the phone, never losing his bewildered look. "And just what, may I ask, was that all about?" he fumed angrily, as he leaned back in his chair and glared at her.

"I'm tired of being tied up on this case. Find something for us to do. Any case, I just want to go out and try to solve something. The time away from that case will do us some good. I've been thinking about it so much, it was starting to take my mind down the wrong roads."

Bishop sat in silence for a moment, taking in what all was going on. Sofia had managed to come up with a very solid plan on her way back from the morgue. She was using the excellent mood that Lucian had put her in, combined with the fact that she occasionally did like to work a separate case to change pace and clear her head. Sofia did this to make it seem as though she had had some personal breakthrough regarding the case. She had also indirectly addressed the thoughts that she knew Bishop had been having since her scene earlier that morning. After considering things for a few seconds,

Bishop began nodding his head in apparent approval at Sofia's new attitude as he looked at the mess she had created.

"Lemme take a look at what all we have goin' on and we can hit the road." His head continued to bounce around as he looked through the numerous manila folders.

"Preferably nothing too involved. How about an easy one? Any suspected suicides or something along those lines?" She bounced from foot to foot, clapping her hands slightly as she waited for Bishop to comply, huffing slightly each time he took a break from looking in order to spit into his giant Styrofoam cup.

"Even suspected suicides take forever with you." Bishop chuckled. "I've got a homeless guy we can check out. That way, even if we don't figure it out, who cares?" Suspecting that he was testing her, Sofia responded just as she normally would when he made such a callous and insensitive remark.

"Hey!" She looked at Bishop angrily as she stopped her anxious bouncing. "Why do you have to go and say something like that?" Knowing that she would give herself away if she acted too anxious to go along with just any case or anything that Bishop said, Sofia felt it was in her best interest to not be too permissive with him.

"Yeah, yeah. Get your gear and let's head out." His response made Sofia feel as though things had gone over well, and had successfully eased some of Bishops concerns. As she gathered her things, Sofia began to think forward to her rendezvous with Lucian and her earlier feelings of jubilation instantly returned. Snatching up her things, Sofia jogged up to catch Bishop just as he left the building.

27

As a day filled with tracking down leads and following the trail of evidence finally came to a close, Sofia and Bishop strolled back into the precinct satisfied with their day's work. They had unwittingly worked into the early evening hours and the sun was just beginning to set. The case had already run relatively cold, but they were able to make some solid progress on the matter. For what it was meant to be, the case had done exactly what Sofia had hoped. It had gotten them out of the office, their minds off the stale feel of the other case, and created some very positive feelings flowing regarding her police work. Even with all of the wonderful things that were happening between her and Lucian, Sofia had been unable to shake the fact that she was being outsmarted by these lunatics. But today, she found some renewed faith in her abilities as an investigator. Another bonus of working the homeless man's case was that it made the day absolutely fly by. Had she been able to, Sofia would have sat at her desk all day bouncing back and forth between thoughts of her evening with Lucian and the case, and the time would have crept by. Now, the workday was nearly over and she couldn't have been more excited.

"Good plan today, kid. We may need to try that again next week." It was no shock to Sofia that Bishop was suggesting another day away from their primary case.

"Maybe so. I want to see if this jarred some things loose. If not, we may have to try something different," Sofia said, knowing there was no chance that the next week would be devoted to anything other than working that case.

As she went to leave, Sofia leaned over to Bishop. "I know your feelings on the whole thing, but at least give the case some thought over the next few days. Today may have really helped us both out. I'll see you Thursday."

Bishop bobbed his head robotically as she made her way to the door, but Sofia hardly noticed. She was already locked in on getting to the morgue to get Lucian so they could make their way home.

Lucian had wrapped up everything for the evening and was ready to leave when Sofia burst into the morgue. Startled slightly, Lucian jumped up from his seat at her abrupt entrance.

"Good Lord, woman!" He reached for his heart. "What's all that about?" Sofia put on her best puppy-dog eyes.

"Oh, nothing. Just glad to be done working, I suppose." She skipped across the room. Lucian laughed to himself as he checked his desk for his things. Snatching up his house keys, he scanned the room quickly to make sure everything, and everyone, was put away properly. He headed over to greet Sofia.

"I'm excited to see you, too," he said, as he squeezed her, still smiling from her entrance.

"How was your day?" Lucian asked. Sofia wriggled free from his embrace.

"Not so amazing that I can't tell you while we walk." She pulled at his arm to get him to leave. Lucian just smiled, laughed, and pretended to resist as she all but dragged him from the building.

28

"I didn't hear much out of you today," Lucian said, as they made their way out into the warm evening air.

"My phone battery died earlier. I must have fallen asleep last night and forgotten to charge it. I meant to plug it in when we were in the car today but I got so caught up in what we were doing that I forgot. Could you remind me to plug it in tonight?"

"I certainly can, but you may want to go ahead and do that right when we get in. I'd hate for you to forget…you know…if you get preoccupied or something."

"You might be right." She pulled him down to her by his jacket for a passionate kiss. "Can't we get a cab?" Sofia whispered, hoping that he would break his normal routine just this once for their special night.

"Nah. Look how amazing the weather is outside. We can't waste a night like this. It's going to be way too hot to walk soon enough, and we can get a cab then. And how can you think that driving at this time of the day is going to get us there any faster than the train?"

Sofia had learned that Lucian's hatred for the city traffic was not limited to his displeasure with driving in the traffic, but also riding in it. He said that he preferred the scheduled stops because he knew just how long the train would take as opposed to the huge question marks involved with driving. The walk and the train ride on from the station to his place weren't too terrible, but they did take some time. Tonight, that was almost more than Sofia could bear.

"Come on!" she whined. "Just this once?"

Lucian just flashed his beautiful grin. "Cool your jets, woman.

There's no need to rush. We'll get there soon enough."

"I hope that's something you learned while practicing," she said, with a smile.

"Look at you!" Lucian cried out, approvingly. "You can laugh about it! Good job." Switching instantly to a satirically serious tone, he added, "And yes. Yes I did."

It had gotten later than Sofia had realized. She was usually less aware of the time when she left, as she was willing to work for hours on end with little to no breaks in order to follow a case. Today was different. Normally, Bishop would never have let them work late without at least making some comment. Today he had allowed them to work on into the night without the slightest grumble, presumably attempting to allow Sofia to get so comfortable with staying off their primary case that they would be able to do so more often. Although her intentions had been to fly through the day, get in early, and head straight to Lucian's at a break-neck pace, she had to admit that the mood created by the evening was far more fitting.

The full moon shone brightly and provided an amazing backdrop for their evening stroll. Huge, billowing white clouds glided slowly across the night sky, guided by the cool breeze. Everything seemed so perfect when she was with Lucian. She couldn't believe how happy he made her.

"I've been meaning to tell you, I have really enjoyed spending time with you lately," Lucian said, casually. "I don't think I have ever enjoyed someone's company as much as I have enjoyed yours." He leaned down and kissed her softly on her head as she looked up to him with a smile.

Lucian slowly caressed her back as they continued with their walk. His presence made everything seem so wonderful to Sofia. She could see no wrong in the world when she was with him. It was unlike anything she had ever experienced, and for good reason. Sofia had begun surveying every situation she entered to evaluate the possibility for danger many years before, and for good reason.

She knew it was much harder for her to get caught off-guard if she did so. When she was with Lucian, she found herself at-ease enough to let such concerns escape her.

29

In her usual state of hyper-awareness Sofia would have easily noticed the group of men that had locked onto them and were now following them towards the train station. Normally she would have noticed such a sketchy looking group even from a distance, but Lucian's hypnotic presence had blinded her so much that she hadn't noticed them leering from across the street when they passed them.

They had fallen in behind the pair and followed them at a distance until they found the perfect time to strike, and that time was now. The men stealthily picked up the pace as Sofia and Lucian made their way around the corner and on to a particularly secluded side street. They were on top of the two before they ever realized what was happening.

It was clear that these men were adept at this sort of attack by the way that they made their move. One of them came up behind Sofia and quickly muzzled her by shoving a large piece of cloth into her mouth, preventing her from screaming or taking a chunk of his hand with her teeth. One major problem that this caused was that it was now impossible for her to announce that she was a police officer. The other men focused on Lucian. They knocked him to the ground and began attacking him mercilessly.

The man holding Sofia was quite large and very strong, which left no room for her to maneuver away from him. He wrapped his other arm around Sofia's arms and chest and squeezed her tightly, limiting her movements, as well as her breathing. He had rested his enormous frame on her back. This prevented her from lifting a foot to try to kick him in the crotch, as he was much taller. Her training had prepared her more for a situation where she was lifted from the ground, which would have allowed for more attacks on her part.

Sofia's first thought was to take the man out by head-butting him directly in the face. Leaning forward quickly, she slammed her head back with as much force as she could. Her efforts were perfectly countered by the man as he lowered his own head and took the blow to the top of his forehead rather than his face. The blow clearly shook Sofia much more than it did the mindless clod holding her captive. Her head began to pound and she struggled to focus her eyes. Pain radiated forward from the point of impact in the back of her skull. Partially blinded by pain, Sofia could hardly tell what was going on. She continued thrashing in an attempt to hopefully break free and reach her gun. However, the man was much too strong.

While Sofia fought her captor, the other men had surrounded Lucian and were now beating him relentlessly. As she continued to battle the man, Sofia was able to turn in such a way that she could see what was happening to Lucian. Seeing Lucian's futile attempts to fight the men off among the barrage of kicks and punches caused her to fight more violently than before. The man's grasp only grew tighter. Sofia's screams for Lucian were muffled by the filthy piece of cloth that was crammed into her mouth. She could see that the violence was escalating as the men beat Lucian into submission. She knew what that meant for him. Her efforts were becoming less productive every second as the man was now squeezing her much more tightly, taking her wind and making it nearly impossible to move or breathe. As she struggled less, she couldn't help but to catch a glimpse of Lucian's face through all of the madness. Her heart broke as she looked at him through the melee. He was looking directly back at her now. His beautiful hazel eyes had never seemed more vibrant to her as he stared unwaveringly back at her. As the men continued to abuse his defenseless body, he kept his eyes trained on hers.

Sofia felt herself losing consciousness and her eyes began to close. Shaking them open quickly, she saw that Lucian was now doing everything that he could to reach his feet, but the men would not stop. Sofia tried to cry out to him, to beg him to give in and give them what they wanted, but it was useless. Between her muzzle and the limited amount of air she was receiving, it was all she could do to lift her head to look at him.

As the men continued to beat him, Lucian began to crawl towards her. This small sign of life caused the young brutes to begin grabbing anything within reach with which to assault him. Sofia was forced to watch as the men continued to beat poor Lucian, without ever speaking so much as a word. Amazingly, Lucian was able to continue to pull himself closer to Sofia as they continued their onslaught.

Sofia began feeling wooziness return and could see the blackness beginning to creep in around her field of view. Her struggling was little more than intermittent wiggling at this point, with an occasional half-hearted kick. She scanned the windows and walkways for signs of help, but no one was there. As she began to feel herself losing consciousness again, she returned her eyes to Lucian. Watching him crawl to her amidst the pummeling that he was taking was more than she could bear.

A large knot formed in the center of her throat and her vision blurred as tears filled her eyes and began to stream down her face. She had often kidded Lucian about his size and physical ability but now he seemed larger than life to her as he continued to make his way towards her. His unwavering gaze locked on her. Sofia stared back into Lucian's eyes, the wonderful moments that they had shared racing through her mind. She knew what was about to happen, and hardly even flinched when she heard the gun go off. She watched Lucian lurch forward, his arms folding beneath him and his face landing solidly on the concrete. Sofia was more than willing to allow herself to slip into unconsciousness at this point. As everything went dark, Sofia began to pray that no matter what hell these men put her through, when they were through, they would take her life as well.

30

Sofia's head throbbed as she awoke. Her eyes fluttered open, her lashes scraping across whatever fabric had been wrapped around her eyes. Dim light crept in beneath the bottom edge of her blindfold. She looked down at the bottom of the material to see if she could tell what sort of fabric it was. Waves of pain radiated outward from behind her eyes as she moved them, which only made her already pounding headache worse. As she went to reach for the source of the pain at the base of her skull, she quickly came to the realization that her hands were tied behind her.

Her arms were lashed behind her and were secured to some sort of object that she could not yet define. She considered tapping her head against the object to determine what it was. Thinking better of it, she decided not to test the density with her already desperately sensitive head. Judging by its texture and shape, Sofia felt it was safe to assume that it was some sort of pipe.

Judging from the texture, stiffness, and distinct musty smell that filled her nose, she assumed that her abductor had used an old sock to cover her eyes. In the mere seconds that she had to understand her current situation, she had dismissed the discomfort that she felt all around her face as a side effect of the overwhelming pain in her head; she now realized that she had been bound from head to toe.

There were no corners that she could use to work the material that bound her hands. It was cold to the touch where her arms rested against it. Her feet were bound and placed directly in front of her, so she believed herself to be seated on the floor, which was clearly cement based on her unbelievably sore tailbone.

Oddly enough, no gag had been placed in her mouth, which was a clear indication that there was no hope in screaming, not that she was about to do so. Screaming for help would only alert her captors to the fact that she had awakened. She needed as much time as she could manage to sort the situation out in her head.

It took every ounce of restraint for Sofia not to panic as she began to recount the actions that had taken place prior to losing consciousness. It didn't take long for her to remember exactly what had happened. The image of Lucian crawling towards her began running through her mind. Sofia tried to shake the thought out of her head, but it was useless, it was all she could think of. Without the ability to focus her eyes on something else to help her replace the image of his beautiful face staring at her as he took such a savage beating, she simply stared into the darkness and replayed the horrifying image over and over. Sofia knew there was no chance the attackers would have allowed Lucian to live after such a brutal attack, especially once they located her badge that they undoubtedly came across while searching her once she passed out. She could hardly keep herself from breaking down.

Sofia knew that if she was being monitored, or if one of her captors was nearby, showing them a sign of weakness at this point could be her undoing. Regardless of her efforts, a single tear squeezed its way free from her eye and sped down her face. Leaning her head down, she pressed the blindfold against her shoulder in an effort to soak the tiny escapee before someone was able to see it. There was a quick hiss as the dry fibers contracted to absorb the salty fluid. Sofia felt a great sadness overcome her. It was the same feeling she had felt immediately before losing consciousness and she began considering what the fastest way to get them to kill her would be. How could she provoke enough of a response to have them take her life quickly without torturing her first? As she ran through the scenarios, she began to imagine the different possible outcomes. Each was more horrifying than the last.

Eventually, she came to the realization that there would be no justice for Lucian if she allowed herself to die now. The thought that the men responsible for taking his life could potentially go free, combined with the level of fear she was experiencing thinking of what these men were capable of doing to her, was enough to give her a reason to try to escape, at least.

Sofia took a minute to compose her thoughts, try to block out the pain that was radiating from her skull, and began to try to visualize her situation.

From what she could tell, she was alone in the room, but she could hardly trust her judgment at this point. She began to test the strength of the material that was binding her hands by pulling her hands away from one another. She tried twisting her hands and feeling around with the tips of her fingers in an effort to evaluate what the material was that was around her wrists. The smooth finish of the material was unmistakable. She began to wriggle and contort her hands in an effort to loosen them, but quickly realized how futile this course of action was. For all of her wriggling and writhing, all she was rewarded with was raw skin courtesy of what she was certain was duct tape. Without the use of her hands, she was clearly going to have to work towards a different method of escape.

Sofia knew that she needed to have a working idea of her whereabouts in case there was any opportunity to run. There was little chance that they were going to unbind her and make that possible, but she had to hope there was a chance for escape. Their attack had been far too calculated for this to be their first time. A crew with a history of this sort of activity was likely to have taken precautions to ensure that escape was impossible. It was at that moment, when she was realizing the level of involvement that had gone into the attack, that Sofia considered something new. The attack could have been a planned maneuver by the very group that she and Bishop had been trying to find.

As she recounted the events of the attack, she understood just how calculated things had been. They had picked a perfect spot to attack the two. Had they realized what was happening, it still would have proven very difficult to escape. The giant that neutralized Sofia was overkill for most women, but not for a person as well trained as she. Murder did not seem like their original intention, but when Lucian resisted, they made the decision to kill him quickly. After killing Lucian, they must have drugged Sofia in order to move her. There was no way she would have been unconscious long enough for them to transport and bind her without waking her up. Passing out from a lack of oxygen simply wouldn't have such a strong effect.

A group that attacked that precisely, that had the means to drug, and move, a victim that quickly, and with a location they knew they could take someone, without the threat of being found, was a group that had a plan and an agenda. If this was the case, Sofia knew that her odds were much worse than she had originally expected.

Knowing that this group was far more intelligent than the street thugs that she dealt with on a daily basis led Sofia to believe that they would have taken her to a relatively remote location. She may be some place in the middle of one of the worst parts of the city. In doing so, they would give themselves plenty of time to recapture her or change locations in the event that she was able to escape. No one would be able to hear her screams for help for some time; or in the event that they had stayed in the city, no one would listen.

Sofia listened for any sound that might give her some idea of her location. The complete lack of airplane noise gave her a very good indication that they were nowhere near the airport. The lack of traffic noise from the time that she had awoken indicated that they were far from any of the major interstate or highway. These two facts were enough for Sofia to deduce that if they were still in the city, they were nowhere good. To Sofia's dismay, this was the most likely possibility. In an area where the gang had established themselves, and were known by locals, they would be nearly untouchable.

While she was doing everything she could to remember her training and not panic, it was impossible for her to ignore how dire things had become. Sofia slowly began to realize how hopeless her situation was as she went down the ever-shortening list of ways that she might be able to escape, and nothing sounded possible. Regardless of how impossible the situation seemed, she was now determined to do all that she could to obtain justice for Lucian.

She had never allowed herself to feel hopeless before and she wouldn't make an exception in this case. Her life had started with struggle, so she knew she had it in her to resist the urge to give up.

An only child to village workers in Columbia, Sofia had seen more injustice, devastation, and evil, in her childhood than most people could see in five lifetimes. A childhood wrought with as much personal loss and difficulty as hers would change anyone, whether it changed them for the better or worse depended solely on the person. The people of the village that Sofia was born into were used as slave labor for local drug lords. Sofia had watched many of her loved ones work their lives away for these men with little more than a small tin shack to show for it.

As bad as the living conditions were, the working conditions were worse. If and when someone passed out from exhaustion in the fields, the overseers would simply drag their bodies away in order to make room for the next person. Those who had collapsed were left lying in the dirt to recuperate for the remained of the day. In order to dissuade the others from following suit in an attempt at receiving a break, those who had passed out were considered free game for the field bosses. The abuse ranged from spitting on them as they lay in the hot, dry dirt, to urinating on them. Occasionally, they would see how close they could shoot the dirt around their limbs without actually hitting them.

The use of the laborers as target practice was rare because whenever one of them was foolish enough to hit the target, things usually turned out very badly for whoever was responsible once it got back to the big bosses. Although cruel and heartless, the lords knew that a crippled laborer was incapable of being productive in the fields, and replacing a field boss was far easier to do.

Regardless of the attempts the lords made, several of the people that Sofia grew up around were killed right in front of her for various reasons. Some were accused of stealing, which couldn't have really been true, as they were hardly allowed to wear more than rags to cover their private parts. Others were accused of trying to inform the authorities, which was also a ridiculous concept, as every villager knew all too well how useless the local authorities were.

Mainly, Sofia believed that they were usually just killing them for sport, but the field bosses would always come up with a way to justify their actions to the lords. Regardless of the accusations placed against them, seldom was there any proof of guilt. They were simply murdered in cold blood, out where the entire village could see. Whenever Sofia witnessed such injustice, her mother would indicate for her to keep her focus on the work that she was doing, and not look at what was happening.

On the nights that followed such events, her mother would come into her room and, cupping her hands around her ear to ensure that no one would hear her talking about their plans to escape, she would whisper to her about her father's plan to get them out of Colombia. She would tell her about how they were going to escape to America and start a new life where they would never have to be afraid of such injustice happening to them. America was a nation of laws that, when broken, held great consequences. As she grew, and the violence increased, Sofia drew from the many acts of cruelty and injustice that she witnessed as inspiration to do the right thing and make a positive difference. She never allowed herself to accept that this was the best that life had to offer her. Those nights when her mother would whisper to her of their future, she would listen to the wonderful stories that her mother would tell her, and she would dream of the fantastic life that they would have once they were gone. Those nights became the only time that she could find happiness because she knew that she could never tell anyone about her family's plan to leave Colombia.

Most of the other people of her village saw the drug lords as powerful and aspired to be like them. They would also take advantage of any situation that would get them into the good graces of these men. They hoped for a promotion from field laborer to some level of boss. If the news of her family's desire to leave the village became known to the wrong villager, or God forbid, one of the low-level bosses, Sofia and her parents would surely be killed in order to make an example for the others. Knowing that such information could get someone a more prestigious job in the production lines, Sofia never uttered a word to anyone. Sofia's mother and father had very different opinions of their tyrannical overseers than did the other villagers. Her parents saw them as evil dictators that took advantage of the people in their village, and this is what they taught Sofia. Sofia would listen to her parents' stories and watch what was going on with her village. She developed her own opinions about what she saw. While she hated their tyrannical leaders for the torture that they inflicted upon everyone, and all that they were responsible for, there was one group that she despised even more.

The local police would regularly come through her village on their way to the nearby mansions. They would stay for hours, drinking the finest liquors and smoking high dollar cigars with them. They would eventually leave, taking with them bundles of cash and other handouts, and never looked twice at the suffering that was going on all around them as they sped through the village. Her mother's stories about justice in America, and seeing how those responsible for keeping law and order in her village shirked their responsibilities, drove Sofia's decision to focus her life on stopping injustice and helping people in any way that she could. Sofia pledged that once her family successfully escaped from the cruel dictatorship of their village and migrated to America, she would devote her life to helping those who needed it by punishing all who deserved it. This became her passion.

One night, when Sofia was nine years old, the stars finally aligned in their favor and Sofia's parents set their plan in motion. Sneaking out during the night, they hid in a number of predetermined locations in order to evade all of the perimeter security sweeps. They had planned the locations based on the pattern of stops they had witnessed the guards making throughout the years they had been observing them. After sneaking out of the village, carrying nothing but the clothes on their backs and a few sacks containing some stale bread they had saved, they escaped safely into the jungle. They stayed in a series of makeshift huts that other escapees before them had built and left behind. It didn't take Sofia long to realize they were taking an escape route that had been used by numerous escaped villagers before them.

She later found out from her father that it was a path able to be kept secret by the fact that one villager at a time knew about it. Whoever learned about the passageway could only tell one other well-trusted villager of its existence on the eve of his own departure. Even then, the next man knew only of the first stop on the route and what to look for to get him to the next location. The trail only took the people to a point that made it possible to find safe passage out of Colombia; it was not a guaranteed exit. Every day that they were in the jungle, her father would go out and locate the next indicator telling them which direction to go. They would sneak along through the jungle at night to keep from being detected by the small search parties that had undoubtedly been sent out to find them. They knew that if they were found, the drug lords would use them as an example of what would happen to others if they tried to escape.

After what seemed like months in the jungle, Sofia and her parents found themselves on the outskirts of Cartagena, a major port city in northern Colombia, where her father procured them a spot on a freightliner. They rode in the cargo hold with the families of several other stowaways. Although the confines were tight and unpleasant, Sofia would always remember it as the greatest trip of her life, based solely on the possibilities that lay on the other end.

As she sat in the darkness thinking of how much of a struggle her parents and she had endured to get to America, Sofia found hope. Feeling a surge of resilience, she began to run every possible scenario that she could imagine for what was about to happen. As she repeatedly ran option after option through her head, she heard a sound that she had hoped she would have had more time to prepare for.

She heard footsteps approaching.

31

Sofia made no attempt to conceal the fact that she had regained consciousness, since these people were not likely to wait for her to wake up if they had questions for her. It was more likely that one of them would send a boot to her face or some other form of abuse than it was that they allow her to come to on her own. She felt that her best defense at this point was to try to get one of the members to listen to what she had to say in hopes that they would realize that keeping a detective hostage would ruin whatever they were working towards. The footsteps drew closer, echoing around the spacious room. It sounded as though only one person was approaching, and the lack of welcoming voices gave her a feeling that they were alone, which worked in Sofia's favor. Getting a single member to listen to her was far more likely if they were alone.

"I'm a detective," she blurted, as the footsteps drew nearer. The walking stopped, but no one spoke.

"My shift starts soon and people will know something is up when I don't show. Everyone knows that we have been investigating your gang, and this will be the first place they check." She wasn't so sure.

"I seriously doubt that," came a gravelly response.

Regardless of how unsettling the man's voice was, she was able to find a tiny speck of comfort in the fact that he spoke to her. The voice sounded like that of a man, but determining an upper age limit was impossible. More than likely, he was in his mid to late twenties as maintaining usefulness in a gang became less common beyond thirty. He spoke in a harsh tone and with a raspy voice, but the words came out just above a whisper. He was approximately ten to fifteen feet from her, and his voice echoed from the walls as the footsteps had before. This let her know that they were in a sizeable room with hard, uncovered surfaces. She assumed that it was a warehouse or an auditorium of some sort, or maybe an abandoned gym; although it was impossible to rule out the chance it was a very large basement or storm shelter. These facts continued to narrow the possibilities for where she was being held, but not enough to give her a solid idea. She needed to keep him talking in order to learn as much as she could about her surroundings, as well as keeping herself alive.

"Doubt it all you want. That isn't going to change the fact that you and your crew are in deep shit once my 'boys' from the station head this way."

"That is very true, but the fact that you don't work tomorrow will. I mean, how will anyone know you're missing if no one expects to see you for the next two days?"

Chills shot down Sofia's spine and brought the hairs on her neck and arms to attention. They had not even scratched the surface of who this gang was or where they were located, yet they already knew who was working the case as well as her schedule. She was terrified, but knew she couldn't let him know that. One thing that had worked in her favor was that her eyes were covered and he could not see the shock and terror that lay within them.

"Even if you were working today, I doubt very seriously that anyone would be looking for you here." He circled around in front of her, finally finding his place directly in front of her.

"Why do you say that?" She realized that she had just missed her opportunity to refute the fact that she was not working that day. These were mistakes she could not afford to continue to make.

"For one thing, you don't even know who you're dealing with. You don't have a single piece of evidence that could lead you to me. You don't know who I am or what I'm doing. Second, you don't know where we are, nor do your 'boys' at the precinct."

From the work that they had done on the case, Sofia knew that there were no weak links in this gang's chain. Regardless of the speaker's position with the group, she knew he would be too smart for her to bluff, especially when she had absolutely nothing to use against him. Her safest bet at this point was to keep him talking while she tried to devise a plan.

"So, you know who I am, and what I do. You know my schedule. You seem to think you know what I have on you. What else do you know about me?" She was struggling to keep it together. She did everything that she could to keep from giving away how truly horrifying this situation was to her. She began working her wrists again, only much more slowly this time in an effort to keep from drawing his attention. She knew it was a futile attempt at escape, but things were going as far from her way as she could have imagined.

"I know a great many things about you, Sofia. But that is not the purpose of this meeting."

"This meeting? Are you telling me that you planned this? That you planned to attack my boyfriend and me in the alley? You planned to kill my boyfriend and take me hostage? Keep talking, buddy. That's called pre-meditated murder and it carries a nice little death sentence." She spoke as confidently as she could, considering the subject matter and her current situation. Sofia was doing everything that she could to keep herself calm, but she felt that her nerves were beginning to show.

"Your charges do not scare me, Detective Milena."

Sofia's heart sank. His comment shredded her last hope that Lucian had been spared, or possibly gotten away, or that she could have been wrong about what happened, since she hadn't seen the bullet wound. She had been knocked out right after hearing the gunshot that she believed to have killed Lucian, so she was never completely positive of what had happened to him. She knew that it was a long shot for such a violent group to spare any possible witness, and now that she was able to look at the situation with no delusions, she realized that it was never a possibility. They had nothing to gain from letting him live. They would never let Lucian get away and warn anyone that she had been taken.

She was beginning to feel the true pressure of the situation, but continued to keep her outward composure.

"I'll be honest with you, I don't know if I should be flattered or disappointed." Sofia was trying to bait him.

There was a long pause before he replied. "What are you talking about?"

"Well, we were operating under the belief that you were a group of methodical and calculating men. I had honestly developed a little respect for you. Your attention to detail, and ability to remove all trace evidence from the scenes, has been nothing short of incredible. The way that you have kept us confused and completely off your trail to this point is commendable. But now, after this, I just don't know."

She had decided that in a last ditch effort she was going to try to flip the tables on him. She was going to play against his vanity in hopes of proving that he had damaged the group's reputation in her eyes. At the thought of this, he might let her go in an effort to redeem their name. She also realized that there was a much easier option for him to consider. He could just kill her, as they hadn't disgraced themselves in anyone else's eyes. This was a risk she was ready to take. Although catching those responsible for Lucian's death was a motivation for her to escape, being certain he was gone was bringing her back around to the idea of giving up. Not only that, but she knew that getting past Lucian's death was going to be next to impossible. Their connection had been short-lived, but more intense than any she had ever felt before.

"Please, feel free to continue," the voice finally replied.

Sofia's tension eased ever so slightly. She knew that in getting him to ask that question, she had struck a nerve on some level. She just had to keep picking at that thread.

"Well, I just mean that you have given me more in this conversation than your entire gang had given me in months. It just shows me that you're not as good on your feet as you are with a plan. You guys are smart, but apparently not very quick." She was being completely condescending at this point, but she didn't care.

"And what do you presume that I have given you?" he asked, rather gruffly.

Sofia grew bolder with every word that she spoke. She felt as though the conversation could end a few different ways, and she was really fine with most of them. Live or die, she was not going to let this guy terrorize her. She had come to the conclusion the he was not overly violent. He sounded well-spoken and had not taken to beating her as she attempted to raise doubt in his mind, so she felt confident that he would be more susceptible to submitting than many of his peers would be. Sofia knew that she needed to make something happen quickly, before the others returned.

"Well, there are a few subtle things and a few that were more obvious. You know who I am and what I do. You have an intimate knowledge of my schedule and some knowledge about what we do and do not know regarding your case. Also, you have been masking your voice this entire time. There is no doubt in my mind that I know you, or we have at least met on a regular enough basis that you believe that I would be able to identify you by your voice."

There was a brief silence at this, giving Sofia cause to smirk. She felt as though she had gotten under his skin. She just knew that she had broken his concentration and his cool. He would begin to unravel at this point. Her confidence began to creep back into her body as she continued with her analysis.

"You have been keeping your distance from me this entire time, which lets me know that you're uncomfortable with women or possibly intimidated by a police officer; or maybe there's something about the way you smell that you believe might give away more about who you are. From what I can tell about our location, I know that we are nowhere near the airport and likely not by an interstate. The room is very large and has an echo, so I can start eliminating buildings that don't include rooms that match that description for your hideout. See what I mean? You guys really shouldn't have come after us. The only thing that has been working in your favor is the fact that you've been knocking off criminals. That man you killed last night was a great person and a friend of every officer in town. Killing him was the worst thing you could have done, especially when you couple that with the fact that you have abducted an actual police officer!" As she spoke of Lucian, she couldn't keep her emotions hidden. The tears welled up in her eyes. She again pressed the blindfold against her face to absorb them before they were able to break free.

"What happened last night was impossible to avoid." His voice had not become frantic, as she had expected. He spoke calmly and even sounded somewhat apologetic. "Sadly, it is now I who feels disappointment in you."

Sofia didn't like the sound of this. She momentarily stopped mopping her tears and tried to figure out where she had gone wrong. What was she seeing that was not there? The confidence that she had felt before was now gone. She had an awful feeling in the pit of her stomach and felt as though she would be sick. The smirk was no longer smeared across her face. She quickly bit down on the inside of her lip in order to try to regain her focus. It was her only chance at warding off the waves of panic that were radiating throughout her body.

"You see, I was an admirer of yours as well. You have done quite well in your career and I believed you to be a top-notch detective. While it is true that you and I have come in contact with one another, the logic that you used in order to reach that conclusion is weak. You presume that we are close because I know your name as well as what you do. News flash, honey, you were unconscious for a while and you carry identification and a badge. You think that we are friends because I have knowledge of your schedule, but in all actuality, anyone that watched you from afar would know that you work a schedule where you're off every Wednesday. I'm keeping my distance from you because I like my personal space, and I see no reason to make myself uncomfortable in an effort to intimidate you; I imagine this situation is enough. As far as the case is concerned, I know every move that has been made on this end, and none of it has gotten any publicity. That tells me that you don't know that the deaths are any more than a rash of gang-related activity. If you had any idea what direction you needed to be going, you would have been feeding information to the news outlets in order to change the pattern or warn the public. Finally, the location that I have chosen for this meeting is of no importance other than the fact that it is a place that I knew I could conduct this sort of activity without fear of being bothered."

At this point, Sofia had no idea what direction things were about to go. She did everything she could to remain confident, which became more difficult every time the voice came out of the darkness. She had been wrong about him. He was highly intelligent and very quick. Nothing that she had said to him had worked at all. The only thing that she had seemed to achieve was to have lowered his opinion of her, which was probably the only reason she had been left alive to this point.

"Now, since we have determined that I know all about you and your work...." He had moved incredibly close to her without her realizing. His breath was hot on her ear as he told her, "Let's hear what you know about me, and mine."

At this, Sofia considered another option about her captor that she had been forcing out of her mind throughout the encounter. She had hoped that she was dealing with a low-level crony or mid-level boss, but his words all but solidified the fact that she was dealing with a mastermind. The fact that he had referred to the acts as "his" work, and he had made no reference to his cohorts, made things very clear that he was in command. The thought that she was dealing with the person that had choreographed these beatings, killings, and mutilations, had been too terrifying for her to even consider. Now, all bets were off. She didn't care about trying to escape anymore. She knew that whatever she was doing there was by design and there was no hope for escape. Her entire body began to shake with fear. There was nothing that she could do to control it any longer. Sofia decided that her best course of actions was to do as he asked, and hope that someone would find her, or that by some miracle, he would decide to release her. She took a few breaths in an effort to regain some composure, and began telling him what she knew.

32

Sofia recounted everything that had happened regarding the case right up until the moment that she awoke in her current position. She faltered a little as she went over what happened in the alley. It was all that she could do to get through without completely breaking down each time she mention Lucian's name, much less while explaining his death. The scene played itself over and over in her mind as she neared that point, and it continued once she finished. The darkness provided by her blindfold made it nearly impossible for her to keep from seeing Lucian crawling across the alley floor to reach her. She now sat in silence and darkness behind the filthy, dry blindfold, unaware of what might come next, and once again unsure whether or not she cared. She had told him everything that she knew. She had even allowed herself to let slip that some of the officers were in favor of the swift brand of justice that he had been inflicting. It was at that point that she felt she had done herself the most good as she mentioned how the death of an officer would quickly change the minds of every single man and woman on the force who had sympathized with their vigilante efforts. Now all she could do was wait in the darkness and the silence.

After a few minutes, the voice finally returned, although it was now much more apprehensive and far less confident. "I need for you to remain calm. I am very sorry for all of the stress that this evening has caused you, but I had to make sure that I knew everything. I'm going to remove your blindfold now. Again, I'm so sorry. This was just something I thought I had to do." Caught off guard by his comments, Sofia sat in silence as the man approached. Sofia's muscles tightened in anticipation of his intentions as he drew near. Reaching behind her, he pulled the knotted portion over her head and removed the stale rag from her face. The light attacked her unprepared and overanxious pupils as she attempted to look directly at her captor. Wincing from the burning pain that overwhelmed her eyes, she peered through the tear-induced haze, finally staring directly into the face that had caused her so much pain.

A knot formed in her throat so tightly that she could neither swallow nor breathe. As he moved away from her, Sofia was able to see him more clearly. Lucian was still wearing the jeans he had been wearing when he was shot. His shirt was different. He had been wearing a blue button up when they left work, but now he had on a fresh t-shirt. Sofia had no idea how long she had been out. From what she gathered from the conversation, and knowing that passing out from a simple lack of oxygen alone wouldn't have taken too long to recover from, she had deduced that it could not have been more than a few hours. Regardless of whether it had been two hours or two days, there was no way that he should be standing before her, much less standing there showing no real evidence of having just been through such a traumatic event.

Sofia swallowed the painful lump in her throat just long enough to squeeze out the words, "It was you?"

Lucian looked into her eyes and nodded his head.

"Not like you're thinking, but yeah," was all he said.

Her head swirled with questions. Sofia wasn't sure if it was terror, relief, or confusion that caused the tears to well up in her eyes, but they came nonetheless. She had been dealing with the loss of Lucian during this trauma of this entire event and now he stood before her, relatively unscathed. There was no explanation, which would not only keep him alive after the shooting, but also allow him to have walked away from the incident with such insignificant wounds. She sat in awe of what she was seeing when suddenly she realized what this meant. There was only one scenario that allowed for him to live through the attack, for her to have been spared from unthinkable events after losing consciousness, and for them to have just had the conversation they had just finished having. Lucian had to be leading the gang responsible for the attacks and had to have staged the event in the alley.

How can that be? She ran through all the possibilities in her mind. Could he be the leader of this gang that was responsible for the vicious, heinous crimes we've been tracking? How could that be the case? How could the man with whom I've spent so much time, that I've learned so much about, be capable of carrying on two completely opposite personalities?

Lucian had been so tender and caring with her in the time that they had spent together, but the man that was responsible for carrying out such brutal murders could never have been capable of anything other than hatred and evil. She wanted so badly not to believe it. She wanted nothing more than to jump to her feet, run to him, and hold him, pretending nothing had happened. She knew that she would never be able to live her life with him with these sorts of questions looming between them.

Lucian wiped away the tears that were now flowing freely down her cheeks. It did little good as they weren't about to stop. He gently stroked her face, hoping to offer some level of comfort, terrified of what she would think of him when he had told her the truth. Sofia continued to stare at him with unwavering eyes. She was silenced by her utter dismay at what he had just said to her. The man that she loved was not dead, but he was no longer the man that she loved. As she sat there crying, she wondered if she should even be happy that he was alive. Wouldn't the world be a safer place without him in it? The thoughts and emotions continued to churn inside of her until she felt as though she would be sick.

Finally, she was able to speak. In a quivering voice, she replied, "I don't understand."

"I know, baby. I'll explain, but I need for you to keep an open mind and I need you to know that I'm not what you think. I'm not gonna ask you to promise me anything, but I do want you to listen with a very open mind. Now, you know I'd never hurt you, so when I untie you, just be cool. Okay? I'm gonna untie you now. Just relax, and I'll try to make it all make sense."

The idea that he expected her to remain calm and "be cool" was ludicrous but she had no plans to leave that room without an explanation. She was both physically and mentally exhausted from the attack and the emotional drain of her situation. It was actually very likely that she would not do anything. She knew that Lucian wasn't lying when he said that he would never hurt her, so she remained physically calm as he began to release her from her binds.

Lucian finished removing the tape from her wrists and tried to rub them gently for her. Sofia pulled her hands away from him quickly, handling them herself before addressing her tear soaked face. Slowly rising to her feet, she paused a moment to let her aching knees and backside adjust to standing. Lucian was completely unsure of what to expect. As he awkwardly attempted to help her dust herself off, Sofia punched him hard, squarely in the ribcage. Recoiling in pain, he retreated and gave her plenty of room to address her needs.

After finishing dusting herself off and stretching for a moment, she looked around the room for a place to sit comfortably while she listened to Lucian's explanation. She noticed a stack of crates that showed some potential and walked over to create a makeshift chair. It pleased her ever so slightly that she had been correct regarding a few things about her surroundings. They were in fact in a large, wide-open room. The walls were made of poured concrete. It appeared to be the basement or bunker of an abandoned house. She had gotten that right, as well as clearly knowing her captor. Sofia laughed a little to herself at the thought of this. It came as no surprise to her that she found something humorous about the situation. She had told many women who had been victimized over the years, when in high stress situations, the emotions are at the surface. Any one of them could present itself. She positioned herself so that she was facing Lucian, eased her sensitive backside onto the crate, crossed her arms, and waited.

Lucian approached her cautiously. The look on her face told him that he needed to get on with the explanation or things were going to get ugly. She had clearly moved from being concerned about the situation to angry and impatient. Lucian had tried to prepare himself for this moment. These were not the circumstances he had hoped for. In the short amount of time he had to formulate a plan, he had decided that the best course of action was to come right out of the gates at full speed.

"I'll get right to it because I know you probably just want to leave. First of all, I don't consider anything I've done as wrong."

Sofia's expression did not waver.

"You know from your investigation, from the work that you and Bishop did, that those men were evil. I never led you in the wrong direction when you came to me, and I never tried to stop your progress. In all honesty, I wanted you to find me. I just never anticipated that it would be this way."

He was not wrong. Sofia knew that each of the men that had died were accused of terrible crimes, multiple times, but each had found a way to use the system to their advantage. Their crimes varied, but each victim had committed at least one violent or reckless act, and had shown no signs of remorse. Several of them had been gang members that had steadily escalated in their brutality with each crime that they committed. Nearly all of the men had served time at some point, but all of them had repeatedly slipped from the grasp of the police.

These exact issues had caused so much dissention amongst the officers at her precinct lately. Sofia had stayed firm in her belief that the system was the way to get justice. She had never seen death as the way to deal with a criminal. She truly believed that people should try their hardest to rehabilitate criminals, and she believed deeply that everyone deserved a second chance. Regardless of these opinions, she listened as he continued.

"I can't imagine that's your biggest issue right now, though. I figure it's a toss-up between why I'm not dead, and the stuff that's been goin' down with the bodies." Lucian could tell by Sofia's aggressive body language that he needed to get to the point quickly. Even when exhausted, Sofia was able to put off an utterly terrifying vibe.

"Well, the answers are really one in the same. You see, I have a unique body makeup that requires a few things of me in the ways of maintenance. At the same time, that makeup affords me a few very unique benefits." Lucian was very uncomfortable with trying to explain the situation to her. It was becoming very clear as he fidgeted about as he spoke.

This type of behavior was not something that Sofia was used to seeing from him. He was always so eloquent and sure of himself when he spoke. His discomfort and inability to get to the point was now beginning to make her very uneasy as well. Even still, Sofia offered him no help nor did she attempt to make herself appear any less agitated to allow him any level of comfort.

"What I did to those people wasn't me tryin' to make some disgusting statement or establish some sort of territorial thing. I was just doin' what I had to do…" Lucian trailed off as Sofia's puzzled expression gave him some idea of just how odd what he was saying sounded. "I guess that doesn't really make enough sense, huh? See, what you have to understand is that if I get into a fight or overexert myself, I use up an exorbitant amount of energy. I use so much energy, that I gotta replenish it real quick or my body starts to feed on itself. When that happens, I got very little time before it starts causing me a lot of discomfort. So in order to keep myself from having to deal with that, I take advantage of the situation that I have before me. I need to give my body something to burn to replenish my energy, and…you know… they're dead…so…." Lucian moved on quickly, knowing that he had not given her anywhere in the vicinity of a reasonable excuse.

"Plus, when I'm fully enraged, I get a little frenzied. When I get like that, there's little that is going to keep me from finishing my task. Do you understand what I'm getting at?" She did not, and that was no surprise to Lucian. He knew exactly the words he had to say in order to get her on the same page with him. Knowing all too well what her reaction to the words he was about to say would be, he began pacing back and forth in front of Sofia.

"Okay. Don't freak out when I say this, because it's really not what you think. You also might like to know that I really like you and care a lot about you. You may not want to hear that right now, but it's the truth." He began to wring his hands a little.

"Alright.... Here it is...and understand that there are a great many things involved with this that are completely inaccurate and that have been taken completely out of context throughout the years."

Sofia was growing impatient with his fumbling and was becoming very confused.

"Okay. Now, I'm not a vampire, per se...."

Sofia's eyes opened wide at his comments as she drew in a deep breath through her nose. This was not the way that a valid explanation started. Even at this, she maintained her silence, although at this point it was more from the shock than her stubbornness. Placing her thumb and forefinger against her eyebrows, she closed her eyes tightly and began rubbing them. Seeing her reaction, Lucian began to try to explain things much more quickly.

33

"Don't freak out! Just listen! Just listen!" He coaxed, pumping his hands to try and calm her.

"Now, what I mean by that is, my body makeup is the common thread between me and all of the others before me, that the myths of the vampire are based on." He spoke quickly, but paused so that she could absorb what he was saying. Lucian had not had to explain this to someone in this way before. He had only actually explained it one other time, and it was nowhere near this difficult. He knew from experience that if she was going to understand what he was trying to tell her, she would have to comprehend each component independently.

"What I mean by that is, throughout history many other people have actually experienced the same body composition that I have. Those people have struggled with coming to grips with their body's abilities as well as its demands. They learned to cope with the demands as they experienced them. Many times, their actions were witnessed by others and when that happens, the explanation is rarely sought out and is more often created in the minds of the witnesses…."

"Stop," Sofia interjected calmly, holding her hand up in the air at Lucian. "Are you being serious?" she asked, in disbelief.

Lucian's face filled with a look of weariness as he realized how difficult this was going to be.

"I can't believe you!" Sofia blurted, instantly becoming more aggravated at Lucian's expression. "I cannot believe that you are trying to explain away murder by saying that you're a vampire!"

"Not a vampire. You're not listening. I know what you think of when you hear that word, and that's not what I am. It's crucial that you understand that!"

"This is too much, Lucian! This is too much for me to absorb! You expect me to believe that you killed these people because you needed to feed your overexerted body so that you wouldn't experience some discomfort?! Does that sound like a reasonable exchange rate to you? Someone loses their life so that you don't have to be uncomfortable?"

"Well, it's really uncomfortable." In an unadvisable attempt at lightening the mood, Lucian opted to take a shot at some oddly timed humor. Sofia's unwavering stare let him know that his shot had missed.

"Plus, that's not what I said," he quickly rebounded. "I killed them because they were evil. Make no mistake about that. I knew what I was doing when I killed them, and I will not deny that. They were evil and the world is a better place without them. I fed on them because of the discomfort."

"You're unbelievable! This is unbelievable! I cannot believe that you're trying to get me to buy this crap, and you are trying to make jokes!" She stood, fuming, for several moments until she could no longer hold it in.

"You let me think you were dead, you son of a bitch!" she shouted at Lucian, her voice cracking with emotion.

Lucian lowered his head, ashamed of how upset she had become throughout the situation.

"I made a mistake with that, and I'm sorry. The way things went down, I just kind of thought things up on the fly, and I thought I needed more information.... It was just a bad idea." He watched her wiping her face from where he stood, wanting nothing more than to console her, but he didn't dare approach her. He stood just out of arm's reach from her and waited patiently as she took a minute to catch her breath. Unable to do any good, Lucian decided to press on to try to get her to understand what was going on.

"I truly am sorry for upsetting you, but I need to try and make you understand. I know how hard this is to believe, and I know you don't want to hear it, but I'm not the monster you think I am. The thing is, nearly everything that you believe about what I am, is wrong. I can explain most of it, but some of it is still a mystery even to me. I'm not really sure where to start, so why don't we do this: ask me whatever you want and I'll answer it with one hundred percent honesty."

Where could she even begin? So many things had just happened. Beyond believing that he was dead, he was now clearly insane! He was expecting her to follow him down the ridiculous road that he had laid out for her. She could only assume that Lucian was about to tell her some twisted tale about being involved in some "vampire" cult, and how all of this had been a part of an initiation or some other warped nonsense! Nothing was making sense. This sort of thing would have happened before, if it were some sort of initiation. There would have been a rash of similar killings, but there had been nothing even remotely similar to what he was doing. While she didn't want to indulge this ridiculousness, she felt compelled to dig further for the truth.

Sofia continued to bounce the information around in her head, trying to make some sense of it. She wasn't able to come up with a single explanation that could hold water. As she continued considering ideas, she grew more and more anxious. As she grew more anxious, her foot began to bounce on the floor. The excessive bouncing of her foot had drawn Lucian's stare as he sat waiting for some response. As she glanced up at him, she noticed that he had focused his gaze on her rapidly bouncing foot.

"Oh! I'm sorry! Is this bothering you?" She stopped the bouncing and slammed her foot down. Lucian's focus remained on the spot where her foot had been bouncing.

"Um, no. It wasn't bothering me at all. There was nothing else to look at. Are you ready to calm yourself and have a conversation?" Lucian's mood had hardened and he spoke very firmly. He was more serious than he had been before. In fact, he had a more serious look on his face than Sofia could ever remember having seen before. His directness caught her off guard, but only caused her to grow more annoyed with him.

"Are you under the impression that you are in a situation to demand anything of me?" she growled.

"You know me pretty well at this point, with the exception of a few things that have just come to light. You know full well that I'm not about to sit here all night while you mull things over. I don't like for problems to sit, unresolved. I'm ready to tell you anything that you wanna know, you just need to ask. If that's not gonna happen, I guess we need to figure out the next step."

Furious, but all too aware that he was being perfectly honest about ending the conversation if she didn't make a move, Sofia took a second and figured out what she needed to know first.

"Well, I guess the first thing that I want to know is, what makes you think that you can take the law into your own hands and go all 'vigilante justice' on these men?"

"Oh!" he said, with some level of surprise, as he took his attention off the floor and finally looked up to meet her gaze. "So you don't have any questions about the other thing?"

"The vampire thing? Well, I assume you are going to feed me some garbage about being in a group with some lunatics that think that they can drink blood," she countered sarcastically. "So, no. I'm not wasting my time on that."

Lucian was visibly becoming frustrated, and made no attempts to hide it. He had known that this was going to be difficult, but had hoped for some level of cooperation. A subject as touchy as this one, mixed with an attitude like Sofia's, was going to add up to a difficult situation every time.

"Well," he said, with a deep sigh. "That's why I told you to listen and then ask questions. So, rather than wait for you to ask, I guess I'll just tell you what I need to tell you and hope I remember to cover everything. What I am is not so easy to explain, and even harder to understand. I should've figured you would think something like that. I mean, that's a very logical explanation. But, I'm not in any group. It's just me. Like I said, I am what the legends of the vampire are based on. I'm not the person that they are based on, but I'm just like the dudes the legends were created about. See, my genes cause my body to create a larger amount of testosterone and adrenaline among various other chemicals in my body. When I'm injured, my body's response is quick and exact. It finds and fixes the problem. Boom, done. I don't know how far I can go before my body gives out. I can tell you that nothing that I've run into up to this point has killed me, of that I can assure you."This was another small attempt at humor that failed to land even the slightest smile on Sofia's face. Instead, she reached out and scratched him as hard and as deep as she could on his arm. He had given her the perfect opening, and she had plenty to be angry about.

"What the hell!" Lucian cried out, reaching for his forearm.

"Go ahead vampire man, heal away," she mocked sarcastically.

"That ain't how it works, woman, damn!" She had taken a layer of his skin with her in the attack and left deep scratches that ended in four perfect crescent shaped holes where the skin was now peeling back. Sofia hadn't actually meant to dig in quite as deep and was a little nervous with how he might react. When he turned his attention down to his arm, she cringed at what she had done, but returned to her icy stare seconds before he looked back at her.

"What did I tell you?" Lucian's demeanor had quickly reverted from anger back to his usual calm self. "Are you going to work with me or should we just end this conversation now? I know you well enough to know that you're going to need to hear the story. So why don't we cut the bullshit for right now?" He had not been wrong. Sofia would never be able to leave without hearing enough to satisfy her curiosity, especially knowing that he had been behind the murders. She maintained her heated attitude, but allowed him to continue.

"See, you have to know the answers. You can't sit through half a movie and switch to something new. Hell, you can't even give up on a bowl of cereal. It's what makes you a good cop, Sofia. So, do you want to ask me some questions and hear things at your pace, or do you want me to let it pour out like an open faucet again?"

Rather than waste any more time with his feeble attempts at explaining himself with no direction, Sofia determined that it was time for her to just go along with his game. He clearly had a great deal to say which is why he was struggling to figure out where to begin, but where was he supposed to begin with such a topic? She refused to let him think that she was buying in to this garbage, so she unloaded sarcastically, "So, you want for me to believe that you're a vampire? Alright. But what about the fact that you go out in the sun all of the time? I mean, you have a tan for God's sake!"

"There we go!" Lucian shouted back. "That's one of the things that I'm talking about. That's actually one of the stupidest things that I've ever heard. What you see in the movies—where they burst into flames as soon as the sun hits 'em—how the hell does that make any sense? That's actually one that I do have an answer for, though. As I was saying before, most of what's been said about us is what was witnessed. Those accounts were probably accurate at some point, but over time they got all jacked up and formed the myths that go around now." Lucian began growing more enthusiastic as he spoke, ecstatic that Sofia was listening.

"Now this goes way back, so hang in there. See, the earliest of our kind weren't worried about hiding what they were 'cause for all everyone knew, they were just the baddest of the bad. They were just very powerful, smart, crazy talented people. Being that they were so highly functioning, they were often the subject of many people's fascination. Think of them as the top athletes of their day. Being so visible in daily life, many of their habits were witnessed by locals. The idea that we cannot exist in sunlight actually came from the fact that many of them would do a full day's work and then go stay up, and often out, all during the night. The reason being, with the high levels of chemicals that course through our veins, we sleep far less than normal people, as in almost never. So, some of them would remain out all night and inside working all day. As the people began to form stories of their exploits, this became more embellished, and became the myth about being 'creatures of the night.'"

"Worked all day, huh? What happened to all of the riches that vampires are supposed to have?" she quipped sarcastically.

"That one is probably closer to fact than most of the myths, but not really the case anymore. See, broods were the reason for the great wealth. These guys would group together and form small communities, pooling their wealth and resources. The fact that we sleep very little leaves a great amount of opportunity to make money. But, ever since the 'Ancients' were formed and our race was thinned out, that's not really the case anymore. Well, it's not exactly the case."

"Garlic, silver, crosses! Do they kill you?" Sofia was becoming very frustrated with Lucian. She realized that she was far more frustrated because he was able to give logical explanations for everything she was asking than anything else at this point. She had hoped he would make it much easier for her to debunk his lies than he was doing.

"Well, garlic has some truth to it, in a way, but not directly. See, what causes our bodies to operate on this high level also magnifies our personality traits. Think about it like this: your allergies are your body's physical and chemical reactions to a foreign substance. Our bodies operate on the same basic principles, just a higher level. So, when we have an allergic reaction to something, it's intense, to say the least. The thing about garlic killing one of our kind may be completely factual, but it's not the norm. Imagine a peanut allergy only magnified exponentially. The cross thing is a flat out fabrication and so is holy water. That one is based on the idea that we're some kind of demons that can be dispelled with holy talismans or relics. When the stories started gettin' out of whack, people who didn't know the truth needed ways to feel secure. Those ideas were created by churches to help the members of their congregations feel safe. It was a commendable effort, but completely false."

"How about fangs, Lucian. Do you have some wonderful little explanation for that one? Did some guy just have larger than normal teeth and that's what that comes from? Or no, wait. It was the churches, again. They decided to tell people that your people were descendants from Satan, and that he spawned them while disguised as a serpent? Am I close?" Sofia was more than frustrated, she was angry at this point. She was shouting at him as she flailed her arms around, illustrating her thoughts.

Lucian began to laugh as he considered her explanations. "Those are actually really good, but no. The fangs are a weird issue. My canines do actually extend when I'm really goin' at it. I got nothin' for that one. I suppose you can chock it up to evolution. They damn sure come in handy on a predatory level."

Now it was Sofia's turn to laugh, only instead of being a jovial sort of laugh, it was maniacal.

"That's it?! What happened to all of your logic, Lucian? You have all of these elaborate stories about everything, and then it's 'Oh, my teeth just grow?'" She spoke in a very strange, condescending tone as she taunted him.

"I don't think that's fair," Lucian responded calmly. "I mean, teeth are a mystery anyways. They grow for a while when you're young, then a second set comes in, pushing the first set out, then they never do anything ever again, aside from falling out. Certain teeth come in to every person's head around the same age, and in the same order. It's all very weird. I don't think anyone can explain what's going on with teeth, so don't expect me to know what's going on with that one."

She stood in silence with her arms crossed. She tried to come up with something to say in rebuttal, but she had nothing. Walking back over to her chair, she sat down and motioned for him to go on.

"I'm not gonna go over everything. I just wanted you to have enough information to know that I'm serious. I just want to tell you a little more, and then I want to get you home. I know you must just want to get home." Sofia did want to go home, but her overwhelming curiosity wouldn't let her. She had to hear more.

34

"Like I've already said, it's my body makeup that makes me the way that I am. One of the most useful and most obvious effects that I experience is that my body heals very quickly compared to normal people."

Sofia's eyes shifted down to his arm, which was still red and clearly not healing and then back up at him.

Lucian addressed her unspoken comment, "Okay, now I'm going to heal from that faster than you would. If I was worked up, it would be almost instant. When I get my blood pumping really good, it's damn near impossible to do any serious or long lasting damage to me, and from what I've found, impossible to do permanent damage. This is the source of the vast majority of the myths about our amazing strength and speed, as well as the fact that it is extremely difficult to inflict any long lasting wounds. Our bodies generate T-cells and antibodies much faster than the body of a normal human being. Our bodies run all the time as yours would in a moment of extreme duress. By that, I mean extremely, extreme duress, and that's just when we're at rest. When we're provoked, things escalate quickly."

Sofia was entranced. She didn't know if she should let him continue or not. He was so convincing that she feared if she let him continue, she may begin to lose her intense anger and disgust, and that was something she wanted to hold onto. She knew that she would need to keep that going if she was ever going to be able to take him in to the station. However, she had to admit that what he was saying was too intriguing to stop him.

"No, go on. I mean, I would hate for you to have prepared this great elaborate story and have no one to tell it to." Although she was attempting to appear very sarcastic, she couldn't deny that she genuinely wanted to hear more.

"It's hard for an intelligent person to let go of their beliefs and buy in. I understand that. What I'm going to do is give you the main facts, that way you'll know some things. Then, there will come a time where you will either choose to believe me or simply be unable to deny that what I have told you is the truth." Lucian began to recap in an effort to ensure he had given Sofia enough basic information to make a decision.

"So, I was telling you about the healing thing. I think that just about covers that. I believe I covered the reason that I ate parts of the body, but I imagine that you would like to know a little more about that particular part."

Sofia breathed deeply, resituated in her seat, and crossed her legs and arms. "Sure," she sighed. Sofia was making her discontent with the entire situation very obvious, but Lucian no longer cared. He had her listening, so he continued.

"So, I take the muscle off these guys for a good reason. Once I get like that, I have a very urgent need to give my body something to feed on. Once I've burned off the energy provided by food I've eaten throughout the day, my body turns to the fat. You may have noticed, not a lot of fat here." He indicated to his lean physique.

"Once it burns through the zero percent body fat that I have to offer, it starts breaking down muscle, and that shit hurts. It's like the feeling you get in your stomach when you're really, really hungry, only it's all over your body, and much more intense. So, rather than give my body time to turn on itself, I start eating. The reason I focus on the muscles is pretty obvious. I mean, a gob of fat in your mouth is pretty gross, regardless what it came from." Sofia's face wrinkled with disgust. She quickly shook the image from her mind as she continued.

"So is that the way that you get the blood that you need also?" Sofia asked, in a sarcastic tone, but was unsure if she had asked that question mockingly or if she actually wanted to know the answer.

Lucian's face slowly dropped until it was painfully obvious how disappointed in her response he was.

"No." He shook his head slowly. "No, that's not...uh...that ain't real. That's one of the most irritating myths."

Seeing his frustration caused Sofia to become very arrogant. She was pushing his buttons, so she decided to continue. "What? You don't drink blood?" She maintained her sarcastic tone.

"Nope." Lucian's mood was beginning to reflect his irritability. He placed his hands on his hips and lowered his head. "See, the thing that I do, eating the muscles, that's more along the lines of what one of us would do when it comes to it. That's not something that I just came up with out of nowhere. I mean, that shit's gross; I'm aware. The first time it came down to it, I had a hard time comin' to terms with it. But if you ever felt that pain, that 'hunger,' you'd do it. Had it been up to my emotions and my reactions the first time that I lost control, I would've had no idea what to do. My mentor had to teach me about what was going on and how I should go about stopping the pain. But, that's just how we have to do things to rebuild our energy.

"Actually, the way that I do it is my own adaptation of how it's normally done. They used to just devour whatever they needed until the pain stopped. I mean, honestly, I could probably run into the woods and kill some kinda' animal and get the same effect; but I don't live in the woods, and these dudes are dead. As far as drinking blood is concerned, that's just a ridiculous mutation of the truth. In the original stories, people had it right. Someone saw what happened and they told other people, and their stories reflected that. Then you get some jackass that wants to be a storyteller, and they change things up. By the time the stories made it into television and movies, they tried to make that part of things a little less gruesome and a little more 'sexy.' It was much easier to look at a person with two tiny holes in their neck than it was to look at a person that has been ripped to shreds.

"The biggest problem I have with it is that drinking blood makes absolutely no sense whatsoever. People don't drink blood! If you did, it would make you sick! That same fact is true for us. Plus it's gross and creepy. So, there's that.

"We are humans first, Sofia. That's what I want you to understand. We're different, that much is true, but we're fundamentally just people. If you took nothing else from this conversation, I would hope it was that."

Lucian maintained his intensely serious look. He even looked hurt in a way.

Sofia wouldn't allow herself to feel any remorse for him, so she continued to probe. "So how old are you? Are you one of the first? Have you been around for hundreds of years and lived all over the world? I mean, you must be since you know these things, right?"

"No, no, no, but those are excellent questions!" he responded with some renewed excitement in his voice. "I'm actually not. I'm still relatively young, depending on how you look at it. I'm forty-seven years old. Contrary to popular belief, we're not immortal. We definitely do live longer than an average person, and we don't show age as quickly as normal people, but we do eventually die. The reason I know the things I know is because I've been tapped... er... selected, as the next ancient." Lucian paused and scratched at his head, realizing how deep his explanation had to go in order for Sofia to understand.

"Okay, for you to understand that, I need to tell you this: a long time ago, there was a civil war among my people. It wasn't long after the English settled in America. Many of our kind gathered and formed a colony in the new land. For a long time, everything was cool and they flourished. It didn't take long for people to hear about how well the town was doing and start showing up. When they first showed up, they were received with open arms. My people had, after all, lived among the normal humans for many years before coming there. After a few years of allowing settlers to join the colony, some things started goin' sour. Basically, some of my people were gettin' pissed that the normal people couldn't offer as much to the community as they could. Typical stuff: some people doing all the work, others were benefitting from it. Anyway, through no fault of their own, they were causin' some issues.

"Over time, the anger increased and began to infect others, eventually causing a split in the community. Those against the normal humans began to think of themselves as gods. They saw their abilities as a sign that they were far superior to the regular humans and felt that they should receive more respect. The others saw those same abilities in a different way: choosing to believe that they were a devolved version of man because of their primal needs and predatory urges. Those who believed this also believed that we should be the protectors of men, that we were born to be Guardians, not gods. That's the way they started identifying inside the community, the gods and the Guardians.

"After several years with a few minor dust ups between the groups, the gods started making some aggressive moves. At one point, a few attacks occurred against some of the humans. Nobody died, but it was enough to cause some concern among the humans as well as among the Guardians. In the end, the humans were driven out by the gods. The Guardians, who felt that it would be far safer for them to leave because of the way things were escalating, encouraged the humans to leave. The bulk of the humans left, but there were several who had married members of the Guardians, so they stayed. Even though most of the humans were gone, the Guardians knew it wouldn't stop there.

"Some time went by, the groups never really broke up, and ideas kept flyin' around. Eventually some of the gods got it into their heads that humans were put on Earth to serve them, which was enough to push the Guardians to take action. Eventually, civil war broke out between the two groups. One believed that normal humans should be enslaved, or eradicated. The other believed that they should live in peace with them and protect them."

Lucian's mood became a bit more somber as he continued. "No clear winner. Most of our people died. Those who survived believed that all of the gods were killed. The survivors decided they had to do something to prevent such a thing from happening again and elected a group of elders. The elders would be in charge of maintaining the history of our people. Everyone promised not to pass along the knowledge of how to unlock their hidden powers and reach their full potential, once the council formed. The elders then decided to take the story of what had happened in their community back to their homelands and share with the broods of the area in an effort to prevent such a thing from happening again. Every elder knows the story of our history. When they start reaching the end of life, they select an heir to teach it to and carry on. The elders became known as the Ancients.

"There are tons of people in the world that are like me, but don't know it. Even though they were never taught to tap into it, the potential is there. They just know they're better at things than everybody else. It can show up in tons of different areas. Some of us are physically gifted due to the extremely high metabolism that accompanies our chemical composition. Some are just ridiculously smart. As I said, the potential is there, they just don't know to release it. I mean, if you were the most athletic person around, would it even occur to you that you hadn't even touched your real potential?" Lucian didn't wait for a response for fear that it may end the conversation when he was so close to the end.

"Anyway, once they've been taught to unlock their ability, they truly become one of my people. The thing is that the Ancients are the only ones who know how to make that happen. The only reason I know any of this is because I was tapped to take over for one of the Ancients. The current Ancient is the man I referred to as my mentor. He's the one that unlocked me so I can take over his responsibility when he's gone. That's why I know so much about all of this."

"This mentor is the guy you talked about at the museum?" Sofia questioned unenthusiastically, as she rolled her neck after the extensive explanation.

"There ya' go." He pointed at her approvingly.

Lucian's story was so well thought out, and he told it with such conviction, that it was almost believable. He had answers for so many questions. It was all based on something so fantastical that Sofia would never allow herself to buy into it. She knew that no matter how well thought out a story was, there were always holes to be found. Continuing to draw his story out was the only way that she would be able to expose them, so she continued to ask questions.

"All right, so how is it that you took out so many people at one time? Some of those crime scenes consisted of several bodies. The group that attacked us in the park, how did you manage to handle that? I mean, I hate to offend you but you're not what I would call physically imposing by any stretch of the imagination."

"Yeah, I kind of glazed over that a little. It really goes back to how fast my body regenerates tissue. If I tear my muscle tissue in any way, it immediately begins to rebuild. My muscle tissue can rebuild incredibly fast. So, when I start tearin' muscle, I get ripped quick. Part of my training with the Ancient is about learning different techniques that he's learned, so I'm ready if something like the gods and Guardians thing ever goes down again. Some of those techniques are about increasing my natural speed. So, whenever I'm full form, I'm really fast."

"So, give me a test drive. Do some pushups or something. I would honestly really like to see that." Sofia's comments were once again sarcastic. She saw no need in masking her feelings about it. Whatever was driving her to sit and listen to this madness, whether it was curiosity or her attachment to Lucian, wasn't going to keep her from trying to get some viable proof of what he was proposing.

"That seems a little silly. If I do that, then I gotta go through the pain after. Like I said earlier, once I burn up that energy and build up some muscle my body's gonna start looking for payment with the quickness. That's the reason that I stay, as you have so kindly pointed out, so physically unimposing. I really don't care to go through that just to prove something to you that you're eventually gonna believe anyway."

"You seem awfully sure of that. A little overconfident for someone who has failed to provide one single bit of tangible evidence that what he is saying is true."

"I suppose it does come across that way. I guess I just feel like you're gonna have all the proof you need at some point and I really don't need to put myself through that to prove it right now." Lucian's eyebrows bolted up his face as he realized another point. "And I would say surviving that little situation in the alley would serve as some of your reasonably tangible evidence."

"You mean the situation that you set up in the alley, with your buddies? You had one knock me out while you pretended to take a beating and had them fire blanks at you. There's a logical explanation. I assume this is some elaborate thing you have put together to try and 'turn me,'" she mocked him, as she peered at him through squinted eyes.

"I most certainly did not set that incident in the alley up!" Lucian replied angrily. "I had absolutely no desire to put you through the pain and anxiety that I saw you go through! I only allowed it to go on in hopes that I would have a better opportunity to get us out of it without you seeing anything."

Once again, his mood softened instantly as he continued his rebuttal. "But, you hung in there until there was no way to deny what happened. When the gun went off, I knew there was no other way. And I hated putting you through the torture that you were going through when you were tied up earlier. Like I said, I think I made a bad decision. I just thought I had to make sure I knew everything, and I needed to be able to make an informed decision about how to proceed. Seeing your reactions earlier when you talked about me gave me reason to believe there might be some way for us to be together, even if you know the truth."

Lucian's words were sincere, of that Sofia had no doubt. She resisted every impulse to reach out to him and try to console him. She just stared at him for a few moments in silence before asking her previous question again.

"So is this the part where you turn me or ask me to join you or something?"

"No." The abrupt way that he answered actually hurt Sofia's feelings a little. She didn't believe what he was saying, but it bothered her that he wouldn't want her to be like him.

"Why the hell not?" she snapped.

"Can't do it," he said, bluntly.

"It doesn't sound like you're going to make such a great leader of your people. I mean, in a crunch you can't even recruit new prospects?" She was lashing out in response to the rejection she felt from Lucian's responses.

"I understand it's gonna take some time for you to get this, but the least you can do is ask me questions without mocking me, 'cause it's highly likely that you're saying something stupid."

Sofia was taken aback by his words.

"I cannot turn someone because that is not possible. People are born this way. When we are born, our bodies develop the same as yours until around puberty. Once our bodies begin to change, they generally develop at an earlier age and at a faster pace. Most of your 'early bloomers' possess the attributes that would allow them to become one of my people."

Sofia sat on her chair with a look of disbelief on her face as she tried to process everything that Lucian was telling her. It was all too much. Every question had an answer. Every comment had some response, that, although completely insane, was perfectly logical. She could hardly focus on what he was saying anymore. The biggest issue that she was struggling with was that the man she had been developing such deep feelings for in the past weeks, was clearly insane.

"I've heard enough. I want to go home now." Sofia rose from her uncomfortable seat and dusted herself off as she began to scan the room for the exit.

Lucian, surprised at her abrupt desire to leave, but aware of how tired she appeared, nodded in agreement.

"I understand. This's been a bad day. I can get you a ride home."

"No, I'll walk. I have absolutely no desire to be near you. You're a murderer! What about me makes you think that I would want anything to do with you?" Sofia glared at Lucian as she started towards the exit across the room.

"Sofia, I understand that you're angry with me, but this is no place for you to be alone at your best, let alone at night when you're exhausted. I didn't bring you to the suburbs for this. Just let me get you home, or at the very least, let me walk with you." Lucian pleaded with her as he followed her towards the door, finally reaching out and taking hold of her arm gently.

Sofia yanked her arm away from Lucian, and turned. "Stay away from me, Lucian. I don't want anything from you. Everything that I've been through today is because of you." She spoke calmly but firmly and glanced at his hand, which was all the warning that he needed. Lucian knew that she would not give in, so he allowed her to leave.

35

Completely oblivious to her location in the city, Sofia stormed out into the dark night, onto the sidewalk and began walking. Her knowledge of the city was extensive enough that she knew once she saw some landmarks she would be able to get herself going in the right direction. Her only concern at that moment was to get as far away from Lucian as she could.

Completely oblivious to her location in the city, Sofia stormed out into the dark night, onto the sidewalk and began walking. Her knowledge of the city was extensive enough that she knew, once she saw some landmarks, she would be able to get herself going in the right direction. Her only concern at that moment was to get as far away from Lucian as she could.

She began processing everything that she had been through and heard in the past twenty-four hours. The physical drain that she had experienced over the past several hours became more apparent as she walked. Her feet felt heavier and her back began to ache. Her knees, still stiff from being straightened out so long, further impacted her stride. She wanted nothing more than to lie in her bed, wrapped in her sheets. As she contemplated that scenario, she couldn't help but think of Lucian being there to hold her.

She had grown close to Lucian in such a short time. He had really shown her a side of herself that she didn't know existed. She was actually having fun outside of work for the first time in years, and felt a real connection with him. She struggled with the idea of how she could have allowed herself to feel anything for someone who was capable of such things. Her job was to notice the sort of details that would have led her to see what he was. She rolled around all of the insight Lucian had given her, and tried to remember him ever actively trying to throw them off the case. As drained as she was, she felt confident that she could accurately remember their conversations regarding the case. She couldn't recall a single time where Lucian had tried to misdirect their investigation. One thing did make much more sense now that she knew the truth about his involvement. It now made perfect sense why the crime scenes had been completely stripped of all trace evidence. Lucian would have known exactly what to look for, and what to remove, or cover up.

Waves of embarrassment continued to wash over her as she walked on. The idea that she had allowed herself to be not only outsmarted, but completely ensnared by the very person she had been chasing was humiliating. She had never allowed anyone so close to her and that was why she had always been such an excellent officer, and how she became the best detective. Every other case she had worked on had gotten her full focus and undivided attention. When others would leave work and head home, she had always put in the extra hours, finding crucial pieces of evidence that were missed. She had risked everything that she had worked for on the very person she was supposed to be tracking. Every step that she took made her more furious. Then Sofia realized that she had been walking for several minutes in an effort to distance herself from Lucian, but with no real idea of where she was, or what direction she was heading.

When she began to look around, a cold, unsettling feeling came over her. He had not been wrong about her not needing to go walking off by herself. She was in one of the most dangerous parts of Atlanta. The area had been completely overtaken with gangs, and there was no real police presence at night. Pulling out her phone, her heart sank as she realized she had never charged the battery from the night before. Taxis did not run through the area either, so finding some transportation was out of the question. The streetlights had all been broken. Although the moon was full, it was completely hidden by the thick clouds that had earlier provided such a serene setting for their walk home. The roads were dark, making visibility a huge concern for Sofia.

Her heels clicked loudly as they met the concrete and echoed for what seemed like an eternity off the run down, windowless houses. As she took notice of the loud clicking, she stopped abruptly and removed her shoes. She knew that the last thing she needed was to draw attention. As she reached down to remove the shoes, she caught a glimpse of the clean, albeit very wrinkled sleeve of her shirt, and realized just how badly she stood out from her surroundings. After a quick glance around to make sure she hadn't drawn anyone's attention, Sofia slinked off of the main road and began to try and devise a quick disguise to help her blend in to her disheveled environment.

Sofia began by tearing one of her sleeves and letting it hang from her shoulder. Carefully moving over to the yard of what appeared to be an abandoned house, she searched for anything useful. Scanning the dilapidated porch that hung off the front of the house, she failed to see anything in the darkness that she could use for self-defense. Knowing there was a very good chance the house was actually filled with a bevy of drug addicts, she elected not to search inside for anything.

As she turned to make her way back to the sidewalk, she nearly tripped over a large cement pot that she saw just in time. The pot lay on its side, the dried up soil spilled out in front of it filled with weeds. Realizing that her best bet at this point was to blend in, she grabbed a handful of the dirt and rubbed it into the skin on her arm to see if it would have the proper effect. Sofia had always taken care of her skin, which had given it a soft texture, which was not the look of a vagabond. The dusty dry dirt did just enough to give her skin a more "weathered" appearance. Accepting that she could only do so much with what she had at her disposal, Sofia began rubbing the dirt on all exposed portions of her skin, focusing mainly on her face.

As she continued to perform her dirt scrub on her face, she realized how hard she was trying to keep the dirt out of her hair. She knew that no matter how hard she focused on making her skin look dirty, her hair definitely did not reflect the same haphazard style of living. Begrudgingly, she began smashing handfuls of dirt into her hair, rubbing it in down to her scalp. She did all she could to crimp and kink her hair in every way in order to get the preferred level of grime that she needed to pull off her disguise. Finally accepting that her skin and hair could hold no more filth, she began to work on her manner of movements.

Taking a few seconds to make sure she could act the part, Sofia began attempting the slow stroll of a heroin addict. She worked to get her head and neck trained to reflect the limp nature of those she had become all too familiar with from working as a beat cop. After taking a few minutes to practice her new walk, Sofia began looking for some reflective surface to see how her costume had turned out. She wanted to make sure that she was prepared in case a situation came along that required her to blend in or even disappear.

Playing the role of a homeless drug addict would be ideal for any such situation, as they were commonly overlooked. Sofia was not surprised to find that there was no glass to be found in any of the surrounding buildings, so she had to make due with an old soda can that she found in the gutter. Sofia twisted the can in half several times and was able to create a large hole in the side of it. She then ripped the pieces apart and peeled the can back to reveal the shiny interior. While it did not provide an accurate reflection of the way that she looked, Sofia could tell that she didn't look the part. No matter how much she tried to make herself look like a disheveled mess, she knew no one would buy her as homeless or an addict. Her clothes were too crisp and too new. Her skin, while now very dirty, showed no signs of the tremendous wear and tear that she had seen on the faces of the miserable souls she came across on a daily basis. She knew that the only way that she would be able to blend in was if she covered who she was completely, not attempt to mask it.

She continued down the street in a much more cautious manner now that she was aware of her surroundings. This was an unfamiliar situation for her, which left her feeling very exposed and vulnerable. Sofia didn't have to look far before she came across a group of homeless people entering one of the old buildings. She followed them in and began to search for someone who might be able to spare an overcoat and toboggan that she could use to cover her clothes, face, and hair.

Locating a woman with the appearance of a street veteran, she offered her the thirty dollars that she had in her pocket as compensation for the woman's full-length overcoat, skullcap, and the shoes on her feet. The woman was hesitant to accept the offer, looking at Sofia as if she was trying to pull one over on her. Sofia knew from her dealings with street people over the years that they were always wary of a deal that seemed too good to be true. She also knew that mentioning that she was a police officer in trouble was more likely to get her thrown out of the building than it was to get her any closer with her goal of striking a deal. Referencing a shelter where she had seen a similar jacket, and pointing out that the skullcaps and shoes were virtually everywhere, gave the woman a much more suitable offer. The woman took a few seconds to consider the offer before eventually accepting the deal and snatching the cash Sofia offered her.

36

Sofia left the building, donning her newly purchased street urchin outfit. The coat was entirely too heavy for the weather and the skullcap was completely unnecessary, but they served their purposes perfectly. Sofia had noticed the stench of the coat before she had purchased it. It reeked of urine, booze, and years of body odor, which accumulated into an amalgamation of filth that took Sofia several minutes to get used to. She had considered going for the less offensive jacket of the woman nearby, but thought that the stench might be helpful in keeping others from taking a closer look at her, potentially blowing her cover. She placed the heavy, moist coat on over her work shirt, causing a puff of the horrid stench to come rushing out. Not wanting to offend the woman as she was still within view, she did all she could to keep from gagging and pushed on to put on the cap.

The thought of placing that filthy cap on her head made Sofia's stomach churn. She continued to try to recover from the overwhelming urge to vomit from putting on the coat. The only thing that kept her from losing her composure was the awareness that these things could potentially save her life. She flipped the hat inside out as inconspicuously as possible and inspected it for lice. Although there was a great deal of white flaky dandruff inside the wool cap, she found no signs of the tiny parasites. After patting off as much of the dandruff as possible, Sofia balled up as much of her hair as possible, and shoved it in.

The shoes were a no brainer and much easier to deal with than the other pieces of the outfit. There was no way that she could walk in the shoes that she had been wearing, and barefoot was out of the question. The constant clicking on the concrete was enough of a reason for her to do away with them. There was also the fact that she would never have a chance to escape if she did encounter a problem. She had a long way to go to get to a point of safety, and her feet were as likely to give her away as her hair was. Forcing her sock into the shoe, she struggled momentarily as the moisture inside slowed her progress. She had noticed the woman's feet were slightly smaller than her own, but preferred tighter shoes to larger ones in case she had to make an escape. While the smaller shoes would cause discomfort, larger ones could cause a very untimely fall.

Emerging once more onto the sidewalk in front of the tragic little house, Sofia covered herself as best she could and began making her way back towards safety. The most difficult part of exiting the area was that she was unable to walk directly out. She had to take the right streets or she would be in danger of running into gangs with members that knew her face. The path that would lead her out was a maze of back roads, side streets, and alleyways. That alone would keep her from passing all major hangouts and bases of operation of every small and large-scale organization in the area. She couldn't afford to run into anyone she had met or arrested before. While she had always treated her suspects fairly, that didn't always matter to them. She knew that most of them would hold a grudge for simply being questioned. If she happened across someone who had been a suspect in an investigation, it could result in a very bad situation for her. Jumping fences or cutting through yards was also out. Local gangs did not tolerate trespassing. It wouldn't matter who she was, or how out of her mind she appeared to be. Besides, it was highly unlikely that anyone who saw her jump a fence would ever believe her cover.

Sofia navigated the streets, keeping her distance from every person she passed, no matter how innocent they appeared. As she walked, she wondered why Lucian would have brought her to such a dangerous area. Not only that, but he had allowed her to leave with very little resistance. She had not given him much of a choice, of course. Nevertheless, if he cared about her, he simply would not have let her go into the area alone. She hadn't imagined the bond that they had formed. It was real and it was strong. Although the time-span that they had spent forming their relationship had been short, they had come to know one another intimately. She knew that Lucian could tell by the look on her face, as she left, that she would not be dissuaded. She still felt like he should have followed her. Considering the lengths he had just gone to in order to get information from her, following her home when she was angry with him didn't seem like too far a stretch.

She had looked back several times to see if Lucian was following at a distance to keep an eye on her, but there were no signs that he was there. While it was very hard to put anything past him at this point, Sofia couldn't believe that he was capable of tailing her without her knowledge, or surviving in the area if he were ever located. He had talked a big game about all of his nonsense, but when push came to shove, he was too small to ever fight off even a single member of any of the local boys. Sofia didn't care. Lucian had taken up too much of her time and efforts, both personal and professional. She forged ahead alone.

It hadn't taken long for Sofia to come across a situation where her cover was necessary. She had successfully slipped in and out of it several times, and was becoming rather good at becoming "invisible" when needed. Rather than allow herself to focus on the insanity that had just taken place with Lucian, she had focused all of her energy on the task at hand in order to keep her mind occupied.

Now, as she rounded one corner, she noticed a group of men standing down the street beneath what seemed to be the only working streetlight in the entire area. They had taken notice of her as soon as she turned onto the street. Recognizing the uniform of a street dweller, they turned their attention back to the conversation and away from her. Having already been noticed, Sofia knew that she could not cross the street or turn back without drawing some suspicion. If the men sensed fear, they were likely to come looking for trouble. She knew that her best option was to try to pass by them without drawing too much attention.

Knowing that she needed to get past them as quickly as possible, Sofia considered changing personas in order to allow for faster movement than the capability of a typical junkie. She had seen enough of both as a beat cop to know the major differences between the two. A drug addict on the street had no shame and no sense of danger. They would ask anyone for money, or drugs. It may be a tourist, a businessman, or even a gangster. A drunk, on the other hand, would generally just wade through foot traffic en route to their destination. The crazy ones were even more likely to wander past people, without paying them any attention, lost in their own thoughts and ramblings. Drunks asked for money too, but far less often than the drug addicts. They tended to show a little discretion when they could tell there was no hope. The reason being, drug addicts were always looking for their next fix, but as long as the drunks were drunk, they were happy. Also, the crazy drunks were almost as likely to attack you for talking to them as anyone, whereas the drug addicts would take a beating if they thought someone might give them money for doing it.

Sofia ventured on, adding an occasional sideways step to her walk. She then began muttering to herself incoherently, occasionally raising her voice loudly, while effectively saying nothing.

For a brief moment, she was reminded of her first date with Lucian and their experience on the train. Her heart sank as she thought of that perfect evening. Forcing herself to concentrate on her survival, Sofia shook her feelings for the moment, forging on. Staring at only the concrete before her and raving like a lunatic, she approached the men. They continued speaking to one another and paid her very little attention.

She planned to pass the group by going out into the street to go around them, but as she began to turn toward the street, a car approached the boys and stopped. The men in the car began talking with the group, and the affiliation was apparent. The three men who had been leaning against the building approached the car to join in the greetings that were now going on. This left a small gap behind all of the men, large enough for Sofia to walk through. Seeing the opening, she redirected herself and hastily tried to pass the men.

Sofia was nearly beyond the group when one of the younger men turned around to locate the source of the stench that had just crept into their area. He shoved her harshly, knocking her into the wall. Sofia had seen his intentions, just prior to him making his move. She was able to tuck her head and roll towards the wall, keeping her face out of sight.

The boy began taunting Sofia about her smell and pointing at her. Sofia's heart began to pound at the thought of what may happen if they looked beyond her thin disguise. The other men took notice of their partner's actions. Laughing, they chimed in with their own comments about her foul odor, but no one approached her.

Sofia knew that looking them in the eye could give away too much or possibly make them combative, so she began to babble a little louder as she made her way past them. She knew that she had to keep them away from her without getting them angry and without allowing them to see beyond the filth. The boys continued to mock and shove her as she slowly made her way past them. Any attempt to defend herself, or strike back, would surely result in a much more violent reaction, so Sofia took the abuse and did everything that she could to maintain her cover.

As she was about to pass the last man he curled in against the wall, blocking her exit. He had clearly missed the substance of the comments about her as he began to make a move to grab her. He quickly realized what the others were referring to as he caught a whiff of Sofia's coat, and recoiled in disgust, falling back against the car that his friends were in. The others began to laugh and turned their attention to him as he jokingly slid down the back of the car, holding his throat as if he were choking to death. Sofia saw her opportunity and moved away from the men as quickly as she could.

She stumbled on down the street as fast as she could, doing everything in her power to keep from breaking character. That was the closest that she had ever come to being victimized. She could hardly keep herself from breaking into a dead sprint, but somehow she managed. After what seemed like an eternity of bumbling down the sidewalk, she finally reached the corner before slinking around it and nearly collapsing.

She had never felt such anxiety. Never before had she been in such a situation with no backup, no weapon, and such a feeling of being overwhelmed. The attack in the alley with Lucian had been different because it happened very quickly and she had no time to think about it. Also, what was happening to Lucian was taking enough of her focus to keep her from thinking about what might happen to her. She had been considering the possibility of something like what had just happened since beginning her trek out of her dangerous surroundings. Vulnerability was not something that she had learned to deal with because she so rarely had to worry about it. She breathed deeply as she leaned against the brick wall. As she sat and gathered her wits, Sofia realized that the laughter and taunting of the men had stopped. The sound that replaced it paralyzed her with fear. It was the sound of several men running in her direction.

37

There was little she could do to recover her drunken alter ego as they approached. She cowered down into her filthy coat as the first man quickly rounded the corner. The apparent leader of the group grabbed her by her jacket and looked directly into her face.

"That's what the fuck I thought!" he roared as he looked back at his crew. Ripping the skullcap from her head, he brushed her hair away from her face. "You 'bout got away with it," he growled. "Forgot about that sweet-ass perfume, huh?"

Sofia had done everything that she could to cover up any trace of a clean smell and thought she had done quite well, but she had forgotten about her perfume. After all of her walking around in that stinking heavy coat, she had begun to sweat quite profusely. The sweat must have reacted with the perfume and rejuvenated its fragrance. She hadn't noticed its sweet smell as she was so used to it from regular use.

He squeezed her face tightly as he pulled her closer to him.

"I didn't notice it till you was gone, but after you took that stankin' ass jacket away I smelled that sweetness on you. And don't no piece of street shit smell like that. So, that means you gotta be hidin' something. And look at what you been hiding." As he squeezed her face, his other hand began to make its way around her collar. He ripped her jacket away from her and threw it to the ground.

"Now look at that!" He looked over Sofia's sculpted body in her form fitting clothes.

"That's what I was hopin' for!" Her heart sank as she looked around at her captors. There wasn't a remorseful or concerned look among them. Each face held the same ravenous expression. Like that of a jackal that had stumbled across a fresh kill.

The man who held her continued to paw at her and pull her close to him, pressing his crotch into her leg. Complete helplessness consumed her. She was outnumbered and unarmed and there was not a chance that anyone in this part of town was going to answer her screams for help.

She knew there was no hope in doing it, but she blurted it out anyway, "You don't wanna do this, I'm a cop!" She managed to get the words out despite the pressure he was putting on her face.

"Do the right thing here; just walk away!" Sofia pleaded to her captors. Knowing that this could only go one of two ways, Sofia prayed for the best.

Her prayers were not answered in time, since the man's face quickly changed to a look of sarcastic surprise. "Oh, ho, ho, ho. We got ourselves an officer of the law here, boys." His breath stank as he mocked her. "Well, I guess we need to show this officer the same respect they show us."

The group began to laugh and call out in agreement. This was what Sofia had feared since the moment she realized where she was after leaving Lucian.

She cringed as he repositioned his hand around her throat angrily. His other hand quickly found its way to her breast, which he groped violently. Sofia knew that it would only make things worse to fight his advances, but she struck out at him anyway. Using her right palm, she struck him against the side of his left eye socket with all the force she could manage.This freed her for a brief second allowing her to grab both of his shoulders as she threw her knee up as hard as she could into his crotch. He screamed out in pain and dropped to his knees, holding his face and groin. There was no place for her to go. The others immediately closed in on her.

One of the men grabbed her and struck her in the face, slamming her head into the building that was pinned against her. Her head struck the building in the very spot where she had attempted to head-butt her giant captor from the alley fight with Lucian. The pain exploded from the back of her head out to her face. She began to slide to the ground, but the leader stopped her. He had recovered slightly but continued to hold his aching crotch. Holding her throat, he slid her back up to her feet. Replacing his hand with his forearm, he held her against the wall.

"Try that again, and you die!" He shouted his warning only inches from her ear.

Sofia's attack clearly caused him some distress, as he was unable to open his eye. The other boys watched as he blindly fumbled at her pants, staring her in the eye. They began cheering him on and calling dibs on who would be next. Sofia had seen the results of attacks like this too often to have any misconception about how this would end. Without a single sympathetic or concerned face in the bunch, she knew that she had no chance of surviving this.

She tried to clear her thoughts, and be somewhere else in her mind, but it was useless. There was no way she could keep her mind off what was happening. She had done all she could to defend herself. She stood no chance against the group of men. Her tears flowed freely. After the strain from the events of the day, Sofia was too exhausted to fight anymore and had no breath with which to scream.

The tears poured down her face as she gasped against the pressure of his forearm against her windpipe. She hated herself for showing weakness and letting them beat her. Crying was a clear indication that she was submitting, and that was something she had never intended to do. Sofia knew this was the end.

As the man continued to try to remove her pants, he began to press harder against Sofia's throat, inadvertently cutting off her oxygen. With the rest of them focused on who was next and what they would do with her body, no one noticed that she was choking to death. At this point, she considered that it might be a blessing. Sofia wished that she could just allow herself to die, but her body and mind refused. She began to fight to move the man's arm from her throat, but it was useless. She was unable to make a noise, and her attempts to fight him merely struck him as her resisting his attack. As he continued to press harder and harder, Sofia felt herself slipping into unconsciousness. Sofia knew this was the beginning of a horrible end.

Her vision became blurred. She saw the blackness creeping around the edges of the men as it had before. Her head pounded and the sound of the blood rushing through her brain was like a freight train in her ears. That was it, as soon as she passed out her fight would be lost. Sofia almost welcomed the darkness.

38

As she stood pressed against the red brick of the building, fading out of consciousness, she heard something over the rushing blood in her ears. The faint sound of hurried footsteps and someone shouting echoed through the street. Someone was coming, but she doubted whoever it was could help against the throng of men. The man holding her snapped his head around to see what was happening. When he did, he loosened the pressure against Sofia's throat. Breathing deeply, she could feel the oxygen rich blood surging into her face. Although blurry, her vision returned. The rushing sound eased and her pounding head became bearable. Sofia glanced around in an effort to see what exactly was going on.

She couldn't make out any features through her tears, all she could see was someone moving very quickly in their direction. The others had turned to face him with their weapons drawn. One shot rang out and Sofia saw the approaching figure recoil as if struck in the right shoulder, yet the person continued to move toward the crowd. Seeing that the first bullet hadn't stopped him, a second shot rang out, followed by a third. While the figure did recoil to some degree, he continued forward.

Seeing him continue in their direction, the others joined in and began firing. A barrage of gunshots rang out. The hard surfaces provided by the surrounding buildings and streets only amplified the ungodly blasts. The combined explosive clatter of the guns being fired simultaneously reminded Sofia of being in the firing range, only now, she didn't have her earphones and the sound was deafening.

Covering her ears as best she could and wincing with each shot, Sofia tried to see what had become of the man through the smoke. She hoped, at the very least, that the commotion they were causing would force them to scramble from the scene and they would leave her. Just as Sofia began to question just how long they could continue firing, she heard several of the men begin cursing as their weapons ran out of ammunition. As fewer gunshots rang out, the noise became more bearable. Sofia began to open her eyes wider and wider, albeit quite slowly.

As her eyes began to adjust to the darkness, the first thing Sofia could see was that the man who had been attacking her before was turned around, staring in the other direction. She hadn't realized until now that he was applying nearly no pressure to her throat any longer. Seeing that his attention, as well as the others, was completely off her, Sofia began to prepare to make a run for it.

Just as she was about to try to escape his hold, Sofia once again glanced down the street towards where the person had come from. Expecting to see a body slumped down in the street, lying in a pool of blood, Sofia was shocked to see the figure still standing. They were now close enough that she could see that it was a man's figure. He was making no effort to defend himself, nor was he reacting to the number of wounds that he must have suffered. He stood in the street motionless, his arms by his side and his head hung low.

One by one, the hoodlums ran out of bullets, and ceased firing. Once the firing completely stopped, everyone, including Sofia, waited for his bullet riddled body to collapse into the street. Mesmerized by the unbelievable act of bravery and demonstration of strength the man had just displayed, Sofia temporarily forgot about her idea of escaping. Now, the only thing she was able to do was wait to see how long the man could stay on his feet.

The firing had stopped for several seconds and the man still stood, unwavering, a few yards away from the cluster of trigger-happy assailants. Slowly, the statuesque figure raised his head and continued to make his way towards them. At this, the man that had been holding Sofia reached down for his weapon, completely releasing his grip on Sofia's throat. Sofia quickly snapped back into the moment and turned to run for freedom.

As she leaned into her left leg for leverage to begin running, she was blindsided by a wave of dizziness that sent her sprawling onto the asphalt. Looking back at the melee, she prepared herself to be pounced by at least one of her captors, but nothing happened. Not one of them even looked in her direction. They were all concentrating on the man who was now only feet from them. He was no longer moving towards them. He was just standing before them, almost daring one of them to make a move.

Each of the men had unloaded their weapon firing at him, and now stood looking at one another in amazement. Their lack of training coupled with their poor technique had caused many of the bullets to miss their mark. Although, judging by the tattered remains of what was clearly at one time a shirt, many of them had not. Sofia struggled to move into a position where she could better see the extent of the man's wounds. As she did, one particularly ballsy individual reached out to strike the man with the butt of his gun, clearly thinking that a man with so many bullets resting inside of his torso would be too weak to resist. He was wrong.

The movement was swift and smooth as the dark figure reached up and stopped the young man's arm before he could so much as begin his forward motion to strike. He moved so quickly and so precisely that it was as if he was able to read the thug's mind. Pausing just long enough to look into the young man's eyes, he quickly swung his left hand up underneath the unsuspecting thug's elbow. Forcing both of his hands skyward in a twisting motion, the vigilante ripped the arm completely out of its socket.

The young man squealed out in pain as he reached for what should have been the muscle of his shoulder only to grab a pocket of soft skin that dangled in its place, holding the inner workings of his arm like a gunnysack. As he held his flaccid, useless appendage, tears of pain filled his eyes. The others jumped back instantly, shocked by what they had just witnessed. They stared at their injured companion in awe for a moment as they tried to grasp what had happened, but they did not hesitate for long.

Two of the older members who clearly had a great deal of experience in fighting as a single unit quickly turned their attention back to the juggernaut, as he took a moment to enjoy the pain he had just inflicted. One dove at him from behind, locking his arms around the hero's biceps and torso. The other punched him fiercely in the gut, causing him to lean forward. The attacker from the rear rode the champion to the ground as he collapsed to his knees. This was just the opening the others needed in order to pile on, too.

They began to beat him mercilessly about his neck and back as he rested on his hands and knees. Sofia was now on the same level as her hero, and the two had a clear view of one another for the first time. It took her a second to realize what she was seeing. The clean-shaven face she had grown so accustomed to, and had seen only a short time ago, had a thick shadow of hair coating it, which she never thought he was capable of growing. The remaining air left Sofia's lungs, as she was no longer able to deny the truth.

As she looked into Lucian's eyes, there was only one explanation for what she was seeing. He had been telling her the absolute truth, and now she had no choice but to believe it. The amount of shock on Lucian's face was unexpected. As he looked up at her, his expression had turned from one of concentration to one of surprise. Now, his face gnarled into an intense scowl. The muscles in his jaws tightened as he ground his teeth and his breathing quickened. Looking directly into his eyes, Sofia couldn't help but notice how intensely the green portions of his irises shined in the darkness.

He slowly began to rise to his feet against the full force of the crowd as they pummeled him, finally standing upright in the center. He seemed to grow stronger with every blow as he stood there; and then Lucian began to retaliate. What followed was the most brutal and unbelievable thing that Sofia had ever seen. Lucian had been shot countless times, but also beaten by the group for several minutes as well. Yet he seemed completely unscathed as he began to dismantle the group.

His first strike was to the man who had been holding Sofia captive. It was a brutal punch to his sternum, followed by a powerful strike to the ribs, which caused a series of loud snapping sounds. The combination left the man breathless for several seconds. The others stopped their own attacks for the moment, in awe at the quickness and power Lucian was able to generate. Considering the amount of abuse he had received to that point, what he had just managed was nothing short of spectacular. The man fell back against the building and slid down the wall until he sat gasping for air next to Sofia.

"I'll be talking to you in a minute," Lucian huffed at the man angrily. He then turned his attention back to the others and continued his masterful retaliation.

As he fought, his movements became faster, more precise, and more powerful with each strike. Each attack becoming more brutal than the last. At first, based on the sheer number of attacks thrown at him, Lucian was still absorbing a huge number of blows. Within a few seconds, he began to block the vast majority of them, with limited energy output. His movements were unbelievably fast and fluid. When the fight began, he had been surrounded on all sides. Each member of the group seemed to be waging his own personal war on Lucian. Now, the men continued to surround him, but the number of successful punches on the behalf of the crowd drastically declined.

Realizing that they were doing no good, many of the thugs began opting for more calculated attacks rather than an unbridled onslaught. As they waited for him to leave an opening, it allowed Lucian time to strike instead of block.

The first to leave an opening was a man of medium build wearing oversized black shorts that hung to nearly his ankles, a crisp, oversized white t-shirt, and a pair of black sneakers that he had left untied. Lucian struck him with a lightning fast kick to his chest. The strike contained such force that the man flew out of his untied shoes, and into the wall. He landed on the other side of the first man Lucian had attacked. The sound of his head smashing into the wall was all that Sofia needed to hear to know that he was dead. It hadn't made a normal hollow bong, like that of a coconut. There was a distinct crushing sound, followed by a short splat. Bouncing off the wall, his face smashed into the ground and he remained perfectly still, confirming what Sofia already knew.

Looking up at the wall where he had hit, Sofia could see that several of the bricks had caved in the area where his chest and head had made contact with the wall. By the time she looked back to the fight, Lucian had already taken out three more of the men. The blows that had taken them out were equally deadly, as they lie scattered around in twisted heaps. As the crowd dwindled, things progressed much faster.

The final blows to the remaining men were very similar, and gave Sofia a glimpse at what she had been searching for in her pursuit of the murderous "group." It no longer took more than a single blow for Lucian to end even the strongest combatant's life. Six men remained, and Lucian hit each with some variation of the same move: a thunderous downward blow to the side or back of the neck, right near the ear. Death was instant for each of them.

Sofia could do little more than watch the murder of her tormentors. As opposed as she was to the idea of what had just happened, she had done nothing to stop Lucian. She had never allowed herself to observe such a situation from this particular point of view. She had never truly seen the criminal through the victim's eyes.

Is this truly the justice that they deserve? she wondered silently. Clearly not in the eyes of the law, but she had to admit it was what she wanted deep down.

The small gang never stood a chance against Lucian once he began to transform. Now, only he remained standing in the center of the pile of broken bodies. Sofia still struggled to believe it, but everything that Lucian had told her was true.

As he fought, she had seen the blood, which was an extraordinarily small amount to start with given the amount of holes in his body, completely stop oozing from his wounds. His body was healing.

His muscles rippled and strained against his skin. His speed had increased every second. His chest heaved as he looked over his conquest. He slowly turned his attention towards the only remaining survivor, Sofia's would-be rapist.

Lucian walked over and squatted down, aligning his face right with the other man's face. Sofia couldn't believe how big Lucian looked. This was not the man that she had come to know. This was a full-grown, well developed, and absolutely ripped individual. His body was exquisite. His muscles bulged as if they were about to tear through the taut, leathery prison of skin that covered them. She thought she could actually hear his skin stretching to accommodate the amount of muscle mass that he packed beneath it.

She could see the blood surging through veins that ran in the thin space between his muscle and skin. Examining the entry points of the bullets that had made contact, Sofia expected to see numerous huge holes. Instead, she saw nothing more than a few small pinholes that closed up and disappeared before her eyes. Although the actions that she had just witnessed were disgusting and abhorrent on nearly every level, Sofia couldn't help how attracted to him she was in that moment. Seeing him in this massive form, mixed with how sensitive and wonderful she knew he could be, Sofia felt a raw, animalistic sexual attraction to Lucian that she had never felt before.

39

"What is your name?" Lucian spoke just above a whisper but it was a nerve-racking sound.

The man attempted to spit at Lucian, but couldn't muster the strength or wind to reach him due to the blows that Lucian had delivered. Sofia was almost certain Lucian had cracked the thug's sternum and broken several of his ribs. His feeble attempt resulted in the spit dribbling over his lips, down his chin and neck, and coming to a rest on his collar.

"What an original response." Lucian struck the man in the face with such force that he all but caved the side of his face in. Sofia heard his facial bones crack beneath the force of Lucian's fist.

A wave of anxiety rushed through Sofia, fracturing her thoughts. She had encountered the sensation before as a child and recognized it as the first stages of a panic attack. When she was young, she went through a time in her life where panic attacks were common. Her family did not have the means to send her to a therapist, but she was fortunate to find a guidance counselor who knew something about such things. The counselor taught her a breathing technique that helped her overcome the attacks, when she was able to catch them early enough.

Breathe deep through your nose. Hold. Out through your mouth. Sofia talked herself through the impending panic attack.

The man groaned as he slid down the wall towards the ground from his seat on the pavement. Lucian caught him as he dropped, and brought him back to his eye level. "How 'bout I just call you Spit? Spit, whatcha think is a good way for Sofia to repay you for your hospitality today? Do you think you should be allowed to live, or do you think she should be allowed to gut your sorry ass? I mean, it's pretty clear that you're not makin' any good use of your life, so why keep it?"

Breathe in deep through your nose. Hold. Out through your mouth. She repeated this in her head as she contemplated what Lucian was trying to say. She was becoming more panicked as she considered that Lucian was about to tell her to kill this man. She had wanted revenge on these demented bastards from the second they put their hands on her, but could she actually go through with murder? Could she go against everything that she believed in and take this man's life instead of allowing him his day in court? But what if she allowed him to live and he got off? If by some chance he were able to get off and go back on the street, he would inevitably do this again to some other woman. Probably to countless other women! She had seen it too many times to pretend that not only was it a real possibility, but a likely one.

These men had funds that they could tap into to get an attorney who would get them off and back on the streets in no time. Even if they didn't, they would go to prison. They had just as many friends on the inside as they do on the street. Prison was no threat to these men. The law meant nothing to them. Nothing phased them because the life that they were a part of was nearly the same in prison as it was on the street.

Sofia looked over at Spit. He had made no attempt to answer Lucian. He just sat there wheezing and fighting for air.

"Nothing to say, huh? Well, Sofia, I believe Spit is leaving the decision in our hands." Lucian reached over and took Spit's gun from the ground beside him. He handed the gun to Sofia. "I say he dies," he said, bluntly.

Sofia stared at the gun. She had held her own so many times and never thought a thing about what it represented. Now she looked at this gun and realized that it represented the end of two lives. While it clearly represented the end of Spit's revolting, undeserved life, it also represented the end of the life that she knew and had worked very hard to achieve. If she fired that weapon, it would mean that she no longer believed that the system would work or that people deserved a second chance. She sat staring at the gun in silent thought as she listened to Spit's labored breathing. Knowing what it would mean if she fired that weapon, Sofia placed the gun on the ground and looked away from Lucian's patiently waiting face.

"I can't do it, Lucian," she whispered. "I don't believe in this. He deserves a shot at rehabilitation." Regardless of what she thought about the prison system, Sofia believed in the judicial process. She believed that some men took advantage of the second chance, and it was because of those people that everyone deserved the same opportunity.

"I know what he was about to do, but he didn't do it. You came in, and saved my life, but he still could have stopped. I'm not this man's judge, and I cannot take his life, Lucian."

Lucian looked at her acceptingly. "I understand, and I admire you for your courage." Hearing this, Spit began to stir in an effort to move to his feet.

"Get off me!" Spit tried shouting the words, but they came out as a whisper and caused him a great deal of pain, which was evident as he fell back hard against the brick wall. Lucian slowly panned his head back to Spit. Tilting his head slightly to the side, Lucian raised his eyebrows quizzically.

"You heard that bi—"

Lucian's hand shot out and clenched Spit's throat, stopping the word before he could finish it.

"What she said was that she could not be your judge. I, on the other hand, have no problem with that position." Lucian tightened his grip slowly, crushing Spit's windpipe and causing his short, choppy breathing to create a gurgling noise. Sofia was horrified. Lucian stared into Spit's eyes with a boiling hatred.

"Lucian, stop!" she cried, reaching out and grabbing his forearm. She pulled at his arm weakly as he continued squeezing and maintained his unwavering gaze. It almost seemed as though he was in a trance, as if nothing Sofia said or did could reach him. Sofia was no match for Lucian's strength, even at her best. Now, at her weakest, she was hardly even noticeable. Lucian continued squeezing tighter. Sofia heard his windpipe collapse. Spit's eyes began to bulge in their sockets as Lucian continued. Finally, Lucian's hand closed so tightly that he was all but holding Spit's spine in his hand. With a simple flick of his wrist, he snapped it in two. Sofia leaned back against the wall once more, covering her mouth with her hand and staring at Lucian. His face was now calm as he continued to stare into the lifeless eyes of his victim.

"Now, you may wanna look away. I need to take care of my hunger and it's not something you're going to wanna see." Lucian remained calm, never turning to face her.

Sofia turned quickly, shifting her face towards the brick and shielding the side of her eyes with her hand. If Lucian had not felt the need to keep her from seeing what he had just done to Spit, she felt certain that he was correct about seeing him eat. The sounds that followed were disturbing, to say the least. Each began with the tearing of cloth as Lucian ripped away the sleeves and pant legs that covered his usual focal points. Sofia expected the sounds to be completely different from anything she had heard before, but they reminded her of the sounds of any other meal. She could identify when he sunk his teeth into the meat as easily as she could identify the sound of the tearing flesh as it tapered off before snapping loose.

Lucian seemed to be doing all that he could to keep from making too much noise, but the sound of his chewing was hard to cover up. The meat was uncooked, therefore extremely juicy and the sound reflected that. It wasn't long before Sofia's imagination could no longer manage to trick her into believing Lucian was simply eating an extremely rare steak of some sort, so she covered her ears. This only provided a small amount of comfort as the smell of blood consumed her nostrils, which completely negated any progress she was making with her breathing technique. Glancing around briefly for some way to mask the smell, she spotted the coat she had been wearing, several feet away from her. Considering it briefly, she opted to see how much longer she could handle the smell of blood.

As badly as Sofia wanted to simply get up and run, leaving Lucian to his disgusting process, her fear of other attackers was too powerful, and her strength drained. Leaving him was not an option. There was no way that she could force herself to get up and go on alone. She knew that she would have to wait for Lucian so that she could proceed.

After what seemed like an eternity of waiting for Lucian to finish this disgusting process, Sofia finally spoke to him.

"What is taking you so long?" She had her head still turned towards the wall.

"It's not a matter of eating because I'm hungry, or I'd be done. This ain't me sittin' down for a pleasant meal, Sofia," Lucian responded. "It's about giving my body somethin' to feed on instead of going directly for my muscle while I'm like this. I have to take it in slowly. I'm sorry, but I gotta take my time. It'll be over soon, and then we can go."

As he continued to feed, Sofia gathered the courage to peek over at him. Lucian had moved away from her and now had his back towards her. She was unable to see him clearly, but she could tell what he was doing. He was not feeding on them as she had imagined. He didn't tear the meat from the bone with his mouth like an animal. He removed the muscle using his hands and fingernails, which appeared to have grown out somewhat, creating more of a claw than a nail. She had wondered why there had been no trace amounts of saliva on the bodies at the scenes of the other crimes, and now she had her answer. He was actually quite careful about how he went about his process.

As she looked on, Lucian spoke. "Please don't watch. This ain't somethin' I want you to see."

His remark puzzled Sofia. "Are you embarrassed?" she asked quietly.

"No. Not at all. But I'm not dumb enough to think you can see this without it messin' with your head. So, please just turn back around," he urged. Sofia hid her head again.

As she sat, pressed up against the cold brick wall, she began to go over what Lucian had told her earlier that evening. The situation was absolutely unbelievable. There was no way that what she had just seen was possible.

"How can this be, Lucian? How can you be a…." She stopped, realizing that she had no idea what to call him, if not a vampire. "What are you?"

Lucian paused to consider the question before answering.

"We've had a bunch of names. Just like with anything, there's a word in every language for us. Here, I guess it's vampire, but that name was given a long time after the truth stopped having any place in the stories. The oldest names were more accurate and there was one for every, like, sub unit…I guess? Like I was telling you, some are physically gifted, others are smart, then there are others. Anyway, the Greeks had names for all of them, but when they were talking about the whole group in general, they called them the Dunamy. It's based in the Greek word that means explosive power, which is dunamis."

He approached Sofia, removing what was left of his shirt. He began using it to remove the blood from his hands and face as best he could, so that he didn't appear to be some sort of monster. Tucking the shirt into his back pocket, he gently lifted Sofia to her feet.

"I can explain anything else on the way home. You really need to get home and get some rest. We have a good ways to go before we're out of this place." Sofia did not resist him, and the two began to walk in the direction of Sofia's apartment.

40

"How can you be a vampire, Lucian?" Sofia asked quietly, as they continued down the road.

"It's just like I said before. I'm just a person, same as you, but with a very different genetic makeup. Our bodies produce the same chemicals, but my body produces more of them and much faster. That's the biggest difference.

"You really have to try to stop thinking of me the way that you think of vampires in general. I'm not the myth. I'm not pure evil, preying on every single blood pumping human being on the planet. I don't have to consume blood in order to survive. I'm honestly not sure if I'm a part of the evolution of man or some sort of devolved version that got skipped over in the evolutionary chain. Sometimes I see the things that I'm able to do and think that maybe I am the next step of the human race. Other times, I look at myself and realize that I'm still very much an animal. Sometimes I see both. What you just witnessed was one of those times where I saw both."

"But you're a murderer," she protested. "A murderer that feasts on the corpses of your victims. Do you see how ridiculous your argument is?"

"But I don't do that because of what I am. Do you see what I mean? I do that because I feel like I have a purpose. I'm only trying to make the world a better place. These guys go out and prey on the weak and the unsuspecting, hard-working, law abiding citizens of the world, so I prey on them and bring some level of justice to the situation; some balance."

"No, that's what I do. It's my job to stop these people and to make them pay for what they do, not yours. Your way doesn't allow for people to repent, or have another shot at life after they've made a mistake. That's the reason that the laws are the way that they are. They factor in some decency." Sofia was insistent, but not angry. She simply couldn't find the energy to be angry at this point.

"So you think that when they're given a second chance, people usually take full advantage of that and make a better life for themselves?"

"You know exactly what I mean. No, not everyone takes advantage of a second chance but some do, and those people make it necessary to give the others a chance as well."

"So you mean that you're willing to sacrifice the many for the good of the few? Is that what you mean? Because that's what I'm hearing. Those very few that take advantage are a good enough reason to allow the vast majority of criminals to go on doing what they do and putting so many people at risk?" Lucian's passion regarding this was undeniable. "Plus, I don't go after people making their first tiny mistake; I don't even go after people who have a chance at being innocent. I research people before I ever make a move," Lucian paused briefly. "That is, unless a situation such as the one we just had, comes along."

"See, why couldn't you have just beaten them up? Why not just teach them a lesson? It's still not what I think is right, but at least they would be alive."The strain of the day had worn Sofia down so much that her accent began revealing itself.

"And what lesson would that be? I can tell you exactly what that's gonna teach them: we need to walk around with bigger guns. That's it!"

"What about the fact that you're killing people? You're taking lives. Don't you worry about that?" Sofia looked over at Lucian, but didn't wait for a response. "What am I saying? Why would you care about any sort of long term effects from your actions?"

"If you're talking about on a spiritual level, which I assume you are, I actually do think about that. I'm not going to get into my personal beliefs on the matter, but I believe that my soul will, inevitably, be condemned for what I'm doing."

Sofia stopped instantly, staring at him in disbelief.

"I really don't want to get in to this right now," Lucian said as he continued walking.

"How do you think we can do that?" Sofia was appalled at the fact that Lucian thought he could say something like that, expecting her to stop pressing him for some reasonable explanation.

"We can just move on to the next subject, or we can simply go back to the last one—pretty much the same way you move around any subject."

Sofia stared at him, her mouth open slightly.

Lucian sighed deeply, knowing that they could not proceed until he had at least tried to explain himself.

"Well, come on and keep walking," he said, beckoning her forward. "No need to stop just so you can listen."

Sofia walked slowly toward him, still glaring at him in disbelief. As she caught up to him, they continued.

"It's like this. Your emotions are nothing more than the feelings that your body creates in response to the chemicals that your brain releases in a certain situation."

"What does that have to do with what you just said?" Sofia interrupted.

"I'll get to it," Lucian replied, calmly. "So, the brain releases these chemicals, and your body and brain, react. Boom! Emotions. Since I have more of those chemicals and they're present at much higher levels in my system, my emotions are much more powerful than yours. All of my emotions. Love, for me, is this unimaginable high. Sadness, on the other hand, is absolutely unbearable. So, the people that I love—those people are very important to me. They're the reason I started doin' this. I decided a long time ago that I would gladly give the ultimate sacrifice for them."

"Lucian, you're not the only person who would give their life to protect someone they love. I, myself, would gladly risk my life for my loved ones. The difference is that you're not risking your life because you can heal from your wounds so quickly, and you're killing people."

"That's why you need to listen, and stop all this interrupting. See, if you're someone who believes that your soul is going to survive for all eternity after your body dies, and the circumstances of that eternity will be influenced by your actions during your life, then sacrificing your life isn't that big a sacrifice. I mean, if you think that sacrificing your life for someone else is going to get you to Heaven, where you will eventually be reunited with everyone you have ever loved, you ain't makin' a sacrifice. You're just trying to jump the line. I don't know what I believe, but I do what I do knowin' that one possible outcome for me is that my soul could be condemned after this life. So, I'm sacrificing my eternity, not my life."

Lucian's comments caught Sofia completely off guard. His logic was insane, and at the same time, an unbelievable testament of love and devotion. Who would consciously condemn themselves for all of eternity? She opened her mouth to rebut his comments, but could honestly think of nothing to say. She decided to turn her attention back to the walk that they had before them instead.

Sofia followed Lucian's lead as he soldiered on through the treacherous neighborhood. He took her down a route he seemed all too familiar with. They ducked down alleys and through backyards of houses. Sofia would have avoided the area altogether had she still been on her own. At one point, they walked past a group of teens, out much later than they should have been. Some of them commented on Lucian's muscles, to which he just smiled and flexed for them. None of them had much of anything to say about Sofia's disheveled appearance. It was too dark for them to see the traces of blood on his clothes and hands, and he acted as if nothing was out of the ordinary.

Finally, they reached a point that Sofia knew was a safe place. She paused for a moment and looked around. Lucian fully expected her to call her cab or suggest he leave so she could flag down a fellow cop for a ride home, but she didn't. After getting her bearing, she worked out the fastest way to her apartment and continued walking. She wasn't going to say it, but she still had questions she needed answers to. She knew it would be impossible to get back into this frame of mind with Lucian. If they parted ways at this point, she would never get the answers she needed.

41

As they continued on, Sofia took notice of how Lucian's body was beginning to change. He was still larger than usual, but he was gradually moving towards his normal size. His skin remained pulled tight around his muscles, but the muscles themselves were changing shape. They were no longer the god-like masculine form they had been before. After his fight with the group of thugs, every single muscle on Lucian's body had been the perfect example of what that muscle looks like beneath the skin. His chest barreled out in full, rounded humps that rested over his tightly drawn abdominal muscles. His biceps were perfectly defined, and clearly separated from his mounding shoulders. His triceps were perfectly cut horseshoes beneath the skin on the back of his arms. Although she couldn't see his legs because of his jeans, she could see where the seams of his pants had been pulled to their limits and actually popped in several places along his thigh. Now, the shapes of his visible muscles were odd and dimpled. She imagined that this was his body tearing down the muscle to account for the energy he had exerted. As his form began to return, Sofia found herself softening towards him again.

"Who was it?" Sofia finally asked quietly.

"What do you mean?"

"No one makes that sort of decision without a reason. No one ever just decides to start a personal war on crime without having lost someone or having some terrible incident that started everything. So who was it?" She regretted asking the question as Lucian slowed his stride. She could almost feel his mood darken. It felt as if the temperature dropped as he walked in silence. The moment passed quickly, and Lucian's face eased. It passed so quickly that Sofia was unsure if his mood had changed or if she had merely imagined it.

"I don't really think any one thing made me do this. I think it's the thought of something happening that really drives me. A lot of times, I'll see the person that I'm checking out commit a crime or I'll think of the pain they're causing. I think about the people they hurt and everyone else who's affected by their actions and it makes me sad. And like I said before, the sadness that I experience is a powerful force. And, just like most people, things that make me sad usually make me mad. That makes it easy to do what I do. Like with what just happened. When I saw those men attacking you, I've never felt anger like that before. Simple enough decision for me. They all deserved to die."

"So, your biggest problem is with men attacking women?" Sofia asked innocently.

Lucian stopped and looked at her, somewhat shocked that she hadn't understood what he meant.

"No! When I saw that they were attacking you I completely lost control!" The look on his face was a mixture of anger and hurt. Sofia could tell that he was thinking of the moment from earlier when he had seen her on the ground. He turned abruptly and continued down the road. Sofia remained still for another few seconds to absorb his meaning, before returning to his side.

"I mean, that's definitely one of my biggies, but it was you! I went into that fight thinking I needed to save some woman from an attack. I didn't realize it was you until I saw you face to face. I mean, look at you. You don't exactly look like yourself. I really just got lucky that I was able to find you at all. See, I really wasn't sure what was going to happen when you left earlier. I knew you were gonna go turn me in. That's just who you are. I thought it out a little, figured I would go pack up my shit and move. I was just gonna head to a new city, make a fresh start. I've left places like that before and started over, no problem.

"But I couldn't do it. I couldn't leave you. I knew I had to make sure I did everything I could to make you understand what I've been doing, and why. So, I took off after you not long after you left. I figured I'd be able to find you quicker than I did, but you went the wrong way. I ended up doublin' back pretty quick when I couldn't find you, but you were nowhere. It was just by chance that I found you when I did, and when I saw it was you on the ground I guess I came unglued. I guess with all we've been doin' lately, and me bein' concerned about how to tell you about all this, I didn't really acknowledge what's been goin' on, but I fell in love."

Lucian looked out of the corner of his eye to see what Sofia's reaction was, but never stopped walking or talking. "I'm pretty shocked that it went down so quick, but it did. Like I said, my feelings grow strong and deep, just not usually so quick. When your emotions can hurt you as badly as mine can, you learn to keep people at a distance. I mean, I knew early on that you were special, but you're really so much more than that. I'm in love with you, Sofia."

Sofia wanted to be able to break down and cry, or go to him, or something, but she couldn't allow herself. He was saying exactly what she had hoped that he would, only it was what she wanted before she knew the truth about him. She had felt the very same way and had found it difficult to believe that she was having such strong feelings about someone in such a short time.

"Wha…I…." Her thoughts were scattered, and her mind in a state of complete chaos. Between all he had told her, what she had seen, and what he was now saying, it was all too much for her to wrap her head around.

"I don't expect you to feel the same after what all has happened. I don't even want that to affect your decision on how to move forward. I can only hope that you'll allow yourself to think about it and decide how you really feel. As far as how we work things out from there, we can figure that out. I just want you to think about things and give me an honest answer."

Sofia's head was spinning from what he was telling her and the conflicting emotions she was feeling. It was probably due to the exhaustion, or the possible concussion she had suffered from the multiple blows to her head, but she was finally able to remain calm.

"How can I even know that, Lucian? How can I know anything? You just told me you were a freaking vampire, or 'Dumany,' or whatever. What the hell am I supposed to know for sure? How can I even know that you're not affecting the way that I'm thinking or how I'm feeling? How do I know you aren't just saying what you know I wanted to hear before all of this happened?"

"It's 'Dunamy,' and it's not like that." He reached out to touch her shoulder, but Sofia shrugged off his attempts to soothe her. She was still very unsure of how she wanted to proceed.

Lucian drew back his hand. "I can't do that. Like I told you, there are a lot of things that you're going to think about me that are simply not true. I can't read your mind and I can't control your mind. That's just not possible. Your thoughts don't work like that. They're not like radio waves that float around for people to pluck out of the sky and listen to." Lucian dragged little imaginary thought waves from the sky as he spoke.

"No jokes, Lucian," Sofia said softly. "Not now." She was in no mood for his little attempts at humor or his endless attempts to deride her comments with his logic.

Lucian quickly dropped his hands and regained a somewhat serious tone.

"What you feel is real. The only way that I've influenced your feelings is by being myself. From there, you formed feelings and opinions as you would with anyone else. So, you just need to search your heart and decide what you feel towards me and what you need to do next."

Sofia turned and headed down the street ahead of Lucian. They walked on in silence, which made the remainder of their walk seem endless. Sofia had so many questions for him, but she couldn't even speak. She wrestled with her emotions and thoughts about what he had told her.

As they approached her apartment, Lucian finally spoke. "I'm sorry for how all this went down. I'd definitely do it differently if I could. But this is how it played out, so we'll just have to move on from here. I can only tell you that I was being sincere and everything that I told you tonight is the truth. I only ask that you consider your feelings before you consider my actions. If you can get past what I've done, let me know. Just to be clear, know that I'm not going to stop. I'll understand if you can't accept those terms, but there are just too many evil people out there for me to stop." After a few seconds of staring at one another, Lucian turned to leave Sofia so she could rest.

"Lucian?" she called out, curtly.

He turned hopefully to reply.

"Do I even want to know why your hair and facial hair are longer?"

Realizing she was only asking to satiate her inquisitive nature, not as a sign of forgiveness, Lucian answered quietly, "Chemical thing. Hair and nails," he held up a hand filled with long nails, much different from the manicured look he normally kept. "They grow when it happens."

"But after the alley—" she began, but Lucian cut her short.

"I shaved. You were out for a while." Sofia looked at Lucian for a few seconds before turning to drag her exhausted body into her building without a response.

42

Sofia slept through her alarm even though it beeped incessantly for an hour before automatically shutting off. It had begun going off shortly after she had fallen asleep but she somehow managed to go into such a deep sleep immediately, the sound never affected her. It wasn't a problem that she didn't get up because she didn't have to be in to work that day, but it was very uncharacteristic of her to not wake up at the smallest sound. She was exhausted from the night's events and barely had the strength to climb into the shower for a very quick, but very thorough rinse. Afterwards, she collapsed into her bed, a towel around her hair to keep from soaking her pillow. Sofia slept as if she had not done so for a week, and didn't wake up until late in the evening.

Her body ached from all of the activity. Sofia continued to lie there, staring out of her window for some time, just thinking of the previous night's events. Whenever she had faced difficulty in her life, Sofia found it helpful to immerse herself in her work. She was able to do some of her best thinking when she was able to focus on something else for a time, and the answer usually came to her out of the blue. The problem with doing that this time was the fact that when she returned to work tomorrow, she would run into Lucian. Even if she and Bishop were to be out of the precinct all day, she would never be able to stop thinking about Lucian. Sofia knew that she had to make a decision about what she was going to do in the remaining hours before she returned to work.

Rising from her bed, Sofia slipped into her favorite pajama pants and made her way to her kitchen. Her steps were deliberately slow and short in order to ease the pain in her legs. She had no idea how far they had walked last night, but she knew she wouldn't be doing it again anytime soon. Sofia was in excellent physical condition but her body was in no way prepared for the variety of abuse she had put it through. In retrospect, it was a terrible idea not calling a cab, or someone else. Why hadn't she just called the precinct and had someone come and pick her up? That would have been a much better alternative, especially considering what all had transpired. Maybe she had subconsciously wanted to protect Lucian, so she had blocked herself from even considering that option. There was no telling. She only knew that she was not thinking clearly in any way, and getting away from Lucian at that moment was her only concern.

She finally made it to the kitchen and selected one of her favorite single serving coffee containers. Inserting the tiny cup into the device, she leaned back against the adjacent counter and waited for the heavenly brown liquid to brew. The aroma of French vanilla quickly filled the small kitchen, giving Sofia the first nice sensation she had enjoyed in over twenty-four hours. As she stood waiting for her cup to fill, she caught a glimpse of her reflection in her toaster. She picked it up and gave her face a good look. She had some bruising around her neck from where Spit had squeezed her. She quickly began checking herself over and realized that she had sustained several bruises on her arms. The area around her beltline, where he had held her and attempted to remove her pants, contained many bruises.

She became angry as she thought of her attackers, the way that they had made her feel completely helpless, and the terror that she experienced when she realized that she was completely at their mercy. Then she thought of how Lucian had come to her rescue. He had helped so many other people who would never know what he had done for them. Could she, in good conscience, stop Lucian from what he was doing when she knew first-hand how much good he was doing at the same time? She knew that she would need to have an answer by the morning. She couldn't see him again or even step into her precinct without knowing what she would do. And, what would she do when she did see him? There was no denying how unbelievably attractive she found him in his excited state.

She continued to run through everything that had happened in the past few days. She couldn't base her decision on just the events from last night, knowing all she knew now. The past weeks had meant so much to her. She had felt such a connection with Lucian, one that she had never expected to feel. It was a feeling that she had given up all hope of having long ago.

Sofia had always placed so much focus on her career that she had convinced herself love was not even something that she wanted. Until now, she had never believed that she was missing out on anything. Lucian had unlocked emotions and feelings that she believed just did not exist for her.

She made herself a cup of coffee, adjourned to her living room, and turned on the television, leaving it on the twenty-four hour news station. She had not intended to watch anything, but preferred the background noise to silence. She noticed a particularly screechy personality was on, so she lowered the volume to just above the muted level. Sofia's muscles screamed as she eased down onto her couch. She slowly laid her head back until it rested on the cushion behind her, staring at the ceiling as she continued to reflect.

Her feelings for Lucian, coupled with the fact that he was actually trying to do good, were the only things that even made her think twice about turning him in. He was clearly going about it in a very different way than she had ever considered, but she could see why he was doing it. She had felt the frustration of watching a man who she knew was guilty of some of the most depraved acts walk free for various reasons. She knew the pain of knowing it was highly unlikely that person would ever pay for his crimes. The difference was that when she saw these things, and felt these pains, she immediately began trying to find a way to make them pay under the rules of the law. She had never considered going outside of the law for justice. Although she had suspected Bishop of operating outside of the rules on several occasions, she had never considered doing the same for a second.

The hum of the television and the faint squelching of opinionated "news professionals" continued in the background as Sofia stared blankly into space, occasionally sipping her coffee. She wasn't really staring at anything in particular; she was just caught in a stare and trapped within her thoughts. Nothing was making this decision any easier. It was as if she actually had a little imaginary angel on one shoulder and a devil on the other, each pleading their case as to how she should judge.

Her moral compass had always pointed true north, guiding her in the direction of good and pure decisions and actions; but this time, it was as if it was spinning out of control. The decision was not as black and white as she had once believed. Clearly, the path to goodness and purity was to turn Lucian in and stop his destruction. However, wasn't it just as good to allow him to operate, saving the lives of so many people who could be harmed by those he hunted? Or was it just the legal path? But was legality as important as morality in these situations? She just didn't see the path that Lucian followed as being wholly evil. Those he disposed of absolutely followed the path of evil. His path lay somewhere in the middle and Sofia was beginning to wonder if maybe that wasn't the purest path of all.

She had no idea how long the knocking had been going on when she finally noticed it. Slowly getting to her feet, Sofia eased over to the door. She braced herself as she peered through the peephole, expecting to see Lucian staring back. To her surprise, it was Shane. She slowly cracked the door, allowing the chain to keep it from opening fully.

"Hi, Shane. Did Lucian send you over?"

"Not really. He mentioned that you were upset about something and that you had had a rough night, so I thought I'd check in on you." His face was warm and genuinely filled with concern, so Sofia closed the door and removed the chain.

43

Shane eased in and gave her a friendly hug.

"You alright?" he asked softly, motioning at the marks on her face. "What happened there?"

"Oh, that was just.... It's nothing. What did he tell you?" She held her blanket wrapped around her, accepting his comforting hug before backing away.

"Just what I said. He mentioned that you had been through something pretty bad last night and that you were upset. That's about it. I didn't have anything going on, so I figured I would check in on you."

"I'm all right. Thanks for coming by." It was actually a nice break from the hours of thinking about everything. "Would you like some coffee?" She eased her way towards the kitchen, selecting a standard coffee mix for the machine.

"That'll work." He eased his demeanor as he tried to lighten the mood. "I'm really sorry about coming by so late. I just figured that based on the time Lucian came in that you might be asleep most of the day."

"Good guess." As nice as it was to see Shane, she was still shaken up badly. Sofia found it difficult to make small talk.

"Like the place." He glanced around.

"Pfft," she sputtered mockingly. "My place is a hole compared to your palace."

"Oh, stop. Lucian and I have been fortunate. You clearly think we're snobs, though. That's real cool. Reeeal nice, Sofie." He joked around, hoping to calm her nerves some.

Sofia handed him his coffee with as much of a smile as she could muster.

"It really is nice of you to stop by. It means a lot."

"It's not a problem. I hope you two are going to be all right. I know how much he likes you. Most times I never meet girls he dates unless he meets them while we're out together."

"Can we not talk about him right now? I'm figuring some stuff out right now, and it's really just nice to have someone to talk to."

"Sure. Not a problem. I can do that...." They both stared at their coffee mugs for several seconds, swirling periodically as they searched their thoughts for a topic that would not lead back to Lucian.

Sofia broke the silence, "So, what is it you do, again? I know that you were a doctor or something, but didn't you quit that?"

"Yes. Yes I did. I decided that I really didn't enjoy it as much as I originally thought I did."

"What brought you to that conclusion?"

"My father died a few years ago. It really opened my eyes to how much time I wasted working and not being with people I cared for. I didn't get to see my parents very much for a long time while I went through school, and while I was getting established in my career. I always thought I would earn a bundle of money and have tons of free time once I did, but he died before I got the chance. I decided then that I wanted to live my life differently. Since then, I have done some things on the side to keep enough money coming in to pay some bills."

"You must do really well with your side jobs to pay half of that rent and have money to spend."

"Actually, Lucian just lets me live there for free. I know you don't really want to hear about him, but he's been really great to me since then. He told me to move in and stay as long as I like, and absolutely refuses to take any money from me. I usually just spend my money on things for the place that we can both enjoy to pay him back. It's a pretty good arrangement."

"Yeah, he's an angel." She spoke with sarcasm as she finished off her coffee. "Angel of damn death," she muttered under her breath, as she leaned away from Shane to refill her cup.

Shane placed his cup on the counter slowly before speaking. "You know, what he's doing is really noble if you think about it."

Sofia froze, holding her coffee mug in place against her lips. She just stared at Shane, trying to determine exactly what he had meant by his comment.

"What do you mean?" Sofia was unsure of exactly how much he knew.

"What he does. It's selfless, and noble, and heroic."

"What do you mean by what he does? What does that mean, Shane?"

"You know exactly what it means. You saw him. You saw what he is capable of, and what he is. The man is a freakin' super hero and has changed an indeterminable amount of lives."

"You… know?" Sofia just stared at him. She was not overwhelmed with disbelief. She was simply surprised. She had considered that Shane might know, but couldn't believe that he did, based on how nonchalant he acted. There had never been an awkward moment between the three of them, which she had concluded that there should have been, had he known. She had spoken about the case with Lucian, in front of Shane, and he had been extremely casual through the entire thing.

"We live together. He's my best friend. Yes, I know."

"Are you involved?" Sofia's mood was no longer playful. She had subconsciously reverted to her instincts as an investigator.

"Are we off the record? That sounded a little like a question that you might be asking as a cop, not a friend."

Sofia eased up a little. At this point, she was more concerned with hearing the whole story than preparing a case.

"Sorry. Of course we are. I just need to hear everything, Shane."

"Well, I do a few things for him, but I'm not involved in the actual 'destruction of evil,' as he calls it. I do most of his research on the criminals, and I fix him up when he's hurt."

"Wait. I watched him heal. What do you mean fix him up?"

"Well, when he gets shot, those bullets stay in there. His body heals up around them, but they're still in there. See, when the bullet goes in, it breaks the skin on the outside first and does damage all the way in. Lucian's body begins healing as soon as it is injured. Naturally, his epidermis is the first to repair and the area surrounding the bullet is last. When he comes in, I have to find the bullets and pull them out. It's not the hardest work I have ever done as a doctor, but it can be a little tricky working in surroundings that are trying to heal over your incisions while you're in there. It's like digging a hole in dry sand that just keeps filling back in."

At this point, there was no reason for Sofia to doubt anything said about Lucian. She didn't even question what Shane was saying.

"So you're the one who decides who he kills?"

"It's easier to think of them as 'evil' and he is 'destroying' them. It helps to process things. But to answer your question, yes, sometimes I do decide who he should track. Most times, he'll have a lead on someone and have me check them out. I find out as much as I can about them. I find out whether there was any hard evidence against them or if they're repeat offenders, what they were accused of, and the likelihood that they're guilty. Once I do all of that, I let him know where they usually hang out or where they live and he spends several nights tracking them. Most times he doesn't make a move on someone without seeing them in the act, but in some cases he'll make an exception."

"When does he make exceptions?"

Shane fidgeted slightly. He was visibly uncomfortable. "When it comes to kids. He doesn't wait for that to happen. He will watch them for a few days. If they act suspicious or put themselves in a lot of situations where they are around children, he makes a move."

Sofia's detective instincts took over once again. "We haven't found any bodies that fit his pattern that have abused children."

"No, you wouldn't. He disposes of them, but doesn't feed on them. He finds them too disgusting to ingest. Can't say I disagree. Those are rough nights. If he can't feed, he deals with some intense stuff. But I can't keep him off those cases. He makes them his top priority and takes them every time. And if I try and keep him away from them for a while, he'll find someone and bring me their information."

"How long has this been going on? Was he doing this before you were involved?" Sofia couldn't believe that this had been going on for any substantial period of time. They had only noticed a pattern and developed the case in the past few weeks. If Lucian had been operating for any longer, surely they would have seen the connection.

"I've never asked him if he was doing this before we got together, but we've been working together for about a year. I became involved after my father died. See, my father didn't just die of natural causes. He was murdered by a degenerate. It was supposedly an attempted robbery. The man was a career criminal and the severity of his crimes had escalated over the years. My father was not the type to fight a man with a gun. He was too smart for that. There were no witnesses so there's no way of knowing how things actually went down, but there was no sign of a struggle. I believe that after robbing my father, he killed him in cold blood. Anyway, he got off on the charges for killing my father. Some evidence was mismanaged and became inadmissible, so he got a mistrial."

Shane's mood darkened for a moment as he thought back.

"He laughed as he left the courtroom."

He paused briefly before continuing. "I was harboring a lot of hate after that. At the same time, I was realizing that I wanted to change my life so that I could enjoy the time that I have with my friends and family. Lucian and I knew each other before that, and he was there for me through everything. When I told him I had decided to quit my job and that I wanted to live a more fulfilling life, Lucian supported me one hundred percent and offered me a place to live. I didn't feel comfortable with the idea of basically becoming a full blown bum. Lucian convinced me that it wasn't only a good idea, but that it would actually help him out. I hadn't been there long before he told me about himself and what he did. He didn't have to tell me much for me to get on board."

"So, he told you about himself and what, you just believed him?"

"No. I'm a logical person, so of course that wasn't the case. He explained all that he could and then he left. He came back a few hours later and was a great deal larger than he usually was, covered in blood. He then grabbed a knife from the counter and cut himself open. As I watched his body heal in a matter of seconds, it was very difficult to deny what he had told me. Plus, I think it was easy for me to believe him because I really wanted it to be true. What he wanted to do, the destruction of evil and all, was something I really wanted to see happen. I wanted to be part of it. Since then, we have worked on a process by which we locate targets and a set of rules that goes along with Lucian's plan."

That was the last piece of "logic" that Sofia could handle.

"Oh, wonderful. You guys have rules for your murders. Well then, I guess that makes all of this all right. I mean, you don't follow the rules of society. You have a separate set of rules that you feel are better than those that the rest of us live by. That definitely sets you apart from other criminals. You guys really are like some sort of super heroes!"

"Okay. I can tell you're getting angry and probably just fed up with all of this information. It's a lot to take in. But before I go, I'm going to lay it all out there. I'm going to tell you something that Lucian would probably rather I not tell you, but I think it's something that you need to know. The reason that you have only been on this case for a short time is Lucian and I decided that we needed the help of someone inside. Lucian is more than capable of doing what he does and never leaving a trace of evidence—not even a body. We operated for several months without your people having so much as a hint of what was going on. The thing is that he wanted access to more information on his targets. He didn't want more innocent people to potentially be harmed before he was able to locate a target. Now, his job is close to the police department, but he can't get to as much information as actual detectives."

Sofia was enraged as she realized what he was about to say. Was this supposed to be calming her down? Finding out that Lucian had only been interested in her so that he could make an ally out of her, and use her to gain sensitive information, was not making her less angry about anything. She slammed her cup into the sink and made her way to the door.

"Please just listen before you lose it."

Sofia placed her hand on the knob and waited for him to finish.

"We needed someone on the inside, and Lucian was positive that it was going to be Bishop."

The death grip that she had placed on the knob loosened slightly at this news.

"He was perfect. He hates criminals and is willing to push the limits of the job to make an arrest. He's a great cop but has more of a sense of what real justice is than most. He was just right for the job. I was ready for him to move in on Bishop, but Lucian could never get past a feeling that he had about him. He would have been perfect for our inside person, but Lucian felt that he could be too easily lured away from our cause. He felt that Bishop would jump at the opportunity to set us up and make an arrest that would make his career."

"So that's when you targeted me?" Sofia interrupted.

"No. We never targeted you—that's the point. Lucian and I were going to make a different plan, go a different way. We had scrapped the idea when Lucian asked you out. Then you two went out and he told me after that first date that he couldn't believe how strong his feelings for you were. What I'm trying to get at is this: he really does care about you. One thing about Lucian is that if you're inside his small circle of loved ones, there's nothing that he wouldn't do to make you happy and keep you safe. And let me just tell you that you are one of the safest."

Shane finally made his way to the door as Sofia opened it. He turned back as he entered the hall. "I really did want to make sure that you were all right. I'm glad to see that you're safe."

With that, he turned and left.

44

Sofia closed the door, locking the deadbolt, the chain, and the knob. She leaned her head against the door softly. Had there ever been a more chaotic sequence of events in history? She had hardly began to get things straight in her head about what had happened the night before, and now she found out that Shane was involved. The only reason that the police had even found evidence of their work was because Lucian had allowed them to. What could she do? Did she go to work the following day and announce that Lucian was the killer? She didn't have any real proof. They hadn't found any trace of useable evidence that would tie him to the crimes. Lucian was too smart to allow himself to be caught by her. He could easily make her look like a jilted lover. He had everyone in the precinct wrapped around his finger, especially Bishop. Honestly, did she even want to turn him in?

She had done a good job of keeping her emotional attachment to Lucian out of her decision-making up to this point, but could no longer pretend that it wasn't a factor. She knew how she felt about him. Sofia had only really just started to believe that he felt the same way after having spoken with Shane. So the question now was if she could turn in the only man that she had truly fallen in love with.

Sofia had operated for so long under the assumption that she would be alone forever because of her great love for her profession. She had never felt that there was something missing from her life, because she truly did not feel that anything was missing. Now she had gotten a taste of what she had missed, and she wasn't sure she could end it just as it was beginning. Then there was her career, the thing for which she had worked so hard, for so long. How could she compromise the beliefs that had made her such a successful officer? It was just such a great amount to consider in such a short time. She knew that she had to have a decision and a plan by the next day when she went to work.

Sofia spent the entire evening and morning going back and forth on whether to turn Lucian in. Each time she thought she had reached the right conclusion, she would find something on the other side that made her doubt herself. Every single point that she could think of had an equally compelling counterpoint. Finally, she simplified her solution down to her emotional attachment to Lucian versus her views on morality. While she had successfully simplified the question, she had all but made the answer simple. The hours continued to slip by as Sofia contemplated her options. Eventually, the time arrived for her to begin getting ready for work. She was no closer to a decision than she had been when she woke up. She wondered if it would have been easier if Shane had never shown up that night. Nothing could change what had happened, and she could only try to make the right decision now. She considered all of the information she had been given.

45

The sky was a beautiful cascade of purple, grey, and white clouds, and it was clear that a spring storm was making its way towards the city. Sofia began her drive towards work against the steady wind that accompanied the dark sheet of rain soaked clouds that covered the sky in the distance. It was actually Sofia's favorite climate—the moment right before a storm arrived. Regardless of her feelings about the weather, nothing was going to pull her out of this trance. A sharp pain was unrelenting inside her stomach as she made her way towards the office. She had no idea how she was going to handle the situation with Lucian.

At each intersection, Sofia intentionally slowed down so that she had no option but to wait for the light to change. She stopped for every pedestrian that so much as looked like possibly crossing the street. Sofia did anything and everything that she could to slow her progression towards the precinct, but she was there before she knew it. Pulling into a spot as far from the doors as possible, Sofia slowly slid off the upholstered seat and eased toward the doors of the precinct.

It felt like a different place as she walked into that building. Before this week, she had never gone more than twelve hours without entering the building. The fact that two days had passed, and she had not so much as seen it, made her feel as if she had been in a different world entirely. The same feelings had occurred to her the week before when she and Lucian had spent both of her days off together, but this was very different. She slowly approached the steps and made her way into the building. As she approached her desk, Sofia felt the pangs of anxiety like needles in her gut.

"Didn't expect to see you today." Bishop called out to her, as Sofia rounded the corner. "Figured we wouldn't see much out of you 'til tomorrow."

Sofia looked at him, puzzled by his comments.

"Or are you guys meeting here today?" Bishop thought it kind of him to keep Lucian's name out of the conversation as he gave Sofia a hard time.

Sofia, still puzzled, refrained from answering. Instead, she attempted to fake a smile and did her best to control her nerves enough to come across as if nothing was wrong. Casually making her way over to her desk, Sofia began perusing the contents of her drawer as she attempted to collect her thoughts. Sensing something was strange about her unusual looks when he mentioned her being there, Bishop continued to press on.

"It's Thursday, kid. You're off today."

Sofia was shocked, but did all she could to hide how surprised she was at that information. "Yeah, I know…I just needed to do something real quick, and then I'm out."

"Why you bein' all weird?"

"I'm not. I just have to do something." She clamored around some more in her desk drawer as she tried to think of something to get to justify having stopped in.

"Have you seen Lucian today?" She did not want to run into him if he was there.

Bishop, still unconvinced that something wasn't wrong with Sofia, moved over to her desk to have a more private conversation. Although they had been at odds lately, he was still very protective of Sofia and wanted to make sure she was okay. Seeing that he was approaching, Sofia tilted her head so that her long black hair fell over her shoulder and covered the bruising that had occurred on her neck. She had applied some makeup to the bruising, but still felt very self-conscious about it.

"Hey." Bishop urged quietly. "You sure you're alright? You seem a little off."

"I'm good. Has Lucian been in?" She kept her head down to keep from looking at Bishop.

"Did somethin' happen with you guys?"

"No. Have you seen him?"

Bishop gently placed his hand on Sofia's shoulder. The soft touch was just enough to cause Sofia to jerk away from him in surprise and fear. She knew it to be a typical reaction for an assaulted woman. Bishop also recognized the reaction.

"What happened?" Bishop demanded an answer as softly as he could. Not wanting Bishop to get involved just yet, Sofia quickly softened and smiled as normally as she could manage.

"Nothing. You just surprised me. I guess I was kind of zoned out."

Bishop continued to look her over for a second before answering her question.

"Yeah, I saw him for a second when I came in, but he was headed out. Said he had to go take care of something and that he would be gone most of the day. He left something on your desk."

Looking down, Sofia noticed a case folder laying there that she had never seen before. A wave of relief washed over her as she realized she had another day to think of what her next move would be, as well as the fact that she wasn't going to run into Lucian.

"What are you doing here, anyway?" Sofia asked Bishop, now much more relaxed than before.

"Eh, where else am I gonna go? Plus, all the stuff from yesterday."

"What do you mean?"

"Our boys hit again last night. They took out a whole group of thugs in Southside. Big mess." Sofia's heart jumped. "Took out some pretty bad dudes. Looks like they were very well connected in the area. All of 'em had priors. Some home invasions, armed robbery, one particularly nasty fella with a habit of raping women." Bishop tossed the pictures of the victims onto her desk. Sofia's hands began to shake uncontrollably as Spit's lifeless face looked up at her. Quickly, she slipped her hands beneath her desk in an effort to conceal her quivering.

"Just another 'attack' that makes me wanna stop looking for these guys." He mumbled beneath his breath.

"Is this it?" Sofia asked, in a puzzled tone.

Bishop looked at her with a confused face. "Isn't that enou…You know what…I forgot you hadn't called in to check. Yeah, there was actually a group the night before, too. Not even far from here. Over towards the train station." He flipped through the pictures he had thrown onto her desk, locating a group of pictures." Sofia didn't recognize the faces as well as she had the others. She knew they were the men who had ambushed her and Lucian. She never really made a point of looking at any of their faces during the attack. She had been too concerned for Lucian.

"Yeah. I tried to call you, but your phone was dead. What, you stopped checkin' your messages on your days off, now?"

Sofia decided not to answer Bishop.

"He didn't happen to drop off his business card. Did he?" Sofia tried her best to act normal. She pretended to scan the picture of one of the men, while keeping her frantic hands out of sight.

"He, who?" Bishop quickly answered her question with a question of his own.

Sofia realized that this was the first time that she referred to the killer as an individual person, in many months of working the case.

"Do what?" She attempted to rebound from the uncharacteristic stumble. "Oh, right. I meant 'they.' The killers, they didn't leave a card did they?"

"Sounds like you got someone in particular on your mind." He was joking, having no idea how right he was.

"Maybe so." She continued to play along as if she was just in a daze. She picked up the case file that Lucian had left on her desk and began to leaf through it, turning her back to Bishop to hide the shaking that was now evident as she held the folder open. "So, nothing out of the ordinary at the scene?" She questioned as she perused the file.

"I didn't notice anything, but I don't imagine my word is enough for you. You got time to head over there?"

Sofia had stopped listening to his response before he had begun. The case file that Lucian had left on her desk was that of a very large man with a very small rap sheet.

Quintin Marks, arrested one time several years before for domestic dispute, was released and had not been entered into the system again since. Quintin was 6'7" and two hundred ninety pounds. Every bit of it was muscle. He looked to be a skinhead but had no tattoos signifying affiliation. He was not affiliated with any of the local gangs. Sofia knew exactly what this folder meant and she knew that she had to stop it.

"Umm, you know what? I don't." She picked up the case file and pictures Bishop had thrown onto her desk, trying to mask the fact that she was also taking the folder that Lucian left for her. "We can look at it tomorrow." She grabbed the keys to her car.

"Okay." Bishop wore a concerned look on his face. No matter what she was saying, he couldn't shake the feeling that she was hiding something.

"Thank you for the concern, but it really is nothing." She was now much more capable of giving him a genuine smile.

"Whatever." Bishop began to make his way towards a group of officers who were congregating for some casual office chatter.

46

As she jumped into the car, Sofia used the onboard computer to find Quintin's last known address. With a soft hum, the computer kicked into action and pulled up the address just as Sofia pulled away from the curb. Even though she wasn't sure what she would do when she got there, she knew she had to reach this man before Lucian was able to do him any harm. She felt recharged as she cruised down the streets, dodging the idiotic pedestrians, continually stepping blindly out into the street. Tracking Lucian allowed Sofia to put all of the concerns that she had been dealing with successfully out of her head for the time being. She was just doing police work, and it felt great. This is what she lived for. How could she have ever doubted that this was what she wanted in life?

She knew then that she had been deliberating over something that was truly not even an issue. She could never jeopardize what she had in her career. She told herself that love could come around again between her and another person, but the passion she had for her job would never come around in another career.

As she pulled up to Quintin's complex, she turned the car off and listened for signs of a disturbance. There was nothing but the sound of airplanes coming in to land at the nearby airport. There was the occasional foreboding caw of the crows mounted on the surrounding power lines. The area was all but abandoned. Most of the surrounding businesses were boarded up and covered in graffiti. Nearly all of the apartment complexes were in the same condition. There were several condemned structures on the block.

In the middle of the block, an apartment complex stood, which appeared to be inhabited, and in decent condition. Sofia took one last opportunity to listen for anything out of the ordinary before opening the car door, but heard nothing. As she exited the car, she took the picture, which was clipped to the inside of the front flap of the folder Lucian had left her. She could show it around in the event that he was not home. As she removed the picture, she took another look at him, taking note of how large he appeared to be. Before entering the building, Sofia took a second to check her weapon and ensure that she had a fresh clip in the gun. She realized how lax she had become in her preparation for such events since her attacks recently. Everything on her gun checked out. Sofia headed into the complex.

Sofia reached the apartment number that she had found in Quintin's file and knocked at the door, looking up and down the hall as she waited. The hallway was filthy and there were holes in the sheetrock everywhere. The hall smelled like a mixture of dirt and mildew. A woman down the hall was picking up some laundry that had fallen out of her basket.

"Do you need a hand?" Sofia asked the woman. Startled, the woman looked up at her and glanced quickly at the door in front of which Sofia stood. She frantically grabbed remaining articles from the floor, nearly knocking her own door over as she ran into her apartment, slamming the door closed behind her. Confused, Sofia turned her attention back to the door and knocked again.

"Mr. Marks, are you there? I have some information I need to give to you. I believe you may be in danger." She realized that if he were inside, he was probably laughing at her for thinking that he could be in any danger. From his picture, she had gotten the feeling that he had never lost a fight, or felt threatened in any way in his entire life. He just had that look about him. She knocked again.

"Mr. Marks. Are you there?" Still no answer. She listened for any sounds to indicate that he might be inside, but heard nothing. Sofia made her way down to the door that the woman had entered with the laundry basket. Knocking lightly on the door, she called out, "Ma'am, can I talk to you for a second about the man who lives down the hall?"

An angry, hushed voice came from behind the door, "No, get the hell out of here!"

"Ma'am, I think he may be in trouble. Is there any way that you can tell me where I can find him? It's really urgent that I get to him right away."

"Keep your damn voice down! You're a cop, you figure it out! He can handle himself just fine if he's in trouble, and if not, even better! Now you gotta go, lady, I'm serious!" The tone of the woman's voice was becoming less angry and more insistent and frightened.

"Can you at least tell—"

"Can't you hear, woman? NO! Now get away from my door." She was now fully panicked.

Knowing a lost cause when she heard one, Sofia gave up and backed away from the door. "I'm sorry to have bothered you, ma'am. I'm leaving now. No one saw me talking to you."

Sofia made her way around the complex showing the picture and asking about Quintin and she received nearly the exact same response from every person that she came across. Each person who saw the picture had the same look of terror on their face when she would show it to them. Each one made it clear that she needed to give up and get out of the complex. Most of all, they just wanted her to get away from them before someone saw them. Most then retreated into their apartments, making sure to lock a series of locks behind them. After having tried to speak with every available tenant in the complex, she decided to take her investigation to the street.

Sofia made her way through the dilapidated neighborhood looking for any sign of life in hopes of finding Quintin in time. She was dealing with a very limited pool of potential acquaintances due to the fact hardly any of the buildings were inhabitable.

47

Finally, Sofia came across a small house that appeared occupied. The little home didn't appear to fit in with the rest of the neighborhood. While run down slightly, it was nowhere near the state of disrepair in which everything else seemed to be. There was some semblance of a maintained lawn surrounded by an old wrought iron fence, as well as some hanging baskets filled with various flowers on the porch. Years of wear were obvious on the wooden siding of the house, and the old white paint was chipping away. Sofia opened the squeaky metal gate and made her way up the little path to the porch. She knocked on the door. A very jolly little woman quickly greeted her.

"Hi there, honey! Don't see many girls as pretty as you around here. What can I do for ya?" The woman's grin spread from one ear to the other.

"Well, ma'am," she began.

"Oh, no ma'am. You call me Mama." She reached out and touched Sofia's hand gently.

The polite greeting was a welcome change from the conversations she had already had that day. "Alright, Mama," she replied, with a smile. "I'm looking for a man who I think is in trouble and I can't seem to get an answer out of anyone." Sofia pulled the picture from her pocket.

Mama took a quick look at the picture and her big warm smile diminished.

She began nodding her head. "Oh, baby girl, you don't need to mess wit' dat man. If he's in trouble, I suggest you leave 'em to it. Lord knows it's gotta catch him sometime."

"Please, Mama. Can you just tell me a little about him so that I can find him?"

Mama looked up at her for a second, and breathed deeply. "Well if I'm gonna tell ya, you best get in here so no one sees me talking to the police." Sofia quickly stepped into the house.

"I didn't say I was with the police, Mama."

Mama walked past Sofia, laughing.

"Baby, Mama's been around a long time. You ain't gotta tell me a whole lot for me to size you up."

Everything about Mama's house, yard, and demeanor was a complete surprise. Given the conditions of the area, it wasn't at all what it should have been. It was a welcome oasis in the deserted and rundown little town. The inside appeared to be kept up nicely. The outside had a wonderful "old" smell to it, which was another welcome change from the filthy conditions in the apartment complex. There were some obvious signs of age such as the creaking floor, old-fashioned furniture, and antique radio in the corner. For the most part, it was just a lovely little home.

"Would you like some tea, sweetie?"

"No, thank you." Sofia stepped onto the linoleum of the dining room floor. "I need to get going pretty quickly. I think Mr. Marks could be in danger."

"Oh, honey. Once I tell you about that man, I don't think you're gonna be too worried about finding him. He's a bad man, baby. Done some bad things to folks 'roun here. Terrible things." Mama pulled out a little wooden chair from her dining room table and indicated for Sofia to sit down as she moved into the kitchen to make them both some tea.

"We don't have any record of him having caused any trouble, at least nothing for quite some time."

"I don't suppose you would. I even know the time you're talkin about. See, back then, this neighborhood was in a little better way than it is now. Now, I ain't sayin it was ever in the greatest condition, but it was much betta' than it is now. Most of the shops was still open and them apartments was full and the buildings was taken care of. Back then, that man had just moved to the area and he wasn't all that well known. Well, it didn' take long for him to make a name fuh hisself. He wasn' a bad lookin' man, and bein' as big as he is, it didn' take long fuh the ladies 'roun here to take notice. Once he started getting his share of attention, it didn' take long fuh him to start takin' his pick and treatin' each one of em howeva he please.

"Anyway, one of em decided she wasn' interested in him no mo, and he didn' take to that notion. He beat that girl up real good. She was a tough one though, not scared like the rest of 'em. Went straight to the police and had him locked up. Then, when he got back from lock up, he showed evabody what he would really do to someone when he was mad. I think he only let her live so that we could see what he had done to her. He made sure that poor girl made her way around the neighborhood plenty for the next few days. She was bad off baby, worse than I eva seen. After a few days of paradin her beaten body around, we just didn' see her no more. No one saw anything or heard anything, but we ain't dumb. We all know what he done. After that, he started terrorizin' everyone. He kep' right on takin' advantage of all the girls. They tried to fight him, but he was just too strong. A few of 'em ended up pregnant, but he didn' let that last long. The boys around here tried to stop him."

Mama's voiced trailed off and her gaze became blank. She sat in silence for a few seconds. "He's just so strong." Her voice was barely a whisper.

Sofia had to shake herself to return to the present. "Did you see something, Mama?"

She had seen that look too many times on the faces of victims and witnesses to let the moment pass without asking her. Mama also needed a moment to snap out of her dazed state.

"Oh, Mama's seen plenty, baby. But we ain't gonna get into that, 'cause I'd never say it on the stand and it won't do you no good to hear it." She patted Sofia's hand gently before shuffling back into the kitchen, returning with the glass jug of tea to refill their glasses. "Anyways, he started shakin' down all the shops for every dime they made. Made it impossible for 'em to operate. That fool didn't even leave them enough money to keep their doors open. Since no one was about to stand up to him, most just did whatever they could to shut down and get out. The landlords of the apartments is too scared to come around, and most of 'em don't care anyway. So everything just kinda fell apart and since he didn't have the shops to spend his time terrorizing, things just got worse for people.

"Oh, sugar." She spilled some tea on the table. She once again returned to the kitchen to get a rag to clean the mess. "So you can see why I say I don't care if that man is in trouble. I dream of the day when this place is free of him. He's done so much damage, we may never be the same as we were, but with him gone, there might be chance for this to become a reasonable place to live again. People around here will never be the same, but we deserve some peace."

"I agree, Mama. But I have to do everything that I can to try and keep this from happening. I can try to do more for your neighborhood now that I know these things. I can even begin to build a case against Quintin so I can get him away from here, but first I have to try to stop the man that is after him. Can you at least tell me where I could find him?"

Mama sighed as she rung the washcloth out in the sink. "I can tell you a good person, baby. Lord knows I can. But you can't help us. Not as long as he's alive. I can't do it, baby. I can't tell you anything about him, and if I could, I wouldn't."

Sofia glanced at the clock on the wall. Mama had delayed her long enough, and she didn't look like she was going to give Sofia any useful information. In a last ditch effort, Sofia changed course from her usual "befriending" style of questioning.

"I would never say a word, Mama. What if someone saw me come in here and discovered I was trying to help Quintin? Say he does get away from the man I'm trying to stop and he finds out that you didn't help me find him so that I could help him. If what you say is true, and I can't help the people around here, what's going to happen?"

Sofia couldn't believe that she was resorting to such tactics to get information from someone, especially someone who had been so nice and inviting to her. She had never pressed someone in this manner for information, but she had to stop Lucian.

Mama didn't even look up from her dishes as she spoke. "I guess I was wrong about you. I'da never figured you for a person that would resort to threats to get what you wanted."

Sofia was ashamed. "Mama, I'm sor—"

"Naw. You done said it. Don't try an' take it back now. Fact is, I don't know what that man does. He rarely leaves the neighborhood, though. If you haven't seen him yet, you're probably headed in the right direction."

"I haven't been able to get anyone to talk to me. What if he was hiding out in an apartment?"

"That man don't hide from no one. If you passed those places and didn't hear any commotion, you probably ain't missed him." Mama left her dishes and moved towards the door. "Now, I guess you betta' get goin."

As she left the house, Sofia turned back. "I promise I will do everything I can to get him off of the streets, Mama. I just have to do this. It's much more important than you know that I stop the man who is after him."

"To you, maybe. But not from where I'm standing."

As Mama began closing the door, something occurred to Sofia. "Mama, why hasn't he done to you what he's done to everyone else?" Mama couldn't meet Sofia's eyes as she closed the door.

As the door shut, Sofia turned and faced the road. She gazed out into the overgrown soccer field across the street as she searched her thoughts for her next move. As she stood there debating which direction to go, she wondered to herself, Should I even care? What will stopping Lucian this one time prove? Even if I found Quintin before Lucian, I would never be able to make any charges stick to him. He would continue to terrorize the people in the area and Lucian would move on to the next victim. I can't spend the rest of my career trying to stop him. Even if I did want to stop him, could I?

As she debated herself on what came next, she heard something that drew her attention from her thoughts. She wasn't sure what the sound was, but it was loud enough to draw her from her daze. The sound reverberated off the abandoned buildings for a moment before disintegrating into the atmosphere. Pausing for a moment, she waited for the sound to return so she could make sure it hadn't been thunder. Sofia looked around to see if there was a reaction from any of the local tenants, but no one so much as came to the window. Not even Mama peeked out to see what the commotion was. Sofia didn't have to wait long for the sound to happen again. This one, accompanied by a second loud clap, was followed by the sound of crumbling rocks. That was enough to clarify that it hadn't been thunder, and Sofia sprang into action.

48

Sofia ran in the direction she believed the sound to be coming from. The blasts became much more frequent and much louder. She approached what appeared to be another old apartment complex. Just as was the case with the rest of the area, the building appeared abandoned, as were all of the surrounding homes and shops. The sounds were constant now. They reminded Sofia of a wrecking ball hammering away at the walls of a building, only much more frequently than any wrecking ball could swing. The entire building quaked with each blast. Tiny pieces of the block wall flaked away with each quake and fell to the ground all around Sofia's feet. The sounds seemed to be coming from around the backside of the building. Realizing that the building did not appear to be structurally sound, she knew she would have to proceed with much more caution. Sofia drew her weapon and ran down the alley which lead to the back of the building.

As she approached the rear corner, Sofia pressed herself up against the wall. She slowly peered around the corner, just in time to see a hulking figure run through a large hole leading into the back of the building. Sofia quickly jerked her head back. For the first time in her pursuit for this man, she became very unnerved by his size. If that was indeed Quintin entering the building, she had grossly underestimated what the numbers in his description represented. The picture and the information that they had at the station did not do Quintin justice. It was possible that he had not grown any, but Sofia had clearly misjudged what a man with those measurements would look like. Sofia had only caught a glimpse of his arm and some of his profile as he dashed into the building, but that was enough to cause her more than a little concern.

As she stood pressed to the wall, she felt the building shake beneath what she could only imagine was a fierce blow from Quintin. Sofia pressed her ear against the cold brick in an effort to see if she could hear what was happening on the other side. She could barely make out what sounded like the grunting and groaning of two men locked in combat. Suddenly, another powerful blow rattled the building, accompanied by the loud cry of one of the men. Concerned or not, Sofia had come this far to stop Lucian. She wasn't about to let him become this man's judge, jury, and executioner. She clutched her weapon tightly, rounded the corner and slowly approached the opening.

Sofia stood at the entrance of the tattered building, attempting to muster the courage to look in. Between what she had witnessed with Lucian and the figure that she had just seen enter the building, the possibilities were terrifying. The fact was, at this point, she wasn't even sure that her presence was even going to make an impact on this situation. Sofia was all but certain that Lucian was the one inside with Quintin. Her only hope was that her presence alone would force him to realize that she was against what he was doing and cause him to leave. She wished that it was in her to just let Lucian end Quintin's tyrannical influence over this neighborhood. However, she didn't believe for one second that she was capable of allowing anyone to stop crime with more crime. From the sound of the loud blasts, the fight had moved towards the front of the building. Feeling confident that she could enter the building unseen, Sofia slowly peered into the gaping hole.

49

The only light in the building was what the various sized holes in the walls all along the hallway allowed through. Heavy, dark clouds had moved in, and blocked out most of the direct sunlight, so there was little to see. Sofia peered down the long, dark hallway. She saw two figures moving back and forth in the darkness ahead, giving her only glimpses of dark silhouettes among the shadows. While she couldn't make out the particulars of the men, she could have guessed which one was Quintin. While both were very large in their build, one loomed over the other by several inches.

One thing that Sofia had noticed when Lucian was fighting the street gang was that though he had packed much more muscle mass onto his frame, he had not grown any taller. She had not mentioned this to him, but assumed that he would have some sort of explanation for it such as, "Muscles are made to grow and shrink. Bones grow to a certain length and then only grow to repair themselves, Sofia." His endless logic on such an unreal situation was maddening to her, even when he wasn't the one making the observation.

The hallway, in the wake of the battle that had just passed through, had been destroyed. All of the doorways collapsed in the melee, so there was no longer a reason for Sofia to clear them before passing. More compromised than before, the building was unsafe. Nonetheless, she did not want to lose site of the men, so she began to make her way down the hall.

Sofia moved as quickly as she was able without making her presence known. She didn't have to be overly concerned with it due to the claps of thunder that were generated with each blow. They were accompanied by occasional bursts of actual thunder from the growing storm outside. She shuffled down the hallway hoping that it would not collapse on her as the men slammed against all remaining supports in the lobby.

The two warriors continued trading blows as she approached, neither having an obvious edge that Sofia could see. She wondered how it was possible for anyone to keep up with Lucian in a fight when he was able to grow to match any opponent. Maybe he hadn't had enough time to reach Quintin's level of strength. Maybe this was the biggest opponent he had ever faced and he was unable to match Quintin. If he just hadn't reached Quintin's size yet, Sofia was in a great position. She'd clearly have a much better chance of reaching them in time to stop Lucian. Conversely, if Lucian was unable to match Quintin's size altogether, she would have to stop Quintin in order to arrest Lucian.

Sofia slipped into the only room that remained intact as she approached the lobby. A hole had been created in the wall, allowing her access to the office that had been built in behind the front counter. From this location, Sofia could see the entire front lobby and had some level of protection from the counter if the fight drew too close. The office stood in a particularly dark area. Sofia, provided with a nearly undetectable hiding spot, could survey the situation and plan how she would proceed. She looked through the door in amazement as she got her first real glimpse of the two men up close. Each was physically unbelievable. Had she not been in the room to see it, she never could have believed it.

Quintin was enormous. His flesh, entirely covered with muscle, did not contain an inch that was not tattooed. His body was a giant canvas, and someone had taken a great deal of time to paint him. His tattoos depicted a terrifying picture that only made Sofia wish she could get on board with Lucian's philosophy for ridding the world of such evil.

Every item tattooed on his body oozed with hatred. Every hate filled symbol and word imaginable had been etched into his skin. There were graphic images of women getting raped, and the bloody corpses of men, all across his back. In the middle of the corpses and battered women was an image of Quintin standing with a giant open-mouthed grin, giving the illusion that he was laughing maniacally at the carnage that surrounded him.

Sofia had never before seen someone completely filled with evil. Quintin showed no signs of caring or compassion for anything or anyone else. Even the worst criminals that she had ever put away had shown some tiny sign that they were able to care about something. Whether it had been their mother, or a dog, or even a motorcycle, they had all found something that they cared for. It appeared that the only thing that Quintin loved was his all-consuming hate. The engorged veins in his body ran across the surface of his skin like a topographical map. They splattered his arms and neck, leading up to, and around, his shining scalp. Tattoo ink covered it, as well.

He was drenched in sweat, which now seeped through the waistband of his oversized, all-black gym shorts. His face was the only place Sofia could locate that didn't have any signs of tattoo ink, but it was now covered in deep lacerations from Lucian's blows. There was no doubt in her mind that this was likely the hardest this man had ever had to fight to defeat an opponent in his adult life. The grimace slathered across his face confirmed her suspicion. She knew from what she had seen in the streets that Lucian would give any man an incredible fight, no matter what size he was. She also believed that Lucian, in all likelihood, could defeat any opponent he came across.

Lucian's size was also stunning, and still so difficult for Sofia to grasp. He was still several inches shorter than Quintin, but his speed was phenomenal. He landed explosive punches in rapid spurts that kept his enormous foe off balance, inflicting serious damage that was beginning to take its toll on Quintin. He also appeared to be using various different techniques as he fought, techniques that would have taken immense amounts of training to perfect, and he was bouncing between them effortlessly. She had seen him for so long as this small, docile, fun-loving man. Now he stood before her as a giant, an animal, an exquisite monster.

His body was massive and packed tightly with muscle, just as it had been before. He looked as though he had reached the limit of muscle mass that his frame would allow. Sofia couldn't help but realize how beautiful he was. She had always thought that he was a pretty-boy, but the way that his body filled out made him look incredible. She had not had the time nor was she in the right frame of mind to admire him the last time that she had seen him this way. Now she had a second to realize how perfect he was when he was in full form.

The most obvious change was his unbelievably chiseled body from head to toe. From the definition of his muscles to the sharp, tight build of his face. Now, his hair was longer than the tightly manicured styles that he normally maintained. His eyes were a vivid green, unlike anything she had ever seen before. Sofia shook the thoughts from her head and attempted to refocus on the task at hand, before the thoughts could influence her actions. She had come to stop Lucian, and that was exactly what was going to happen. Sofia prepared herself to enter the room and took one last look in before making her move.

As she watched for a minute, something occurred to her. Sofia realized that she might have overestimated Lucian's ability. She may not have even needed to be there to help Quintin. Lucian was more than holding his own in the fight, but Quintin wasn't wearing down.

As the fight waged on, Quintin continued landing volatile punches, powerful enough to have killed normal men. Lucian was able to recover from each shot, but was unable to mount any sort of attack for several seconds. Suddenly, pulling from some well of reserved energy, he lashed out with a flurry of blows that knocked Quintin to the ground. Lucian leapt on top of him quickly and sunk his teeth deep into the thick muscle surrounding Quintin's neck. Quintin let out a chilling roar as Lucian pulled away, taking a large chunk of flesh with him. Quintin knocked Lucian away and got to his feet. As Lucian reached his feet, both of the men refrained from attacking long enough to catch their breath.

Both men stood in their respective corners, sucking down wind and checking the amount of damage inflicted on them before continuing. They looked over their wounds, Quintin paying special attention to his neck, and Lucian focusing mainly on his ribs. Quintin's problem was obvious. The blood cascaded down, covering every inch of the right side of his body from the massive wound on his neck. Lucian seemed to have an internal injury that was causing him considerable pain. It seemed likely that he had broken a rib and possibly punctured a lung. Even if he was able to regenerate tissue easily, there was no way that he could mend a broken bone if it had shifted from its normal position.

"Bitches bite!" Quintin bellowed as he looked over the amount of blood covering his hand.

"No such thing as a fair fight, Q-Ball," Lucian mocked. "Not that this was ever a fair fight."

"What the hell is going on? When I chased you in here, you were a little runt. How the hell did you get so big?"

"That's for me to know…and that's about it." Lucian smirked. Placing his left palm against the base of his ribs on the left side, he used the other hand to force his lower rib back away from his lung. There was a grating noise as the bone grinded against itself, as he slid it back towards its intended resting place. Lucian grimaced some before sprouting a grin. He held his rib in place as he stared at Quintin. His breathing quickly returned to normal. He returned to his upright position. Taking his own fighting stance, he leered at Quintin. A smirk crawled across his lips.

"Now, I'm done playin' around with you!" Lucian surged forward at a dead sprint. After all of his talking, Sofia had lowered many of her expectations as to what Lucian was capable of doing. He had mentioned that he was able to move fast, but this was faster than Sofia had imagined.

He didn't move at the speed of light. He wasn't even a blur, but he was close. When he combined multiple moves, it was difficult to catch each one. He caught Quintin in the ribs with a series of powerful punches. The explosive shots rang out around the room just as they had before. Quintin had no time to react. Caught completely off guard by Lucian's speed, he recoiled from the punches and let out a loud yell as Lucian landed blow after blow. Sofia could hear his ribs cracking mixed with the sounds of the punches.

Driven back several feet, Quintin fell to one knee. Sofia was so caught up in Lucian's recovery that she didn't even realize that he had just gone in for the kill.

"I've seen what you have done to this place, and the people in this area. I can't allow these people to have to suffer by your hands anymore."

Just as Lucian reared back to throw the final punch that would surely end Quintin, Sofia screamed out from her location behind the wall. "Lucian, no!"

Lucian's head snapped over to see Sofia running from her hiding place. Seeing her face, he smiled. At that moment, Quintin seized the opportunity to make his way back into the fight. Using every ounce of energy he could manage, Quintin landed a fierce uppercut that sent Lucian off his feet, and sailing into a darkened corner of the room, a few feet from where they were standing.

"Freeze, Quintin! APD!" screamed Sofia. Quintin, who had barely noticed her presence to this point, turned his head and looked at her out of the corner of his eye. He paid her little attention, turning back to look at Lucian. Sofia approached him with her gun drawn. Quintin was still on his knees but remained as tall as Sofia. She approached him from her position behind him, placing her gun against his head as she tossed her cuffs in front of him.

"Put those on! Now!" Quintin didn't move. He was gasping for air at this point and struggling to breath. After that last barrage by Lucian, Sofia had no doubt that he was dealing with some broken ribs as well as possibly some internal bleeding. "Don't you worry about him. I'm taking him in, too.

Just put the cuffs on." Sofia stayed focused on the back of Quintin's head as she waited for him to put the handcuffs on.

Quintin turned his head slowly to try looking at her as he spoke. "Take him where? That fool's done."

Puzzled by his comment, Sofia leaned over and looked around his enormous body to see what he meant.

50

Lucian was lying flat on his back, a long wooden pole from the staircase banister he had landed on sticking out from his left pectoral. Sofia stared at his limp body in shock.

"Lucian?" She tried calling out to him, but was only able to produce a whisper. There was no response.

"Lucian." She spoke much louder this time, praying that he had simply not heard her the first time. There was still no response.

"Lucian!" She shouted this time, choking back the tears that were welling in her eyes.

Quintin began laughing at Sofia's futile attempts.

"You move and I swear to God I'll put a slug in you, asshole!" Sofia shouted as she left her position behind him to check on Lucian. She continued to hold her gun on him as she slowly walked across the room.

As she drew nearer to Lucian, she could see that the piece of tattered railing had gone directly through the center of Lucian's right pectoral muscle. Sofia instinctively reached for his throat and checked his neck for a pulse, but there was nothing. Seeing him lying there, Sofia was unable to keep herself from feeling her truest emotions. Knowing that he couldn't be killed had made her whole investigation of Quintin very easy. Stopping Lucian was her only focus, never thinking that she would lose him. She figured that the most likely scenarios were that he would go to jail, or he would leave. Both situations ended with the possibility that she would be able to see him again. This situation caught her completely by surprise.

"Lucian?" Sofia pleaded. "Come on, baby, you can fix it. Just heal it up. This should be nothing compared to those bullets. You're not a vampire, this can't kill you. You're a Dunamy, Lucian. This is a myth, this isn't real!" She continued to split her focus between Lucian and Quintin. "You have to be alright, Lucian."

Sofia tugged at his massive arm to try to get him to stand up, but it was useless. Quintin's laughter was echoing throughout the room now.

"Shut it, Quintin!" Sofia screamed, as she turned her attention back to Lucian. The wound the banister spindle created had not healed at all. She had hoped that there was some sign that Lucian's body was still working on some low level, but there was nothing.

"Come on, baby! You have to get up!" Sofia pleaded, continuing to pull at him. The tears were now streaming down her face. Sofia leaned down and stroked Lucian's long, sweaty, golden hair. As she looked into his face, Sofia began to relive their first date together. It was the first time that she had ever felt so much happiness and it was all because of Lucian. He had made every second that they spent together wonderful. As she continued to roll the memories around in her head, Sofia realized that she no longer heard Quintin's laughter.

Swinging around to find Quintin on his feet and moving towards the door slowly, Sofia raised her weapon, concentrating her barrel on Quintin's head. She shouted, "What did I tell you?!"

"What are you gonna do to me, cop lady?" Quintin asked, never stopping his progress towards the exit. "That was self-defense and you know it. You got nothing, so I'm leaving."

Sofia knew that he was right. There was nothing that she had on him that she could make stick. She hadn't witnessed the beginning of the fight, so she could never testify any differently. Sofia realized that none of that mattered to her now. She could only think of the pain that she was feeling which was like no pain she had ever experienced before. It burned like acid in her stomach, and Quintin was the cause of it. Even though she had no idea how Lucian had gone about provoking him into that fight, she knew that Quintin was evil. He was the epitome of what Lucian was trying to stop. He was the monster that she had been searching for.

“That’s not what I asked you.”

The sheer tone of Sofia’s voice was enough to stop Quintin in his tracks. It wasn’t commanding or aggressive. It was calm but filled with hatred. He turned and faced her directly, an evil smirk strewn across his lips.

“What? You gonna shoot me, cop?” He held his arms up, inviting her to do so. Sofia hesitated briefly as she considered the ramifications of her actions. She knew that shooting an unarmed man would likely end her career, but she felt confident that she could get around it because of his sheer size and the threat he posed to her.

“I been shot before, and it just never seems to take. So you go ahead and take a shot, honey. I don’t think you are gonna like what happens next, though. Just remember, your boyfriend back there can’t help you now.”

His comments sliced through her thoughts and all but made the decision for her.

“Well, I did swear,” Sofia said.

The shot rang out and Quintin hit the ground, screaming out in pain. Her aim had been true and had done exactly what she intended. She had shot him directly in the kneecap, completely disabling him for the moment. Sofia leaned back down and gently caressed Lucian’s face before leaving his side to approach Quintin. Making sure to keep her distance from him having seen what he did when given the opportunity, Sofia began pacing in front of him. Quintin writhed in agony before her, but ever so slowly, his screams turned into a sick laughter that sent chills down Sofia’s spine.

He shouted, “I warned you, bi—”

Sofia fired a shot into the opposite knee before Quintin could finish his threat. He cried out again, much louder than before. Sofia resumed her pacing, almost as if she were stalking him like prey. He lay on the floor holding one bloody leg in each hand, tears from the pain rolling down his face.

Sofia couldn't help but lecture him. "I don't understand men like you, Quintin. You have so many options in life because of your size and strength, and you constantly choose the wrong path. Why is that?"

Sofia's voice was stern and becoming angrier as she went on. "I came down here to try and keep you safe!" she proclaimed, waving her gun around and using large gestures to accentuate her speech. "I went a long way out of my way to try and protect you. I do all of that, and you take a cheap shot when the fight is over and kill a man. Not only that, you disobey my instructions and threaten me!"

Her lecture was doing little to make an impact on Quintin, but it was doing plenty to get her blood boiling over the matter. She fired another shot into Quintin's shin, causing another pain filled howl. "You don't get to threaten me!" she shouted at him. The training she had received at the academy and the numerous courses and lectures she had attended to prepare her for life as an officer went out the window.

As she continued to pace, Sofia repeatedly looked back to see Lucian's body lying with the large wooden pole protruding from his chest. All that she could think about was the men who had attacked her and how Lucian had saved her. A single tear rolled down her cheek as she slowed her pacing and focused on Lucian. As she stared at his corpse, she allowed herself to accept what she felt for Lucian. Even in the wake of all that she had learned about him, she loved him more than she realized she was capable of loving anyone. Her heart ached as she looked at him. Now Lucian lay dead because of this man, a man who had crippled an entire community with his presence. It was all too much for her to take in. In that moment, Sofia lost every idea of who she was or who she had ever been.

"See, he came here to kill you because he thought you deserved to die for the crimes that you have committed, but I thought people could change if you give them the chance. Well, maybe he was right all along, Quintin! Maybe I'm the one who doesn't understand." Turning her attention back to Quintin, she watched him drag himself across the dirty cement floor towards a nearby wall.

"I guess I should thank you for opening my eyes to how truly evil some people can be."

Quintin began pulling himself up against the wall using primarily his upper body, as his legs were useless. He panted heavily as he glared at Sofia.

"I'm glad I could be of service," he mocked. Most people would have found it impossible to deal with the amount of pain that Quintin must have been experiencing at that moment, but he was actually remaining quite calm at this point.

Quintin continued, "I'm even—"

Sofia never gave him the opportunity to finish. She didn't even remember firing the gun until seconds after it happened. The bullet struck Quintin in the head, an inch above his right eye. His arms relaxed and his body slammed into the wall that had held him up. He slid down the wall and collapsed awkwardly into the corner. A trickle of blood rolled down his forehead before gathering in the thick hair of his eyebrow. His eyes remained trained on Sofia; his expression was one of shock. Sofia stood there with her arm extended, looking back into Quintin's lifeless, soulless eyes. After all of the effort that she had put into her career and her life to lead it the right way, she had thrown it all away.

Sofia knew that there were people who could identify her and people who knew she had been looking for Quintin. Quintin was unarmed and it was clear that he had been tortured, before the cold-blooded murder, from the pattern of shots fired. Even though she knew all of this, Sofia felt nothing. She wasn't concerned about what she had done, nor was she worried about the ramifications of her actions with the department. She had held happiness for only a short time. He had taken it from her, as well as so many others. She knew that she would never find true happiness again without Lucian. Without another thought, Sofia unloaded round after round into Quintin's face and head until the magazine emptied, and the slide of the gun locked up.

51

Turning away from Quintin, Sofia walked over to Lucian's body. She sat on the steps next to him and held his hand in hers. Rubbing her face against his hand, she remembered how sweet he had always been to her. She thought back to the things he had told her as he explained everything to her. She had never considered how difficult that must have been for him. To know that what he was telling her would almost definitely drive her away from him. If the situation had been different, could she have done the same? Could she have told him a secret that dark, knowing that she would likely lose him for doing so? Unable to answer such questions, she hugged his palm tightly against her face and kissed it softly.

Sofia placed his hand gently on the step beside his body. As she looked him over, she became enraged at the site of the wooden dagger that had taken his life. It shined bright with his blood. Sofia realized that she had never seen Lucian bleed. Even in the attack in the street, he had never spilled a drop of blood. She imagined that was just another part of his healing abilities. His injuries usually healed so quickly that there was no time for the blood to escape. There was something different about it, but she couldn't quite tell what it was.

Unable to look at him impaled that way any longer, Sofia lowered her shoulder and pushed against his body. Lucian's enormous frame hardly moved. The awkward confines of the staircase made it difficult for her to get the leverage she would need to push him over, so she went lower in an attempt to roll him over, hoping that his immense body weight would break the rod off at its base. Her new position gave her the edge she needed and Lucian's body began to roll. Placing her feet against the wall, Sofia put everything that she had into one final push. There was a loud pop as the lumber snapped at its base, which sent his body to the floor with a heavy thud. She had to catch herself to keep from rolling right off behind him.

Sofia could hardly see through the tears in her eyes as she walked down the steps and rolled him over onto his back. Grabbing the stake with both hands, Sofia jerked them skyward. The blood that covered the stick caused her hands to slide off, sending her flailing backwards where she landed flat on her back. She began to sob heavily as she lay there. Not willing to have this final right denied, Sofia scrambled to her feet and once again grasped the rail. Taking a much tighter grip, and sliding her fingers between the beveled grooves, she pulled gently and steadily, pulling harder and harder until it began to slide from the opening in Lucian's chest. The wet, suctioning sound that it made as it exited the gaping hole solidified everything that had happened. It was then that she accepted that he was gone, and she could no longer restrain her tears.

The hunk of wood clacked against the concrete into the shadows as she cast it aside. Sofia buried her face into Lucian's neck. She couldn't remember a time that she ever cried so hard, or a more devastating moment in her life than this. Although she had seen a great deal of the people in her life be murdered in front of her in cold blood, she had never truly been given the time to get to know any of them very well. This was the first real connection she had ever made with another human being on this level, outside of her parents. She cried until she became so tired that she lay her head down on Lucian's arm, curled up beside him, and listened to the sound of the falling rain. She finally fell asleep.

52

Sofia had no idea how long she had been asleep. When she finally awoke, her head still rested on Lucian's arm. She glanced around the room groggily, looking for the source of a noise she thought she had heard. Unable to locate anything, she began to wonder if she had actually heard something or if it had been a dream. As the events of the evening began to come back to the forefront of her thoughts, paranoia began to set in. She snapped her head over to the spot where Quintin's body had fallen to rest, to confirm he hadn't moved. A solitary moonbeam shone through a broken window overhead, lighting his corpse perfectly. He was still there, exactly as she had left him, slumped over and riddled with bullets.

Springing to her feet, Sofia ran over to the door to see if someone had happened to come across the crime scene. Aside from thinking that the storm had masked the noise, she genuinely hadn't cared whether or not she was found out during all of the commotion. Now, as things settled in her mind from her slumber, she felt that someone surely would have heard something and come to investigate the noises from earlier. Peeking through the massive doorway, she glanced up and down the street to see if she could find the source of the noise she was now convinced she heard, but there was nothing.

The rain had stopped and the cloud cover had moved on, revealing an all-illuminating full moon. She could see clearly up and down the road in either direction, and there was no sign of movement or life. Not convinced that she had imagined the sound, Sofia walked to the corners of the building and checked down each alley. Still there was nothing. Giving a final glance down the street, she reentered the building as she rubbed the sleep from her eyes. Her tears had made the skin beneath her eyes tight and dry. She rubbed them until it hurt, then she rubbed them a bit more.

Suddenly, Sofia heard another noise. The staircase where Lucian had fallen creaked under the weight of something. Someone was in the room! Reaching for her gun, Sofia realized that she had left it lying on the floor somewhere after shooting Quintin.

"Who's there?" she called out, unable to see anything more than random flashing color orbs and blackness.

"Well, hello, beautiful," a soft reply, from the shadows sounded.

Sofia's heart felt as though it would explode. Temporarily blinded from her eye rubbing, she couldn't confirm where the voice had come from. Why had she rubbed them so long! As her vision slowly returned to her, she began to scan the dark room for life. She looked over to where she had left Lucian's body, but it was gone.

"Where are you?" Sofia whispered loudly. "Is that you? Baby, is that you?" Still somewhat blinded, Sofia was unable to differentiate between shadows and objects in the dark room.

"It's me. I'm here." Lucian's voice came from a darkened area a few feet from where he had been lying. Her eyes continued to adjust to the dark until she finally saw him slumped over on the staircase, with the look of a battered soldier. She stared at him in disbelief, but couldn't help but smile when he flashed a weakened version of his beautiful grin at her.

"How'd I do that?" He pointed over to Quintin's corpse. The feeling of warmth of seeing Lucian left her with disappeared, as she looked over at the lifeless body.

"That was…uh…." She searched her thoughts for a way to explain what had happened, but couldn't find the right words. Of course, there was no need to explain. It was obvious what had happened.

"Doesn't matter." Lucian stretched his muscles as best he could. "You alright?"

"You were dead," she whispered, unable to look away from Quintin. She couldn't believe what she had done.

"That would not appear to be the case," he replied, with a chuckle. "I mean, pretty much, but not entirely." He continued to stretch casually. "I was definitely closer than I've ever been, but I never actually died, I guess. I was still in there. It was just more like a dream than anything. Real weird shit." Lucian closed his eyes for a moment as he tried to search his thoughts to see what he could remember, but it was futile. The memories of what he had experienced while unconscious were just outside the limits of his memory.

"It's like trying to remember a dream when I try to think of it. There are little clips that almost bring it back, but I can't remember it." Searching the dark room for a moment, he located the picket from the handrail that had pierced his body.

He nodded his head in the direction of the blood stained shard that Sofia had removed from his sternum. "From what I could tell, that thing was pokin' through part of my heart. Can't heal if my heart's not workin' right. My guess is that I would've stayed that way for a good bit if that thing had stayed in me. I take it you pulled it out?" Lucian asked, not knowing the specifics of what had transpired after the stabbing.

Sofia nodded slowly, never taking her eyes off Quintin's corpse.

"Well, that allowed everything to start healing my heart. After that, things went back to normal." He tapped his chest lightly. "Stake in the heart: that one clearly has some roots in the truth." He laughed weakly.

"Where's the logic in that?" Sofia asked solemnly. "You said you were basically just a human. If your heart stopped, you should be dead. Unless it's shocked back into rhythm, it can't start beating again." She was caught in a deep stare that she couldn't pull out of, but longed for an understanding of how Lucian had survived, welcoming the logic she had found so annoying before.

"That's true. But I did use the qualifier 'basically' for that very reason. I was out, so I can't be sure, but I imagine my heart was workin' on some really low level, which kept my blood flowin' to some degree. Tell me this: did my body ever get cold?"

Sofia thought back and realized that she had not noticed whether his body temperature had ever dropped. With that thought in mind, Sofia simply curled her lips inward and slowly shook her head. There was no way that she was going to debate him on that issue.

Lucian gave a subtle flip of his hand, adding, "Well, there ya go."

Lucian began inspecting himself for any other injuries that might not have healed properly and began taking notice of how large he had grown during the battle. "Damn! I'm huge!" He chuckled.

His comment eased Sofia's nerves slightly. Breaking her concentrated gaze, she couldn't help but smile as she finally turned to look at him. The wound on his chest was still there, but appeared to be healing. Just like before, he was healing up and there was only a skin-filled crater where the puncture wound had been before, and it was growing shallower by the minute.

"Why do you still look so sad, pretty lady?" Lucian asked, even though he knew exactly what was causing her distress. Knowing that she wouldn't answer him, he continued, "Quintin was a terrible person, Sofia. He's done horrifying things countless times and there was no chance he was ever going to stop. This was the only way to handle this guy. So don't let that get to you. You stopped an unimaginable amount of grief because of what you did." He was hoping to ease her sadness as much as possible.

Lucian pulled himself to his feet, walking across the moonlit room, and placed his massive arm around Sofia's shoulders. Sofia, weary from everything, leaned against him and laid her head against his chest, still covered with blood. She didn't care. She was coming to terms with what she had done. Though overjoyed by the fact that Lucian was alive, she was still far too tired to show it.

"Are you seriously not going to say anything about how huge I am?" Lucian asked softly, causing Sofia to bury her face in his chest to keep from laughing.

She didn't want to laugh. She wanted to dwell on what had happened and continue to be ashamed of herself.

"Stop it!" Sofia pleaded weakly, as she fought to stop smiling.

"No! I will not stop it! This is ridiculous! I am a massive individual right now and you aren't saying a word! I feel vindicated! All of those little comments about how small I am, and now this!" Lucian modeled his impressive physique for her, striking a few poses to show off his build.

Sofia allowed herself to laugh at his silliness for a second, but felt odd about laughing in light of what had happened. Lucian stopped modeling and struck a more serious tone.

"But, in all seriousness, this is gonna hurt like hell pretty soon if I don't manage it, so you might want to get going."

Now that Lucian's death was no longer occupying her every thought, the reality of the situation was settling in with Sofia. She had no desire to be present during the gruesome events that would be taking place when Lucian began to shred the giant corpse for sustenance, but she had no idea what was coming in her very near future.

"What am I going to do, Lucian? I killed a defenseless man. I used a police issued weapon. The evidence is going to show that he was unarmed and that he was tortured before he died. People here are going to be able to link me to this. I'm going to have to go to jail." Sofia's voice began to crack as she considered the idea.

"Stop. You've done enough crying in the past few days." Lucian placed his fingers below her chin and tilted her face up to look at him.

"You need to focus on what this dude was guilty of. You saw him in action. He was a terrible person who deserved what he got. And then some. Don't worry about a thing. I'll take care of the body, and I'm pretty sure you don't have to worry about the people around here going to anyone about what they think happened. They'll probably want to throw you a damn party when they find out this piece of trash is gone." Sofia was listening to him, and oddly enough, she found herself agreeing with him.

"I'll tell you what—I'll call Shane and have him pick you up. I'll go pick up your car later on tonight and I'll have it back to you by morning. That way, you don't have to go back down there just in case someone's snooping around."

Considering everything that had happened, Sofia just wanted to let Lucian take care of things so that she could go home, so she did exactly that. She handed him her phone and didn't resist as he pulled her over and squeezed her tightly.

Lucian realized that it was a good sign that she had allowed him to hold her without any signs of hesitation on her part, but had hoped she would embrace him back. Accepting it as a small victory, he released her and walked a few feet away to make his call. Because he hadn't moved too far away, Sofia was still able to hear some of what Shane was saying and pieced the rest together.

"Hey man. I need a favor."

"You hurt?"

"Nah, I'm good. I'm with Sofia and I need you to come grab her."

"She alright?"

"She's okay, I think. Just needs a ride out of here while I clean up a mess. Can you get her?"

"Yeah. No problem."

"Cool. I'll see ya shor—"

"We need to talk to your brother."

"Why?"

"More Keepers are showing up in my searches."

"From Victor's crew? That doesn't sound like them," Lucian said.

"I know. But it's them."

"Alright. I'll look into it. Let's just take care of this right now."

"Where are you?"

"Still got the info on that guy I told you about?"

"Yes."

"That neighborhood. Call this number when you get close."

"On my way."

"Thanks, bud." As he hung up the phone, Lucian turned back towards where he had left Sofia. She had moved up right behind him and now stood with her arms crossed and her head down, all but begging him to hold her. Without saying a word, he wrapped his massive arms around her and held her snugly against his chest. He could feel the tension in her shoulders slowly easing as he held her close. Her desire for him to hold her made him hopeful that things were going to be all right.

"Is everything alright with Shane? Was there something else he needs you to go do?"

"No, no, no. Nothing like that. He's on his way."

"Are you sure? You can go if it's something more important." Sofia didn't intend to let Lucian leave her, but made the suggestion anyway.

Lucian simply squeezed her gently and added, "There's nothing more important."

With that, Sofia finally relented and unfolded her arms from her chest. Lucian was overjoyed as she wrapped her arms around him as best she could. Knowing the amount of pain he was about to experience when his metabolism kicked in wasn't even enough to make him let go of her as the two stood in the shadows and waited for Shane to arrive.

As they held one another, bathed in the all-consuming darkness, Sofia stared out the framed, door-less doorway she had run to when she woke. She gazed into the stormy night at the distant lightning that lit the dark, heavy clouds. She waited for the low rumble of the accompanying thunder, oblivious to the smile that had found its way back to her face.

About the Author

James R. "Beau" Landrum works as a video production manager for a court reporting firm in Birmingham, Alabama, and lives in a small suburb of Birmingham with his wife, Delilah, and their two children. Rise of the Dunamy, his first novel, is the first installment of his Dunamy Series.

Beau's interest in the world of fantasy fiction began with Greek mythology at an early age and carried on through adulthood. He says, "The most intriguing stories for me have always been the ones that make fantasy seem obtainable in reality; a trait I hope to carry into my own writing."

The idea of the Dunamy came to Beau while watching television in 2008. A show that illustrated the amount of gang violence around the U.S. caused him to question how to keep his soon-to-be-born daughter safe in a world filled with such violence. In the days and weeks that followed, the story of the Dunamy began to unfold; and in the years that followed, the first portion of the story was written, centering around the character of a young, strong female protagonist.

Stay tuned for the next installments in the Dunamy Series.

www.ingramcontent.com/pod-product-compliance
Lightning Source LLC
Chambersburg PA
CBHW070636310726
48982CB00001B/302

* 9 7 8 1 6 1 3 4 3 0 4 3 9 *